The Spy Is Dead

The Spy Is Dead

CHARLES RUSSELL

A Crime Club Book
Doubleday

NEW YORK   LONDON   TORONTO   SYDNEY   AUCKLAND

A Crime Club Book

Published by Doubleday, a division of
Bantam Doubleday Dell Publishing Group, Inc.
666 Fifth Avenue, New York, New York 10103

Doubleday and the portrayal of the
stylized gunman are trademarks of Doubleday, a division of
Bantam Doubleday Dell Publishing Group, Inc.

Library of Congress Cataloging-in-Publication Data

Kelly, Terence, 1920–
The spy is dead/Charles Russell.—1st ed.
p.   cm.
"A Crime Club book."
I. Title.

PR6061.E497S6   1988   88-14927
823'.914—dc19   CIP

ISBN 0-385-24614-5
Copyright © 1988 by Terence Kelly
All Rights Reserved
Printed in the United States of America
December 1988
First Edition

The Spy Is Dead

ONE

"Karl Sodek?"

"Speaking."

"My name's Braley. Harry A. Braley. You don't know me . . ."

"No, Mr. Braley."

"No." The speaker paused. "Mr. Sodek, I was over in San Francisco in the fall, staying with a friend who took me out to Fairhill. I was very impressed."

"That's kind of you."

"No, but I was. And I was wondering . . . Well, I've been thinking it over through the winter. You see, I've got this land near Tombstone. You know? Tombstone, Arizona?"

"I know of it. Naturally. But I've never been there."

"Well, I've got this land. Desert, more or less, but there's water and all the utilities handy and I reckon that if someone could do something like your Fairhill with it, it could be a winner."

"Mr. Braley . . ."

"No. I know what you're going to say. But I'm not trying to sell it to you. Not the land. Only the idea. The way I figure it is that with all the retired people who come to visit Tombstone, if there was the right thing handy . . . You know, golf course, health club, cottages, library . . ."

"Mr. Braley . . ."

"Hear me out, Mr. Sodek, hear me out. I'm not asking you to back it; just help me get it moving. I put in the land and, say, a couple of million bucks to kick it off. That's no problem. But I need someone who knows about these things to put it together . . ."

Karl Sodek heard him out, looking down from his office in Union Street on the boats in the St. Francis Yacht Club glimmering wetly in the dismal day, idly fingering the deep scar on his forehead, which sometimes bothered him when it was dank and clammy with the weather coming in off the western seaboard. It would be dry in Arizona, dry, hot and sunny. And after all they'd never been to Tombstone! His grey-green eyes under his heavy eyebrows twinkled . . . Tombstone! Where Hollywood had won the West! *High Noon* and all that. A Lourdes for every self-respecting American—well, anyway, for a one-time Hungarian who'd gratefully accepted sanctuary.

Braley was going on, "I'd meet all your expenses, naturally, and of course there'd be absolutely no obligation . . ."

Sodek cut him short. "Okay, Mr. Braley, I'll come down and take a look at it. And don't worry about the expenses. It can't be for a week or so. Where do I contact you?"

Braley gave him a telephone number and address.

"Tucson?" echoed Sodek in surprise. "How far's that from Tombstone?"

" 'bout sixty miles. Well a bit less from where I live. You'll stay with me, of course . . ."

"I'll be bringing my wife with me."

"Better still. Stay a week. Stay longer if you like . . ."

2

He telephoned Eva at Kent Woodlands. "Meet me for lunch."

"I can't. I'm . . ."

"Cancel it."

"Karl!"

He understood the sudden alarm in her voice. "Nothing's wrong," he reassured her.

"Sorry. But if you knew what my heart just did!"

"Well I'll buy you a nice lunch to settle it down. Aliotos. One o'clock. All right?"

"I suppose so. Although what will Myra say being stood up at five minutes' notice . . ."

"Myra's a born survivor."

"What is this, Karl? What's happened?"

"It's not what's happened. It's what's going to. One o'clock." And he put down the phone before she could change her mind.

He managed to book a table central to the two lines of fishing boats and cruisers in the harbour below. The water was slate and so still that the relative brightness of the sunless sky threw reflections of their bows and handrails. In the far background one of the uprights of the Golden Gate and the lines of its cables on either hand gave the impression of an enormous tent. He liked Aliotos. It was for tourists but tourism had always been his business. As Sergei Roff. As Michael Downley. And now as Karl Sodek. In Bond Street, London. In the Place Mohammed, Casablanca. And now in Union Street, San Francisco. Only it was a different kind of tourism he handled now; he'd shifted from delivering people for others to accommodate to providing places for others to deliver to him. It was less arduous, less pernickety, more profitable and, above all, much more interesting.

He watched Eva heading across the restaurant, petite, alert, her dark hair cut to a casual fringe over a forehead lined with the years of pain which had led up to, in fact caused, their meeting; her huge eyes dark, expressive, accusing even. She wore a scarlet suit of sufficient style to have heads turn and the eyes follow. How different she looked from that day five years ago when she had first walked into his office in Casablanca and, with a drummed-up self-confidence which had been transparent, asked him for a job; when she'd been Anita; how different and yet, how much the same. He was not in love with her and never had been in love with her but she was very important to him. Women had always mattered to Karl Sodek; now there was only Eva. They had shared so much in the past; now they shared a secret, the new identities which the British Government in collusion with the American Government had created for them. Karl and Eva Sodek, expatriate Hungarians, rich enough to have no need to work, active enough to find idleness unacceptable.

He kissed her cheek, momentarily holding her with firm affection before he drew out her chair. She waited until he was across the table from her.

"Well?" Her brow was deeply furrowed.

"We're going to Arizona."

She expressed no surprise. "When?"

"A week today."

She shook her head. "Maybe you're going to Arizona a week today, Karl. I certainly am not."

"You don't have to be here. Hector can . . ."

"And come back from Arizona to find we've got some sort of Charlie Chaplin playing Garfield Morgan?"

Eva was in theatre; Hector was her company manager; and Garfield Morgan was a heavy.

"You wouldn't have hired Hector if you hadn't enough confidence in him to leave him to a do a bit of casting."

"It isn't a bit of casting and Hector's got his blind spots. Can't you put it off?" But before he could have replied she asked, "How long were you thinking of going for? And what's it all about?"

The waiter came just then. They ordered clam chowder and snapper and a bottle of Chappellet. Then he told her of Braley's offer.

"I thought we could make a week of it," he said. "Get away from all this drizzle." He nodded in the direction of the small armada and saw the still surface of the water had been disturbed by several seals creating oily-looking wavelets.

"Seals," he said.

She nodded; seals were not all that uncommon.

"You won't need a week to size it up," she said. "Why not just go for a couple of days? There'll be plenty of opportunities later if you take it on."

"Okay," he said.

3

Braley met him at the airport, a biggish man in shapeless fawn slacks with a sagging belly caressed by a white T-shirt. He wore dark sunglasses and a floppy sun-hat which, together, hid his character.

"Well, sir, I'm glad to meet you," he said jovially, opening the door of his white station wagon. "Sorry the little lady couldn't come with you."

Sodek shot a quick glance at him. It didn't ring true—not from a man with sufficient land to develop as a resort and a spare two million dollars. But the sunglasses effectively concealed reaction—it was like looking at a wall.

"She felt it wasn't worth it," he temporized. "Not for just a couple of days."

Braley went round the Buick and got in the other side.

"I'm sorry that's all the time you can spare," he said. "There's a lot to see round Tucson. We're pretty proud of it." And then, as if remembering, "To say nothing of the ranch."

"I've made some enquiries," Sodek said, and then, out of courtesy, "naturally." And went on, "There are quite a few developments near enough to Tombstone already. To say nothing of Sun City. Do you really think there's room for another?"

Braley set the Buick in motion.

"Oh, sure, sure," he said. "Just wait until you see it."

"Are we going straight out now?" He was already considering the possibility of returning to San Francisco on the following day.

Braley shook his head. "First thing tomorrow. By the time we got there, there'd be only a couple of hours of daylight left. No I figured we'd spend this evening running through a few ideas I've got sketched out."

Sodek didn't like that either. He was involved in three such projects and all with professionals hired to do the planning.

"Well, okay," he agreed, "but I should tell you, Mr. Braley . . ."

"Harry."

"All right. Harry. I should tell you that if I do get tied up with this, I'd want my own architect."

"Sure," said Braley offhandedly. And without taking his eyes off the road, "You ain't American."

"I am now." He used the formula which by now had almost become a habit. "I got out of Hungary just after the Russians put the uprising down. Into Austria."

"That was a long time back."

"I went to England first. Only been in the States for a couple of years."

He waited for the usual surprise that a Hungarian refugee should so quickly have established himself at such a level of business in a new country. Instead, Braley said, "You never been in these parts before, Karl? You don't mind if I call you Karl?"

"Not in the least. No, I haven't."

"Not been to the Grand Canyon?"

"I meant round here."

" 's the Grand Canyon State."

"Yes, I know."

It was baffling. And obviously a wild goose chase. There was no question of doing serious business with Harry A. Braley. But he could hardly tell him to turn his wagon round and go back to the airport.

"Helluva number of caravans here," he said to fill an uncomfortable silence.

"Snow birds."

"Snow birds?"

"It's what we call 'em. Come down to get away from the snow. When it melts they all head 'back again."

Once started, Braley talked at length about the caravaners and no sooner had he done with them than he switched into a curiously determined discourse on almost everything of note they passed. The land was pancake flat desert interspersed now and then with curious oases which were groups of up to perhaps half a dozen houses, some large, some very large, all on generous plots. Everywhere was cactus, cactus and spiky-looking trees; the sky was a brilliant blue and the distant mountains crystal sharp.

Braley talked about it all. He talked about everything: houses, birds, cacti, insects, trees, mountains, the vehicles they passed, even the road itself. He talked about everything except the project. On the two or three occasions Sodek tried to drift the conversation to it, he veered away from it. Finally they arrived. He pulled the station wagon to a halt outside a low-lying, brick-built house approached by a semicircular drive off the highway. He got out, leaving his door wide open, came round the front, opened Sodek's door for him, waited for him to get out, opened the other door and reached over his seat for his grip, put it down and slammed the two offside doors shut. "Won't be a minute, Karl," he said. "Just slip it in the garage. Gets too damn hot without the air-conditioning on." He went round the front of the vehicle again, slipped quickly into the driving seat, yanked the door shut from the inside, jammed down on the accelerator pedal and, with a screech of slipping wheels on the gravelly surface, drove off round the semicircular drive in a cloud of dust, hitting the highway, turning left on it and heading back in the direction from which they had come.

4

For moments Sodek stood spellbound, dumped with his grip beside him in the dusty, burning afternoon heat in a driveway outside a house which stood quite by itself, with only the passing highway to indicate it had the least connection with civilization. Behind the house rose an unbroken range of distant mountains in air so clear that each ridge, each cleft, each peak was drawn knife-edge sharp.

Braley! No, he could not be Braley! Sodek stared after the Buick, now the merest dot on the dead, straight highway. That wasn't Braley. It couldn't be. He had checked on Harry A. Braley. And Harry A. Braley had been all that he'd made himself out to be. A wealthy man who owned a ranch of immense acreage near Tombstone. Such a man didn't personally collect a stranger ostensibly as a business partner only to dump him with nothing but his grip in the middle of a desert! And yet . . . He had telephoned Braley at his ranch. Spoken to him. Made the arrangements, checked the flight number . . .

Sodek shook his head. There was mystery here indeed. And more than mystery. There was danger.

He turned to face the house, separated from the driveway by a low brick wall. It showed every sign of occupation, drawn-back curtains at the windows, furniture within; every sign of occupation but no sign of occupant. For a moment he hesitated. The wise thing was to wait for a passing car and thumb a lift back to Tucson; every instinct advised him this was the wise thing to do. But the temptation was too great, overriding caution. He could not walk out on this. Not spend the rest of his life wondering.

Decisively now, he picked up his grip and strode through the opening in the low brick wall and along the short path, between a narrow cactus garden, which led to the front door. He pressed a bell-push. From within the house he heard the ringing. But no one came. There was a knocker, of horseshoe shape; he lifted it and angrily rat-a-tatted it. Still no response. He grasped at the door latch and pressed it down. The door, heavy, solid, opened easily. Entering, he found himself in a hall of generous size. At each end was a door; in the wall facing him two more. He opened the nearer of these and discovered a kitchen, modern, superbly equipped, empty. He tried the next and found himself in a room of considerable size. Exposed timber ceiling beams ran the width of it, the floor was liver-coloured fitted carpet broken with large Mexican rugs laid in a strict geometrical pattern.

Sitting easily enough, in a flowered-patterned armchair in the far corner by the fireplace, was a man he had once known over a period of several years, a man who, watching a belly dancer in Casablanca, had, unwittingly disclosed part of his inner nature, a man who had loaned him a London flat that he hadn't owned, a man who had once come to kill him.

George Le Clerc!

He stared amazed, the grip still in his left hand forgotten, the fake Harry A. Braley forgotten, his peremptory deposal on the roadside like so much garbage forgotten. His mind was filled instead with older memories: of George Le Clerc in the Café Américain in Casablanca; the one-time jolly, extrovert, dice-rattling colleague with the booming laugh which went so well with his massive frame; the George Le Clerc who to hide his real character adopted the style of a Sidney Greenstreet; the George Le Clerc who had shown that behind that bland and affable exterior lay a man amoral, ruthless, mean; the George Le Clerc who was a paid hack of the British MI6; the George Le Clerc who had come gun in hand with a posse to a shabby shack in a village called Little Beg, near to Basingstoke in England, to kill him; the George Le Clerc who, by humbling, he had made an enemy of for life.

Le Clerc was the first to break the silence. "You didn't get your nose refixed, I see."

He wouldn't have said it like that in the old days. It would have been: "Well, sir, you still prefer your old nose, I see! And why not, indeed? The British Government will nothing pay for wearing our old noses. I misquote, sir. But I think you take my meaning!" Or something of that order. And Le Clerc would have shaken with mirth with his fat cheeks and his double chin wobbling. But not any more. Because once his disguise has been removed and he is shown to be another character, an actor can never adopt an original part in the play again.

And so his quip was spoken with the contempt of a man determined to establish his superiority, of a man who has not forgiven a humiliation.

"No, George," Sodek said grimly, "I didn't get my nose fixed. Nor this." And he touched the scar across his forehead, less livid now, yet a brand to distinguish him from other men.

He resolved to say no more. Not to seek an explanation. Instead, for long moments he held Le Clerc's rather small eyes with his own, then—unhurriedly putting down his grip and glancing through the sheet of glass which walled between sitting-room and yard—said casually, "Who's the girl?"

"Lovely, isn't she?" Le Clerc responded.

Sodek nodded. "Very."

The girl *was* lovely—a few years more than twenty, leaning against the chrome rail to the swimming pool steps, dressed in a minute bikini, white with black polka dots, slender, tanned, with titian hair swept up from her forehead, held to fall in a kind of ponytail down her back.

"Who is she?" Sodek repeated.

"Your new assistant." For moments it seemed as if after all Le Clerc might fall back on an antiquated role. But he resisted. "Her name," he said, "is an unusual one. Petronella." And, after a pause, meaningly, "Petronella Roff." And he went on to speak in the calm, matter of fact manner of a man explaining the background to an enterprise in which his listener is to be involved—which, indeed, was exactly what he was doing.

"She is not of course supposed to be your wife; except for the purpose of booking hotel bedrooms, buying airline tickets and so on. It is hypocritical to have to go through these pitiful little subterfuges which those they are inflicted on don't believe for a moment, but even these days hotel managers still prefer it. She will leave with you in a few days' time when you fly to Miami where you will take a crash course in deep-sea fishing." He paused. "I take it you aren't an expert deep-sea fisherman?" Sodek shook his head, resolved not to give Le Clerc the satisfaction of asking him questions. "No, none of my researches," Le Clerc resumed, displaying no impatience, "have indicated that. When we are satisfied that you can not only talk big-game fishing naturally but, if necessary, handle a marlin or a swordfish, you will sail with your wife to Grand Bahama . . ."

"What's the girl's real name?" cut in Sodek.

Le Clerc waved a fat, superbly manicured paw. "Harrington. But it doesn't matter."

"Is she English?"

"Yes."

Sodek looked back towards the girl.

"You appreciate our choice?" Le Clerc enquired. And when there was no reply. "We have been to a lot of trouble. A girl of such delicious beauty is an essential part of . . . shall we say the furniture? . . . in the enterprise you are to carry out for us."

"All right," said Sodek. "Let's stop playing games."

"My dear Sergei . . ."

"I am not Sergei. I am Karl. Karl Sodek."

Le Clerc shook his head, the rolls of fat which substituted for a neck shifting like dough.

"You can forget Karl Sodek until you have carried out this mission for us."

"I'm carrying out no mission," Sodek said. "Neither am I risking being poisoned, shot or blown up by re-adopting my own name."

"Oh, you don't have to worry about that any more," Le Clerc said comfortably.

"I'm to take it from that your spy has completed *his* mission?"

"The spy is dead." He said it very casually.

"I see," said Sodek quietly.

Yet he did not see. If the man who for three years had impersonated him, the man on whose account it had been made to look as if the real Sergei Roff had embezzled the funds of Cayman Island company, obliging him to flee to Casablanca with a face dramatically changed by a brilliant plastic surgeon, the man whose work had been so valuable that Sergei Roff, re-christened Michael Downley, had been provided with a Moroccan travel agency as a swap for his own in Bond Street, the man so vital to MI6 that once his cover had been blown the real Sergei Roff was to be tricked into returning to England for the express purpose of being assassinated by the KGB—if that man was dead, and presumably his death and perhaps all the circumstances of the complex plot had become known to the Russians, then what on earth was this new, this ridiculous stratagem all about? If the spy was dead, then his own hold over the British Government, the hold which had made him rich, was lost. All right. But the British Government had no hold on him, no power to force him to undertake missions for them. Yet this was not a game, he had not been tricked to this house in an Arizona desert to no purpose; this had been carefully planned. And not by George Le Clerc; Le Clerc was just a jackal. He would try, because he was that kind of man, to convey that in some part, at least, the planning was his—but it wasn't. And he would try to convey that he was privy to the plot in its minutest detail, but he would not be. No—but there would be much he did know it was important to discover.

"Tell me," Sodek said, "did the Russians discover they had blown up the wrong man? That the man they thought to be Sergei Roff was nothing more than a minor British agent?"

"It is of no account," said Le Clerc—which merely showed he didn't know. But then, as if appreciating to leave it there would underline his ignorance: "So far as we are concerned you can now send a memo on the whole business to them."

Sodek didn't believe this for a moment; but his question had been answered. Whatever the man who had impersonated him had set out to achieve had been achieved or the achievement of it no longer mattered.

"So I can take it that this latest nonsense has absolutely nothing to do with whatever the last nonsense was all about?"

"Absolutely nothing."

"All right," said Sodek. "You win. I'll ask the questions."

"Ask away." (Sodek suspected he all but added "My dear fellow.") "I won't guarantee to answer them."

"I am to go with that girl out there, who is to be posing as my mistress, for a crash course in deep-sea fishing in Miami and then on to the Bahamas to carry out some mission?" Le Clerc inclined his head. "Supposing," Sodek said, "my wife had come with me as she would have done if . . ."

Le Clerc seized on the pause, brief though it was. "If she weren't involved in the casting of a play?" His smile was almost benign. "Well in the first instance she isn't your wife. You never married Anita Fermor—or Eva as you now call her. And in the second she would not have come with you. At the last moment something would have prevented her." And he added smoothly, "We have our little ways and means."

"Yes," said Sodek grimly. "You have your little ways and means. All right. This mission? What is it?"

"You will be informed."

"In other words you don't know?"

"You will be informed."

"All right. We'll let that pass." He thought for a moment. "As I am too rich for bribes to interest me," he resumed, "it would be stupid of me not to realise that you feel you have some sort of hold over me."

"Stupid," Le Clerc agreed.

"And yet you don't."

"We have a hold over Anita Fermor."

Sodek was shocked to silence.

"Anita Fermor," Le Clerc explained, "was a heroin addict . . ."

"I know . . ."

"To satisfy her craving she did what many addicts do, she became a pusher."

"I know that too."

"No doubt. In return for, shall we say, services to be rendered, no charges were brought against her. On the other hand she was not provided with any kind of legal undertaking which protected her from the possibility of future charges. You take my meaning?"

"She is an American citizen now. There is nothing . . ."

Le Clerc held up a hand as soft as air. "That was arranged on representations from the British Government. It can as easily be . . . disarranged." And after a pause, "There are occasions when the British and American Governments, or even sometimes MI6 and the CIA, work together. This happens to be one of them. The American Government is as interested as is the British Government in the little matter in which you are to be involved. Do I make myself clear?"

Sodek nodded. Le Clerc had made himself only too clear. If he refused to help them, Eva would lose her American citizenship, be deported to England and arrested for pushing heroin.

"If I agree," he said, "will Anita Fermor be provided with . . . a legal undertaking that no action will ever be taken against her?"

"Of course."

"And what am I supposed to do? Assassinate someone?"

Le Clerc chuckled. "My dear fellow, no. Nothing so crude." He was enjoying his pound of flesh. "Be patient. All will be revealed to you this evening. And now," he rose, "I think it is time you met Mrs. Roff."

5

The garden was strange with, around its sides, a continuous brick wall about six feet high beyond which the tops of enormous suaros and mesquites could be seen. Around the pool there was expensive terrace furniture: tables, chairs, chaise longues. On one of these lay Harrington—now Petronella Roff.

When they came out from the house she looked up interestedly at her companion for the weeks ahead. She saw a striking-looking man in his late forties with thick, iron-grey hair, grey-green eyes under heavy eyebrows, a broken nose, a badly scarred forehead, and an air of considerable self-confidence. She was much relieved.

"I will leave you," said Le Clerc, with no attempt at introductions, "to get to know each other." And he went into the house.

Roff stood staring down at the beautiful creature lying in the chaise longue, her green eyes coolly appraising him.

"How do you do?" he said.

She smiled. Her cheekbones were high and the smile drew definite folds of skin to the corners of her mouth. Her nose was neat and straight, her lips were very red, her eyelashes long and sweeping. He could detect no flaws.

"How much do you know about this nonsense?" he asked.

"Not too much," she said. "I gather someone will be coming to explain it to us later on."

"Are they paying you?"

She nodded. "Yes. But it's not only that."

Her voice indicated good breeding and a typically English upper-class education.

"What is it then?"

"I'm not to tell you."

"How much do you know about me?" he asked.

"Oh," she said. "Up to a point, quite a lot. Your father was a Russian émigré and was killed with your mother by a V-bomb in the war. You were brought up by an aunt who taught you Russian, which you speak fluently. You had a Bond Street travel agency. You were framed by a man named Laurence Kress to make it look as if you had embezzled investors' funds for a tourist development he was doing in Spain which were held in a Cayman company."

"They've briefed you pretty well."

"Only the outlines."

"Do you want the details?"

She shook her head. "No. Not now. Later, perhaps, when we've got to know each other better."

"All right," he said, and deliberately changed the subject. "Curious garden," he said. "I mean . . . why the wall? With nothing but desert all around?"

"It's to stop children falling in the pool."

"I don't believe it!"

"It's a local edict apparently."

"You seem to know a lot about Tucson."

"I've been coached."

The penny dropped. So that was what the phoney Braley's chat was all about.

"Now why exactly," he mused, "are we to be coached about Tucson?"

"Because we have a house here.

"We're to be involved with someone, or some people, who're to believe it's where we live. Or at least live some of the time. And because we live here we know that crested quail waddle when they walk, and that the local sheriff has four different radios in his pick-up truck . . .

"And that there are thirty thousand students in Tucson University. Yes. And incidentally you don't call that a wall around the garden, you call it a fence around the yard."

"But do I?" he said. "After all, I'm back to being Sergei Roff. And he wouldn't have called it a fence around the yard."

She nodded her lovely head approvingly. "Good point," she said.

"And I'm to call you Petronella. That's a bit of a mouthful."

"You're supposed," she said, chuckling, "to be a very wealthy man who can afford the kind of expensive mistress who's liable to choose that sort of name to go with the image she tries to create in order to be certain that very wealthy men choose her to be their mistress."

"I have to say," he admitted, "that in spite of everything, I'm beginning to find this quite an intriguing business."

Le Clerc came out just then. "I'm going into Tucson to meet a flight," he said. "I shouldn't be gone more than an hour and a half." And with that he left them.

"Curious, isn't it?" Roff said, watching his departing back. "I wonder." He stood abruptly. "Excuse me."

He went into the house and was just in time to see the front door closing on Le Clerc. After a few moments a limousine came into view from a triple garage beyond the bedroom wing. He watched it from the hallway window as it nosed into the semicircular driveway and then turned left onto the highway. When it had gone from sight, he went into the sitting-room and picked up the telephone. The line was dead. He was not surprised. He went out to rejoin Petronella—to find her swimming lazily in the pool, head high so that only the end of the ponytail was wetted.

He waited until she turned at the end, came back and, holding on to the margin, said to him, "Find out what you wanted?"

He nodded. "The telephone's dead. Of course I could always thumb a lift to . . ." But he shook his head. "No, it was only to make a point. They're very thorough."

6

When Le Clerc returned a spectacular sunset of gold and scarlet was lighting a partly clouded sky. There was another man with him, a stranger to Roff, a powerfully built man with hard eyes, a Roman nose, bald but for a well-trimmed fuzz of white hair above his ears, a man whose thick, sculptured lips were clamped tight-close when he was silent and who projected such an air of power as to make Le Clerc, who normally had quite a presence, seem of small account.

His name was Shapland.

They met in the sitting-room—Roff, in his own suit, unwilling as yet to admit total acceptance of the situation by wearing any of the semitropical wardrobe he had discovered provided for him; Le Clerc huge but impeccable in perfectly tailored grey cool-wool; Shapland in a dark-blue pin stripe which would have looked well in a City boardroom. And, against these three men, all formally attired and providing a perfect background to her femininity, Petronella, in slim black trousers and a Chinese-style yellow silk, long cuff-sleeved, neck-buttoned blouse with matching skull-cap tilted to show an inch or so of hair above her forehead and through whose open centre her titian ponytail, released, flowed luxuriantly down her back.

There were few preliminaries.

"Have you heard of Dragon Cay?" Shapland asked of Roff.

"No."

"It is a small island off Abaco. It has been bought by a syndicate which is developing it as a resort for game fishermen. When fully completed it will also have two hotels, many cottages and a golf course and club. But the game fishing is the important thing. The principal entrepreneurs are a Japanese named Yasuo Minahero and a one-time Englishman, now a Bahamian citizen, named . . ." and he paused deliberately, "named Laurence Kress."

"Laurence Kress!" echoed Roff, shaken and amazed.

"Laurence Kress," Shapland agreed. "At the moment Kress is in control, partly through his own shareholding and partly through nominees. For reasons I will not explain that is not a position we can accept. Your task is to do whatever is required to ensure that control passes from Kress's hands. Once that has been achieved it is unlikely we shall want anything more from you and Miss Fermor will be given a document which will ensure that no one, not even the British or American Governments, can prosecute her for any of her past misdemeanours."

"But this is absurd!" cried Roff. "Kress would never deal with me. Not after what happened on the Benevente business."

Shapland looked at him coldly. "Why do you think we selected you? It is *because* of the Benevente business."

"I tell you he wouldn't deal with me."

He pictured Kress, his well-made body, his jet-black hair, his shrewd eyes glinting behind his heavy spectacles. Remembered his charm, his impressive propensities as host, his imagination, his quicksilver mind, his purposeful conversation. There was a string of qualities, rare in a single individual, he could recall when he thought of Laurence Kress. Yes, but he could remember other things about the man. His cruelty to his wife, his contempt for failures, his commercial amorality, his ruthlessness towards any who stood in his way, his pitiless dismissal of those who had served their purpose. As *he* had once. And Roff thought of their last meeting, in a sleazy *estaminet* near Ploërmel; of Kress rounding the half landing of the stairs which led to his garret of a room; of how in the meeting of their eyes he had realised that the relationship between them which had seemed so warm, so filled with promise, was utterly changed. That he, the one-time colleague, having served his purpose, contemptible in failure, had overnight become an inconvenience which, with no more ado, must be discarded.

He said as much to Shapland. "So far as Kress is concerned, I've been written off as nonentity. He wouldn't touch me with a barge-pole."

"You show you do not understand such men," said Shapland wearily. "When he discovers that the man he shipped off to Morocco to run a second-rate travel agency has made himself even richer than he is himself, he will show you nothing but respect."

"Do I explain how I made my money?"

"You explain how you got your start. The money you blackmailed the British Government into giving you. You may tell him as much as you like about that episode. You will go on to tell him, truthfully, that you learnt from him how to put together developments such as those you currently have on hand at the moment, including a very major one near Tombstone, Arizona. He will be flattered; everyone likes flattery but such men as Laurence Kress like it laid on with a trowel. When you have gained his confidence, he will almost certainly invite you to invest in his Dragon Cay development and, especially because you are an enthusiastic game fisherman, you will allow yourself to be persuaded."

"Is there," said Roff ironically, "any limit to the amount I'm to invest in Dragon Cay?"

"In the first instance you may do so up to one million dollars. Le Clerc, who will be with you, although unknown to you, will see to that side of things. If it appears necessary to increase your investment to achieve your purpose you will clear it first with him." He glanced at his watch. "Are there any more questions?"

Roff looked slowly around at the three men: Shapland rocklike, hard as nails; Le Clerc flabby, supercilious, but dangerous all the same; Petronella, beautiful, utterly self-possessed and showing a curious lack of interest in these machinations.

He nodded. "Yes. What exactly is this all about?"

"That is not your business."

"Does *she* know?" He said it with intentional rudeness, nodding curtly at Petronella.

"Yes."

"You expect me to spend weeks with her, pretending she's my mistress, not knowing what this is all about while she does?"

"So long as there is no purpose in your knowing, you will not be told. It will be safer for you anyway. If it should happen that it appears of advantage to us for you to be told, then you will be told."

"And if I refuse?"

"Miss Fermor will be arrested."

Roff felt the bile of anger rise. "She worked for you," he said, somehow managing to keep his voice under control, "for years. Wasn't that enough? Didn't she pay for what she did? She kept her side of the bargain—wasn't it reasonable for her to believe you would?"

"We made no bargain," Shapland said. "She did what she was told to do."

"But not at the end!" There was triumph in his voice. "Is that why you've picked on me? To get your own back on her?"

"We have chosen you," Shapland replied, "because we consider you are the man most likely to achieve what we require to be achieved. So far as Miss Fermor is concerned, except that she enables us to persuade you to co-operate, we have not the least interest in her."

"No interest?" He was very angry now. "No interest, you say? When you've had a whole gang of snoops and informers, like that one . . ." he jerked a thumb at Le Clerc, "prying into her private life, following her around, watching everything she does against the possibility you can use her as a bit of blackmail? She's built a decent life. You know that! You've got a dossier on her, haven't you? You know she's involved herself in theatre. That she's respected by everyone she deals with. That she's happy. As happy as she's ever been in a pretty damn miserable life, which you and your lot are as responsible as anyone for making such a hell till now. And you'd smash up that life. Not because you think she deserves to be sent to prison, but because you haven't got your way with me. My God, what sort of people are you?"

He was on his feet, facing Shapland, every muscle whipcord taut, the anger blazing from his eyes.

But Shapland was unmoved. "Mr. Roff," he said, "it is not our business to deal in the commodities you have listed. Are you or are you not going to do what we ask you to?"

Roff, white-faced, nodded. "Oh yes. I'll do it. What you've asked. Nothing more. On one condition. That I have in writing first that if I do succeed, so far as Anita is concerned the slate's wiped clean."

For once Shapland hesitated. Then he nodded. "See to it, Le Clerc."

"But, sir . . ."

"I said see to it."

"Meantime," Roff said, "may I contact her?"

"Miss Fermor? No. Not under any circumstances. You need not worry. Miss Fermor will be advised that you will be away for a few weeks and reassured sufficiently. You will remain here three more days. During that time the man who brought you here will complete your grounding so that you will be able to convince Kress, and for that matter anyone else you come in contact with, that you have spent quite some time in Arizona. You will then fly to Florida for your course in game fishing and when you have been passed as expert you will sail in a chartered yacht, on which you will live while you are there, to Grand Bahama where Kress rents a house. Le Clerc will see you get the details. If possible you will make your own arrangements for renewing your acquaintanceship with Kress but should there be a problem you may call on Le Clerc for help. Once you have made contact with Kress, you will be on your own. As and when you have done what you have been sent to do, you will come back to this house and wait here until you receive Miss Fermor's contract. Then you may do what you like. Neither of you will be called upon for help again."

He left with Le Clerc. A few minutes later the telephone, mysteriously restored to life, rang. Roff answered it.

"Yes?"

"My name's Crann. Jim Crann. I'm the guy you thought was Harry Braley. Thought I'd let you know I'd be coming along about nine tomorrow to run you out to Tombstone. My wife'll be with me to clean up the house."

"Thank you, Mr. Crann," Roff responded dryly. "That's very considerate of you."

"Don't give it another thought. If there's anything you want, my number's 555-2673. And if there's anywhere you want to go, there's a Ford in the garage and the key's in the glove compartment."

"I suppose you couldn't suggest what we do about eating?"

"You could try the Tanque Verde Ranch. It's pretty nice. Just keep along the highway away from Tucson for about six, seven miles and you'll see the signpost to it on your right."

"Thank you, Mr. Crann. That's probably what we'll do."

He put the receiver down and went looking for Petronella, remembering something strange: that Shapland had not addressed a single word to her and she hadn't asked a single question.

7

Their dinner was served to them with a panache bordering on theatricality, with two waiters and a chef attending and the tomato-red casserole from which it was served placed like a crown on a specially fetched side table.

"Are you going to tell me anything about yourself?" he said.

She shook her head. "No," she said briefly, but with good humour. "But you can tell me about our dinner."

"Creole Jambalaya. It's a Louisiana dish."

She began investigating. "Prawns . . . Ham . . . What's that?"

"Chorizo sausage."

She started to eat. "Delicious."

"Try the wine."

She looked at him over her glass. "You like being rich, don't you, Sergei?"

"I like the freedom it brings."

"Were you very poor? When you were young?"

"Yes."

"I wasn't poor." It was the first thing about herself she had volunteered. "But then I wasn't rich, either. Just well-to-do."

"How on earth did you get involved in this?"

"Don't," she reproved him, "spoil this delicious meal by asking questions."

She felt at ease with him and if the restaurant had emptied about them, she would have scarcely noticed. He was twice her age; he was rich, successful. His iron-grey hair, his generous mouth, his steady eyes, his broken nose, the fierce scar on his forehead, all these together made him a striking-looking man. For all his English upbringing there was something . . . foreign about him. Something different.

"Say something in Russian to me," she said suddenly.

"Ty tak prekrasna, Peta. Prekrasna chto dukh zakhvatyvaet."

"What does that mean?"

"You're very beautiful, Peta. Beautiful enough to take a man's breath away."

She shook her head. "I wish you hadn't said that, Sergei." And she put a hand on his. "The next few weeks are not going to be very easy for either of us. Don't make them even more difficult still."

TWO

Laurence Kress owned a Colonial-style mansion on Lyford Cay and a Nassau office from which to run his complex international affairs—one of the delightful limestone Federal-style houses with white-painted louvres and deep wooden verandahs hanging over the street. And as well as these properties he had rented, for a period to cover the development of Dragon Cay, another house, on Grand Bahama, which was of ultracontemporary design in glass, stone, wood and concrete built out on a bluff known from its shape as Eagle Head and the building as Eagle Rock.

His wife, Dilys, loathed the time she spent on Grand Bahama, which she liked no more than she had liked the Channel Islands—"hell holes both"—and had she been able to have her way she would have stayed in Nassau. But she was not allowed to have her way. What baffled most of Kress's close associates and the myriad of casual acquaintances he made in the course of his high-powered business life was perfectly clear to her. She knew how others saw her—colourless. Her inability to do justice to her husband's enormous wealth frustrated him; at times she positively embarrassed him. Had he been able to sail into a casino with a woman of such elegance and notoriety on his arm, this would have given him as much pleasure as any successfully concluded business deal. His associates and acquaintances wondered why he did not do just that. Why on earth, they would ask each other, hadn't he got rid of her years ago in exchange for a mistress, or a string of mistresses, who did him justice; or married again some woman with the background and aggression to lift him into high society?

Dilys could have given them the answer, but had she done so they would only have laughed at her. Masked from others by the trappings of wealth and determinedly hidden from himself (in much the way a man of God by refusing to admit his lust appears to conquer it) was an inferiority complex which if acknowledged would have made a mockery of all Kress had achieved.

Dilys had been his secretary when, a struggling and not very talented architect, he had started out on the long and initially difficult climb. He had been married at the time and had a son but before too long Dilys had become his mistress—because, as she later realised, she was convenient.

To Dilys, who came from decent but quite nondescript suburban parents, he had been like no man she had met before: ambitious, single-minded, tremendously exciting. Although he never killed the principles imbued in her through childhood, he managed to crush any overt resistance to his own utter disregard of them. He would use, she soon discovered, anything and anybody; he made far more enemies out of one-time friends than anyone she knew by quite ruthlessly using and then discarding them.

And so, as somehow the question of leaving him did not arise, she went along with him, and while he never quite destroyed her own inner convictions, he succeeded in having her put them aside and live her life without them and, in the process, lose all personality.

2

On the morning when Roff and Petronella were arriving on Grand Bahama, Kress had invited Yasuo Minahero (who after himself was the principal stockholder in "Oceanfront," as it was called) together with the architect for the scheme, a rangy San Diego Californian named David Warbeck, and the architect's wife (whom he had yet to meet) over to Eagle Rock for a working lunch.

To most Westerners, Orientals are somewhat mysterious and perhaps the Japanese more mysterious than most. It is certain that those who were taken prisoner by them during the war recount that not only, after three or four years of close proximity, did they fail to work out how they ticked but, even more remarkably, the Japanese would admit that they didn't really know how they themselves ticked. Kress of course had his theories and in particular would draw attention to the long period when Japan, shutting itself off from the world, allowing no one to leave or enter the country, became utterly inward-looking.

Yasuo Minahero had apparently switched into property when shipping slumped and was now, in common with many leading Japanese, diversifying worldwide against the day when Japan's very post-war success brought in the problems. He was in fact a gentle, rather professorial-looking man with thick, silky-grey hair who wore spectacles thinly framed in gold. His principal interest was making money; his principal hobby game fishing on his seventy-foot Knight and Carver fishing cruiser. He also owned an even larger boat—a superb forty-two-metre ocean-going yacht by Picchiotti—the *Tsuki No Hikari* (roughly translated it means "moonlight") which he kept permanently moored in the marina of the Pompano Beach Hotel where he had two permanent suites.

In his early days Kress had developed a formula for welcoming guests who were to be impressed or at any rate shown not to be superior, a formula which was by now become an absolute habit—on no account must he appear to be awaiting their arrival. Accordingly Dilys was despatched to meet the *Tsuki* (as he insisted on abridging her), involving an arduous trip down the stairs from the core of the house (whose considerable living quarters were jacked up to enjoy the splendid view of white sand beach and turquoise ocean) to the pool deck and thence by a sloping path through sweeping lawns of Bahama grass edged with low-cut hibiscus hedges and planted with casuarinas, coconut palms and flowering trees and shrubs. She watched the *Tsuki*'s docking skillfully effected by the Japanese crew and a couple of their own Bahamian staff and then the three guests descend from the glittering white leviathan, Mrs. Warbeck leading, followed by her husband and Minahero. Dilys, observing a comfortably self-assured woman of about thirty-five with an easy mouth and direct, rather penetrating eyes, envied the cool look of her outfit of cream duster coat and waistcoat dress.

"Good morning, Mrs. Warbeck," she greeted her. "I'm Dilys Kress."

"Hallo. I'm Jo," Mrs. Warbeck responded warmly, holding out a hand, equally regretfully taking in Dilys's shirt and slacks and concluding she was overdressed. "What a delightful spot you have."

"Morning, Dilys!" David Warbeck, a big, outdoor-looking man with naturally curly golden hair, a large nose and very friendly eyes, called out. "What have you done with Laurence?"

"In his den," said Dilys shortly. And then, thinking better of it, "Some damn lawyer from the Isle of Man just caught him."

Minahero's small, well-shod feet touched concrete. He was very correctly dressed in a blue gold-buttoned yachting blazer and peaked cap. "Good morning, Mrs. Kress," he said with a quick, stiff little bow. "You really should not have gone to the trouble of coming all this way." He spoke his sentences with little gaps between batches of words. "And it is too hot out here for you. Please lead the way."

Dilys, with Jo beside her, set off on the long trek back with the two men following. Shortly they came to Kress's yacht, an eighty-five-foot Dutch *Moonen*, which by comparison with the *Tsuki* appeared quite a modest craft.

3

"*Konnichi-wa,*" said Kress.

"*Konnichi-wa,*" responded Minahero.

"*Ii o-tenki desu ne.*"

"*Hai. Ikaga desu ka.*"

"*Arigato, jobu desu.*"

"You speak Japanese, Mr. Kress," said Jo, delightedly.

"Just a few words. And, Laurence, please."

"Are you learning it?"

"I think, Jo," Kress replied, "it's a very sensible language for anyone in business *to* learn these days. And, in fact . . ." He broke off as the telephone rang. "Excuse me. Yes?" he answered it. And after a moment, "Yes, all right, Kelly. But no calls after this one." He put a hand over the receiver. "Please *do* excuse me but it's quite important. Dilys . . ." he gestured. "You know." There was a trace of impatience in his tone as he turned away abruptly from her. "Yes, Peter?"

While he listened in silence, Dilys organised the seating of their guests in the huge, light, airy and quite dramatic sitting-room which was six-sided, with each side of a different length and none meeting at right angles. The floor and ceiling were both of wood, the former of rich mahogany with only oblongs of sisal matting to break its surface, the latter of bleached pine. The drapes throughout were of plain pale mushroom, and aluminum sliding windows and floor-to-ceiling doors leading to the broad verandah, which entirely circumscribed the house, allowed the brilliant tropic light to flood into a room furnished very simply. The only primary colours allowed were found in two impressionist masterpieces quietly placed away from the main sitting areas.

"Fine . . . All right, old chap. And don't phone me again before, say, nine this evening, your time." Kress put the walkabout telephone down and picked it up again. "Kelly, put it on to recording, will you? And come up and join us." He turned with an apologetic smile. "Now. If there is anything anyone would prefer to champagne?" He glanced around the company.

"Is there anything *to* prefer?" enquired Warbeck, chuckling warmly.

"Before twelve o'clock in the morning? Not so far as I have been able to discover," said Kress smiling and starting to strip the wire from one of two bottles in an oversize ice bucket.

She looked up as Kelly Brown made her entrance.

Kelly was Kress's Grand Bahama secretary, shared his study with him and worked every day whether or not he was on the island. She was an exceedingly attractive and very efficient Bahamian girl. She was not his mistress— under no circumstances these days would Kress have contemplated confusing his business affairs with those of the flesh—but otherwise she shared an intimacy with him which was crucifying to Dilys—the more so as she had, in effect, usurped the very place she had herself held. Kelly Brown knew, if not all, at least a fair share of Kress's financial secrets; Dilys knew only those which, as it were, were dropped like crumbs from a table. Dilys was not even permitted to enter his study and such knowledge as she had was gleaned from business lunches and the like. Had she the courage, Dilys would gladly have murdered Kelly Brown—but it would have been a waste of time; Kress would merely have replaced her.

In any case generalized conversation did not continue long. Apart from their business interests the three men had little in common; the women too were poles apart. This was a meeting to discuss aspects of the Dragon Cay development and scarcely had the second bottle of Dom Pérignon been broached and glasses recharged than Dilys, hoping to maroon Kelly at one end of the room while the men withdrew to the other, suggested to Jo an inspection of the house—a ploy ill conceived as Kress merely called Kelly over to sit in on the meeting.

Minahero was making a suggestion: "I believe we should consider a separate company for the golf. I think there would be some advantages, financial and psychological. We are agreed the emphasis is on the deep-sea fishing. We must remember that very many who come to 'Oceanfront,' whether as visitors or cottage owners, will not in the least be interested in playing golf. If it is felt that 'Oceanfront' is—what shall I say? . . . all purpose?—then it may not to them seem very different from . . . what? . . . the Ambassador on Cable Beach or our Grand Bahama Hotel and Country Club. And then when we come to consider the financing, if we separate the golf into its own company, there will be advantages. Of course as this would be a departure from our original intention, we would need to pass a special resolution and unless you were in agreement, Laurence, this would hardly be a possibility." He smiled good-naturedly and showed his palms. "So I am in your hands."

Far from disagreeing, Kress was in favour of the suggestion. In fact, not being in the slightest degree interested in golf, he was quite willing to check out of the golf club aspect altogether.

Eventually he said, rather slowly, as if he were working it out as he went along, "I think it would need to be a separate company. If 'Oceanfront' has a subsidiary, it will of necessity become a holding company . . ."

"Will it?" said Minahero.

"Yes," Kress said. "Because of local company law."

Minahero nodded. "Then it is agreed."

"Agreed."

"And the financing?"

It was not the moment to appear too eager. "I'd like to think about it, Yasuo," Kress replied.

"Of course."

Kress turned to Kelly Brown. "Remember we have to give twenty-one days' notice and specify the terms of the Special Resolution."

"Yes, Mr. Kress," she said—as if this was news to her.

They moved on to discuss other aspects of the project, mostly architectural, both well pleased with what had been agreed and with only one subsequent point of discord. They had been discussing with Warbeck details of the fishing-equipment building and shop. Because he rarely fished, Kress could contribute little compared with the Japanese, who was an expert fisherman, and the American, who had been hired as architect principally because of his experience in designing marinas, and thus found himself in the unaccustomed and disagreeable situation of being largely listener. Moreover to be spending so long over matters of detail and little importance struck him as an utter waste of time and when Minahero suddenly introduced a suggestion which was an entirely new departure from anything previously discussed, he was almost ready to disagree on principle.

"Do you not think, Laurence, it would be good to be able to mount the fish?"

Had he been attending closely, Kress would have understood exactly what Minahero meant. As it was he echoed, somewhat automatically, "Mount the fish?" causing the Japanese to ask Warbeck, "That is right?" and the American by nodding to appear to show Kress lacking in knowledge and thus to irritate him.

"When a big fish is caught," the Japanese smiled, making matters worse, "or sometimes even quite a small fish, the man who has caught it"—again he smiled—"or the lady often likes to have it . . . preserved. To put it on a wall. The usual practice is to send it to someone such as Pfluger in Miami. But it would not be difficult, with the right equipment, and the right men, of course, for us to do it here."

Kress was by now positively annoyed.

"Really, Yasuo," he snapped, "we're developing a resort, not going into the business of stuffing marlins!"

"It could be good publicity. Especially for those who come in their own yachts. They could take them back with them instead of waiting."

Minahero could hardly have put it more circumspectly but Kress now found himself in a situation from which it seemed to him he could not (particularly in front of a Japanese) retract without considerable loss of face.

"No, Yasuo," he said courteously but firmly, "I'm sorry, but I can't agree to it. And really I do think we have spent a great deal of time this morning on matters which really are of very small importance. May I suggest we break for lunch?"

He rose to his feet but for the moment Minahero stayed where he was.

"I cannot persuade you?" he said quietly. "It is important to me, Laurence."

Kress shook his head. "No, Yasuo, you can't persuade me." He smiled engagingly. "But then, of course, I'm not really a fisherman. Shall we join the ladies?"

Minahero stared at him impassively through his gold-rimmed glasses, then, very slowly, rose. "Very well, Laurence," he said.

Dilys had heard it all and found it not dissimilar to many occasions in the past when, determined to prove himself and demonstrate that once he had decided to have his way he could be brooked by no one, Laurence had picked on some unimportant trifle and obstinately refused to budge. Nothing from now on *would* budge him, of that she was certain. Minahero would never get his fish mounted on Dragon Cay. And, glancing at the Japanese, calm, but with his small mouth tightly closed, she was certain of something else—that her husband had made yet another enemy.

THREE

Whilst Roff and Petronella were in Miami undergoing his crash course in game fishing, Le Clerc called on them at the Fontainebleau Hotel.

"Come in, George," said Roff, admitting him, remembering, with irony, opening the door to Le Clerc to let him into Hibbert's shabby bungalow in Little Beg; remembering the big black car he had seen drawn up just inside the gateway with the men in it whose job, had he resisted, would have been to drag him out so that he could be whisked off to some secluded spot and quietly murdered.

Difficult this, for Le Clerc, he thought.

Le Clerc entered. He was dressed in a lightweight summer suit which, for all his enormous girth, hung beautifully; his tie was grey silk pierced by a pearl tiepin; on his feet were grey suede Gucci shoes. In one hand he held a Panama, in the other an envelope.

Petronella, in a white trouser suit, was manicuring her nails out on the balcony, which overlooked the swimming pool and ocean.

"Drink, George?" Roff said teasingly.

"I would have thought you would have remembered from our Casablanca days that I never drink in the afternoon," Le Clerc replied.

"Then shall we sit out on the balcony?"

"If you don't mind, I would rather not."

No, of course, Roff thought, he loathes the sun.

"I'll come in then," said Petronella.

Le Clerc waited politely until she had taken the corner of the settee before seating himself in an armchair.

"I have come," he told them, "to inform you of the arrangements made."

"The boat's hired?" Roff said.

"At twenty-six thousand dollars a day you need to be rich."

"She's costing that?" said Roff, abruptly abandoning banter.

"Well," replied Le Clerc, who was beginning to enjoy himself, "with a crew of seven, to say nothing of the cost of running the boat, depreciation, harbour dues . . ."

"Seven!"

"Captain, chief engineer, mate, deck-hand, cook and two stewardesses. And then . . ."

"Just a minute!"

Le Clerc's small eyes hardened momentarily. But then, recovering, he enquired with prodigious politeness, "Yes, Sergei?"

In spite of his resolutions, Roff felt his anger rising.

"There's a damn sight more behind this than I've been told, isn't there?" he snapped. "I just do not believe that the British Government is going to sanction twenty-six thousand dollars a day for the hire of this boat just to enable me to buy shares in some bloody subdivision!"

"It is not some bloody subdivision," Le Clerc replied urbanely, altogether happier when faced by others at a disadvantage; "it is a major development costing well over twenty-five million dollars. Now," he spoke as if Roff's objections had been finally dealt with, "let us waste no more time. You have been given your instructions and you are aware of the consequences which will certainly follow if you do not carry them out to the letter."

But he paused. And Roff read the pause. Le Clerc was trying to provoke him. Trying to tempt him to abandon the project and take the consequences. And he understood why. Because it was not only himself Le Clerc could never forgive, but Anita too. Because Anita had kept that vital paper she had lied to Le Clerc she had destroyed; because Anita had provided the means by which he had been outmanoeuvred. Le Clerc might be polite, might smile, might even joke—but within that mass of flesh lay a hatred which, whatever else might happen in the next few weeks, he must never forget existed.

He took his hands out of his pockets. "All right," he said. "Say what you have to say, then go."

But Le Clerc, victorious, was in no hurry. "Tell me," he said easily, "how is the fishing going? Have you managed to catch anything?"

In fact, for beginners, they had done quite well: kingfish, wahoo, dolphin and bonito had been amongst their catches and Petronella had even raised a marlin but it had slipped the hooks after five exciting minutes. And, for all the constraint which had to lie between a man and woman only one of whom understood the details of a project on which they were jointly involved, a constraint inevitably magnified by their unspoken agreement to keep their relationship platonic however great the temptation, for all of this the days spent side by side in fighting chairs under a broiling sun, learning the craft of deep-sea fishing, and then the shared evenings, had been pleasurable enough for Roff to have no wish to share these experiences with Le Clerc.

"As you'll no doubt have had a daily report of our progress," he answered, "you'll know perfectly well that we have caught fish, what fish we've caught and how we're making out as fishermen. So if there's nothing else . . ."

"But there is," Le Clerc interrupted. "As, except in an emergency, I shall see neither of you while you are in Grand Bahama, for which you will be leaving shortly, the time has come for your final briefing." He was clearly irritated. "Firstly, a mooring has been arranged at the Pompano Beach Hotel marina on the next pontoon to where a Japanese named Minahero—who after Kress is the largest shareholder in the Dragon Cay thing—keeps his yacht, which is even larger than *Fair Lady* and is called *Tsuki No Hikari*. As it is the only yacht there at the moment carrying the Japanese flag you will have no difficulty in recognising it and, having a yacht of roughly commensurate size, in striking up an acquaintance with Minahero which could be useful."

"Does he live on *his* yacht?" said Roff.

"No. He has two separate suites in the hotel, one of which he seems to use solely for entertaining. Secondly, if I want to contact you, I will leave a message, and return telephone number, addressed to Sergei Roff in the Pompano Beach Hotel."

"And if we want to contact you?" asked Petronella.

"If you want to contact me, you telephone Mr. Noel Baker at the Freeport Inn—no, Roff, don't bother to take notes. I will leave you with a dossier you are both to learn and then destroy—you telephone Noel Baker who will always know where I can be found. So far as contacting Kress is concerned, my enquiries lead me to believe that with the first stage of the development, which, by the way, is known as 'Oceanfront,' nearing completion and a full board meeting of the company due to take place about the time you arrive, he will certainly be on Grand Bahama. I hope I shall be able to let you know most evenings where he will be dining but in default you will book at El Morocco, which is his favourite restaurant." He chuckled, his good-humour apparently restored. "Appropriate, don't you think? He normally eats from about ten o'clock. You should have no difficulty in resuming your old acquaintanceship. And you will have much to talk about."

"How do I get into Grand Bahama as Sergei Roff when my passport is in the name of Karl Sodek?" Roff said coldly.

"Karl Sodek," Le Clarc responded blandly, "no longer exists." He reached for the envelope, opened it and, taking out numerous items, placed them on a side table near his chair, then selecting one, passed it to Roff. "Passport," Le Clerc said.

Roff opened it. Studied it. Shook his head, impressed. The passport was dated identically to the one in the name of Karl Sodek already in his possession. It was stamped with visas which, glancing through them, he was fairly sure mirrored the trips he had made over the last two years to Mexico, to Canada and to the Caribbean. Even the photograph was the same.

"Neat," he said, "but if Karl Sodek has been obliterated what happens to his businesses?"

Le Clerc reached for another document of legalistic-looking form comprising several pages. Roff started to finger it but Le Clerc interrupted him: "Don't bother with it now. Read it on the yacht."

"What is it?"

"It was fortunate," Le Clerc said, "that you didn't use your name as a title to your companies. That would have made things more complicated. That . . ." he pointed a podgy, but perfectly manicured finger, "once you have signed it, effectively transfers all the Karl Sodek holdings into the name of Sergei Roff. It has been prepared after consultation with leading American and English lawyers. And you will need these cheque-books . . ."

"My accounts have all been changed?"

"Of course. And these." One by one he announced and handed each item over. "American Express Card! Hertz Rentacar! Driving Licence!"

Roff stared mesmerised at the growing pile. "What about Anita?" he demanded.

"That has all been taken care of." Le Clerc resumed his listing. "Share transfers! Your general holdings on the Stock Exchange and so on. If you sign these before I leave—Petronella can witness—by the time you return from Grand Bahama all your stock holding will have been transferred into the name of Sergei Roff. Visiting cards!—I hope you approve the style of printing. Medical card! . . ."

So it went on. One by one, Le Clerc produced the items which together created the background to, and confirmed the reality of, a man of means. Karl Sodek had been sponged out. By the time he returned to San Francisco not a trace of him would remain. Such was the awful, terrifying power of two governments working in collusion.

"Finally," said Le Clerc, "your dossier. Please read it, learn it—both of you —and then destroy it. Now, if you will give me the equivalent items which a man named Karl Sodek who no longer exists used to possess, I will be on my way."

Roff shook his head.

"My dear fellow," said Le Clerc, very sure of his ground, "aren't you grateful that I have restored your old identity to you?" And when there was no reply. "It's all quite useless now, you know—documention covering Karl Sodek. It's not a question that he isn't any longer; it's that he never was."

Again Roff shook his head. And there was silence. Silence except for the sound of distant laughter from the poolside and the faint sigh of waves on a deep sand beach. And the tension mounted in that comfortable, if unremark-able suite in the Fontainebleau Hotel, Miami Beach. Petronella, watching, waiting, lit a nervous cigarette and the scratch of the match was louder than the laughter and the waves, and the smell of its sulphur was strong.

"I think there is one more document you have to give to me," Roff said quietly. And when Le Clerc gestured to the empty table top, "Don't play games. You know exactly what I want."

"Oh that," said Le Clerc contemptuously. He put his hand inside his jacket and from an inner pocket withdrew an envelope which he threw casu-ally to Roff, who opened it, took out the document it contained, read it slowly through to its end.

"You hated that, George, didn't you?" Roff said. He got to his feet. "All right. I'll sign these transfers and Petronella can witness them and I'll give you all the Karl Sodek material. But I warn you, Le Clerc, if, when all of this is over, harm has come to Anita, or the promises this document makes"—he waved it slowly—"are not honoured to the very last particular, I shall make it my business to seek you out and as God is my witness, I shall kill you."

FOUR

The yacht *Fair Lady* had been built for a Frenchman in the late nineteen-twenties and had known only two subsequent owners through the next sixty or so years before being bought by an international firm of yacht charterers who, regardless of expense, had had her quite superbly modernised in the Pons yard in Barcelona, so that, while none of her style was lost, she was transformed into a classic yacht for modern-day chartering. Nearly one hun-dred and forty feet in length and with a beam of over twenty feet, driven by a pair of powerful German-built Deutz engines there was no ocean she was not capable of tackling with contemptuous ease.

Roff and Petronella, delivered by a chauffeur-driven Rolls-Royce, were ap-propriately impressed.

"You know something, Sergei," Petronella chuckled, "I'm not at all sure I can carry this off!"

"Not to worry," he said, "when it's Emperor's new clothes."

"Eh?"

"The prerogative of the very rich is to behave in ways which in the poor would attract attention. Come on."

They climbed the gangplank. At the top, awaiting them, resplendent in white uniform and gold braid, was the captain, a tall, large-featured man of about Roff's own age with a pepper and salt moustache and pointed beard.

"Good afternoon, madam," he said, with a small bow. "Good afternoon, sir. Welcome aboard."

"Good morning, Captain Stewart. A pleasant day."

"It is indeed, sir."

Stewart led the way, informing them in the easy manner of one experienced in his task.

". . . when she was refitted, the entire upper deck was removed and this saloon was largely constructed from the materials they salvaged . . . This we call the card room . . ."

"Charming," Petronella said.

"Yes, madam, it is a delightful room, isn't it? The principal stateroom is known as the 'Venice Suite.' It used to be two single cabins; all they did basically was to remove the partition. I didn't order your baggage to be unpacked. We do have clients we prefer to do it themselves."

"No, that's all right. Have it done."

"I'll have it seen to directly. When would you like to sail, sir?"

"Oh, more or less right away."

"And meeting the crew?"

"Say in ten minutes. On the upper after deck, I think. And what do you think, Peta? Champagne? Or champagne cocktails?"

"Just champagne, Sergei."

"If you'll ask the steward?"

"Of course. If you'll excuse me, sir. Madam."

When Stewart had gone, Roff held out both his hands to Petronella. "Well done."

"I say," she said, taking hold of them. "Ain't 'arf something, ain't it!"

He chuckled. "Ain't it just?"

They stood a yard apart, arms level, looking into each other's eyes. "I could get very used to this, you know," she said.

He nodded. "It would not be all that difficult."

And suddenly he took her in his arms and, for the first time, kissed her. And she did not resist.

Still with his arms around her, she said quickly, "Look, why don't we go to Nassau first? And then Eleuthera? Why don't we go all round?"

"Le Clerc . . ."

"Bugger, Le Clerc!"

She broke away from him suddenly, surprising him.

"Sergei," she said, "I shouldn't be saying even this much but I'm going to. Only don't ask me anything more. There *is* much more in this business than they've told you. And once we get to Grand Bahama there's . . . well, there's danger. From Tuesday we're supposed to be in cahoots with your old friend Laurence Kress. But today's only Saturday so we've got three whole days. Why don't we use those three days being what we're supposed to be? A man as rich as Croesus and his mistress swanning around the Bahamas." She paused. "While we can?"

2

They left within the hour, at first buoyed up by an almost schoolboy, sense of glee; but this exhilaration was quickly replaced by an odd feeling of presumption which was not so much caused by their temerity at cocking a snook at their masters as by the ridiculous size and opulence of the *Fair Lady*. And, having met the crew, been served their champagne in the sheltered deck abaft the saloon and ordered lunch, both were aware of a curious sense of rootlessness.

"Do you think," she said, "they're in the know?"

"The crew?"

"Yes. I mean . . ." she stared beyond the gentle boil of *Fair Lady*'s wake at the line of Miami Beach hotels, now low on the horizon. "I mean, are they the usual lot? The normal crew? And if they are, how much do they know?"

"I should think," said Roff, "it has to be the normal crew and they know nothing. But it's quite possible they've been tipped off not to disturb us. After all," he glanced at her lying in the chaise longue beside him, "I don't imagine they really believe you're Mrs. Roff."

They raised Bimini before sunset, invited to the bridge by Stewart as soon as the first faint haze of its casuarina trees came into sight. It had been an uneventful voyage across the sixty or so miles from Miami with only the passing freighter or tanker or the odd fishing cruiser in the Gulf Strait to remind them the world was not entirely theirs. It had been dead calm at first, then roughening a little with wavelets flecked with white in the afternoon breeze, then calming down again, so that now the sea was smooth enough for the flying fish to pattern the water and for the bow wave of *Fair Lady* to draw an extending arrow either side.

"Alice Town," said Stewart, pointing towards a collection of

weatherboarded houses sheltered by coconut palms behind a dazzling white
sand beach.

"Do we anchor there?" asked Petronella.

"Entirely as you wish, madam. We can find a mooring in the marina or
simply anchor in the roads. It depends on whether you want to go ashore or
not."

"Is there anything to see?"

"Not really. It's mostly geared for fishing, which is about the best there is
anywhere in the world."

"What do you think, Sergei?" And, before he could have answered, "I
don't think I want to bother with going ashore. Not on our first night." And,
to Stewart, "Can I steer her in?"

He shook his head. "No, madam, I'd rather you didn't. It's quite a narrow
channel." And then, relenting, "Of course if you aren't in a hurry we could
go in the long way round, and then you could."

"We're not in a hurry," Petronella said. "Not in any hurry at all."

"Right then, madam," Stewart said, standing aside. "She's all yours. Keep
her steady as she is until you pass Rabbit Keys—that's those tiny islets where
the land runs out. Then steer on ninety-five degrees. You can read that on the
binnacle beside you. When we've passed South Island, I'll take over, if you
don't mind."

"Yes, Captain," said Petronella with a mock salute and took the wheel.

Seeing the tenseness of her body, the sparkle in her eyes, her hair blown by
the breeze from the open bridge windows playing around her eager face, Roff
was thinking different things: that she wasn't acting her role correctly; that
there ought to be a hardness in her which was lacking; that she exemplified
all that a man could look for in a woman: animation, beauty, gaiety, excitement, joie de vivre; that the touch of her body against his own in that first
kiss had brought into the open something he had refused to admit before:
that he was falling in love with her.

But for the moment she had quite forgotten him. With the wheel in her
hands of a sudden, the magnificent yacht had come to life in a way it had not
been alive to her before. And for the first time she really understood what it
was the very rich grasped which was denied to the balance of mankind and
why they schemed, fought, cheated, blackmailed, even murdered to retain
that grasp. *Fair Lady* exemplified it. Power.

3

They dined by candlelight seated at either end of an elliptical mahogany
table superbly dressed with fine linen table-mats and napkins, branched can-
delabras and a low centrepiece of roses. They were served impeccably by the

steward assisted by one of the two stewardesses and the chef paid them a visit to ensure that everything was perfectly to their taste.

Coffee was served on the open deck space directly below the bridge from which the day awning had been removed. Anchored as they were in the natural harbour formed by the enclosing inner shores of North, South and East Bimini, there were in all directions little scatters of lights of which the great majority were from Alice Town and Bailey's Town and from the bobbing lights of fishing cruisers and other craft tied up to the slips. But the greatest concentration of all was in the sky above. The tide was ebbing fast with a steady, rustling noise along *Fair Lady*'s sides as she strained against her anchors, and from the shore floated the sound of music. Now and then some great fish, hunting nearby, crashed the surface, splintering the stars into dancing lights.

They had dressed quite formally, Roff in white tuxedo and Petronella in an evening gown—it had seemed appropriate—and for a while they sat in silence, Petronella smoking, Roff content to enjoy her company and the magic of the warm, still evening. Then she said, "Sergei. In Tucson you asked me if I wanted the details which led up to you being involved in this. And I said, no—not until we've got to know each other better." And, with her eyes holding his: "We've got to know each other better, haven't we? And we're going to get to know each other better still."

He agreed. "Yes."

"Tell me about it. We've all the time in the world."

"Where shall I start?"

"Where it had been made by Shapland to look as if you'd embezzled the funds of Kress's company."

"No. That had to have been organised by Kress himself. Obviously they had some hold on him."

"You don't know what?"

"No. Anyway, he'll have got a clearance from them as his price. So that side doesn't matter. The reason why they wanted me out—MI6—was so that my place could be taken by one of their agents who, with both of us having plastic surgery, in my case this, and this . . ." he tapped his nose and scar, "could take over my identity. Then, three years later, when this agent's cover had been blown, they wanted me back so that the KGB could liquidate me instead of him!"

"Leaving him free to keep on doing whatever it was that he was doing, with the KGB believing him a goner?"

"Yes. But of course ahead of being liquidated, I had to step back into the shoes that this character had been keeping warm for me."

"You mean go back to your wife?"

"That and more. Go back to the same house in the same village. Drink in the same pub. Chat to the same locals. Of course they all thought I was mad."

"Why?"

"You don't know how they tricked me into going back?" She shook her head. "By faking an obituary of Sergei Roff in a daily newspaper and making sure a copy got to me in Casablanca."

"I don't believe it!"

He chuckled. "You'd better. Sounds damn funny now but it wasn't at the time. Had me crawling round the churchyard looking for my grave! And when I couldn't find it, into the pub, insulting the villagers and spilling my spaghetti bolognese all over them."

"Sergei!"

"Why shouldn't you miss the point?" He waited as a late-returning fishing cruiser passed fairly close to them, its red and green navigation lights reflecting prettily in the water. Someone aboard hailed an "evening" to them. And Roff replied. And then the boat was gone. Momentarily *Fair Lady* rocked gently and then fell still again.

"You see," he resumed, "at the time I hadn't the least idea that someone had been pretending to be me for all those years, living with my wife in my house—well, actually her house—running my Bond Street travel business and all the rest of it. For all of three long years I'd presumed that the moment anyone recognized me for who I really was, I'd be arrested. Of course as the months went by I started to put it more and more out of my mind but the moment I read that fake obituary it all came flooding back. I *had* to go back to England to find out what it was all about even, as I thought, at the risk that the instant I was recognized it would all be up. But, no! Not a bit of it! Everyone greeted me like a long lost brother who'd never been away! Can you imagine what that was like? I was confused, perplexed— and damn frightened! I began to wonder if I was going mad and acted accordingly. But, of course, friend Shapland and company had worked that out as well. Early on, the village had been briefed I'd had a terrible car accident—which explained my face; and a few weeks before I came back, briefed I'd had a nervous breakdown." He shook his head. "You have to admit it was brilliantly put together."

"But," she said, "your wife . . ."

"Wasn't! American actress. In the set-up. I found that out afterwards. When they'd paid her off."

"But you thought you'd married her?"

"Sure I did. Registry office. Witnesses. The whole shebang. Beautifully faked."

"Were you in love with her?"

"Valerie? No, not really. I've only loved one woman in my life. Jennie."

"Tell me about Jennie?"

He shook his head. "No. She died in childbirth. So did the child. A lifetime ago. I was a different person then. There's no point in talking about Jennie."

Petronella knew better than pursue it. "But you married Valerie," she said.

"Yes. I'm the kind of man who has to have a woman to share his life with him. Alone, I'm incomplete. Oh, I can manage. I have inner resources. But I'm incomplete. Valerie? She was interesting. Attractive. Elegant." He smiled faintly. "Matter of fact you and she have certain similarities. Eyes. Hair. Same sort of colour. Only she didn't do her hair like you do." He looked at her gold red hair flowing down her back, and imagined it flowing over her naked body. For he knew that nothing was more certain that they would make love that night.

"And Anita?" she said.

"I never loved Anita."

"And yet you're doing all this for her."

"She did as much and more for me."

And he explained. "She was palmed on me in Casablanca."

"By Shapland?"

"Yes. She was supposed to be working with Le Clerc. Her job was to let him know at once anything important I did. Any change in my appearance. If I grew a beard, as in fact I did, it would be reported back to London so that the other me should grow a beard as well. Or shave it off."

"Did she become your mistress?"

"Yes."

"Do you think those were her instructions?"

"I don't know. I never asked her. And I wouldn't now. Anyway, at the end, when the KGB had blown up the wrong man by mistake and Le Clerc and his bunch were coming to collect me to make sure that little gaffe passed by unnoticed, she saved my bacon because she'd kept the faked copy of the newspaper which she'd told Le Clerc she'd destroyed."

"And which was the last thing they wanted to fall into Russian hands."

"Yes. So there you have it, Peta. I don't love Anita, and I never have. But we get on famously, we've lived together for four years or so and I'm everlastingly grateful. And, until I met you, I never looked at another woman seriously."

She put out a quick hand. He understood. This kind of utterance was not acceptable.

He got to his feet and, going to the deck rail, leaned on it, watching a white light pooling on the sea approaching them, listening to the creak of rowlocks, watching the dinghy all the time until it had gone on past them leaving a phosphorescent wake. "Fishing, I suppose," he said, coming back to his chair. "The sea's writhing with fish. I never heard so many in my life."

And it was true, you only had to sit back and listen and you heard them all the time.

After a while he said, "When we do get to Grand Bahama, you're going to have to be different."

"I know."

"Mistresses of very rich men twice their age are hard as nails. It's a well known fact."

"Is it?" She turned to face him. "Sergei. I'm not going to get sentimental. And you mustn't either. If we're to do what we've got to do . . ."

"Sentiment is out?"

She ignored the smile. "Well sentimentality is. I don't want this cigarette." She stood abruptly, went to the side of the boat and threw it into the sea. There were no fish jumping just then and he heard the brief snuffed-out hiss. "Come on," she said.

"We won't have many nights like this," he told her.

"Damn you, Sergei!" she said.

The card-room lights had been switched off but the star glow and the yacht's riding lights gently illuminated her in the long, sleeveless, oyster-coloured dress, simple but superbly cut.

"When we get to Grand Bahama," he said, "you'll become another person. I may even find it difficult to remember the person you were. I shall have to tell myself that the woman Kress is talking to isn't really the woman he believes her to be. But I may find it difficult to believe that myself. You won't forget that, will you?"

She made a pace towards him and stood looking down at him, her head slightly bent.

"You are a very generous man, Sergei," she said. And, holding out her hands, "come on, I want to be by ourselves."

When they were, in the beautiful stateroom which had been made out of two single cabins, in the wide double bed which had been converted from two single beds, she said quietly, "Stay like that, Sergei. Just for a little while. Don't do anything."

And so he controlled himself and even moved away from her.

They lay for quite some time in silence, both concentrating in the nearness of their bodies, in the being truly by themselves. And then, as if the point had at last been sufficiently proved, she ordered him quietly, "All right, Sergei, make love to me. As if the first time was to be our last and you didn't want anyone else ever to make love to me again."

FIVE

"Don't look now," Roff said, "but he's just come in."

"Thank the Lord for that," said Petronella. "I was beginning to feel conspicuous. Anyone with him?"

"Yes. And she's not his wife."

He watched over her shoulder as the headwaiter bustled across to greet Laurence Kress.

"You'd better describe her," Petronella said, "or I won't be able to resist it."

"She's a stunner. About your age. Local stock, I'd say. Jet black hair. Very high cheekbones. And something of the Orient in her as well. In the eyes."

"I can see her. I thought you told me women didn't interest him."

"That girl would interest anybody."

A waiter was pulling out Kelly Brown's chair. Kress was chatting to the Maître d' who was all attention.

"I can't bear it," Petronella said. She reached for her bag and taking out a compact pretended the discovery of a blemish.

"Got 'em!" she said with satisfaction, viewing Kress through the mirror. "How many years since you've seen him?"

"About five."

"Has he changed much?"

Roff called to mind the first meeting with Laurence Kress. Flying over with Valerie to Jersey and then having to wait a full hour for their host to present himself, enduring Dilys's complaints meanwhile. The relief when

Kress came in: well made, fiftyish, his shrewd dark eyes glinting behind his heavy spectacles. His firm handshake; his voice, warm, assured, welcoming.

"No," he told her. "Hardly at all."

"Do you think he'll recognize you?" she said.

"Probably not."

"He never saw you after you'd had your plastic surgery?"

"No."

"And he probably didn't know what they did to you. I mean . . ." She hesitated. "I mean when you think of it they probably wouldn't have wanted him to know what you *did* look like when they'd finished with you, would they?"

A waistcoated waiter topped up their wineglasses. When he had gone, Roff said, "One of the things that always puzzled me is why he agreed to frame me. I would have thought if anyone was too smart to have put himself in the position of being blackmailed, it was Laurence Kress."

"Too smart now," she said.

He nodded. "That's probably it." He stared at Kress, not thirty feet away, and caught his eye.

"Doesn't recognize me," he told her. "Which means it's up to us." He came back to what they had been discussing. "Yes. He'd have learnt the hard way, I suppose."

"D'you know how he made his money?"

"Well it was in property. I knew that much. But he played his beginnings pretty close to his chest. I think he liked conveying the impression he'd more or less always been successful."

"Which you didn't believe?"

"No. Because of Dilys who hadn't developed with him—the ordinariness which must at one time have been acceptable to him was still there and he didn't like it. He treated her like dirt. It was the one strike I had against him at the start—the way he treated Dilys. In every other way he was delightful company." He thought for a moment. "There was something else too," he said. "He was inclined to overwork the business of being a tycoon. Of having experience and knowledge of things where lesser mortals would have been thin on the ground. Wine. Food. Hotels. Restaurants. Travel. That sort of thing. Men who've *always* had money don't have to prove it."

"Sounds like an inferiority complex."

"You wouldn't think so looking at him now."

"He's probably lost it. It's wonderful what having a lot of money for a lot of time can do for you." She chuckled. "Give me a month on *Fair Lady* and I'd run even Elizabeth Taylor close." She reached for a cigarette. "D'you mind?"

"No sweet?"

"Just coffee."

"In other words you want to get it over with."

"In other words I'm burning with curiosity."

They paused as they passed Kress's table.

"Good evening," Roff said quietly.

Kress, busy with his starter, looked up.

"Sergei Roff."

Just for a moment, Kress's eyes half closed in disbelief. But his recovery was remarkable.

"My dear chap!" He seemed to discover Petronella. "I'm so sorry!" He rose to his feet.

"Darling," said Roff, "I should like you to meet an old friend . . . a very old friend. Laurence Kress. Laurence, Petronella."

Kress bowed. "Delighted to meet you, Petronella."

"How do you do?" said Petronella with contrived uninterest.

Kress gestured. "My secretary, Miss Kelly Brown."

"Hallo," said Kelly.

"Waiter!" Kress called.

"No, we mustn't disturb you," Roff said. "I remember you once told me that to interrupt a man in the middle of a well-chosen dinner was even worse than interrupting him in a game of chess."

Kress waved away the passing waiter and remarked, "You have an excellent memory, Sergei. And, as I recall, whenever we did play chess, you always beat me. Probably because your memory *is* so good."

"Yes," Roff said. "I have an excellent memory."

Petronella was exhibiting impatience. "Sergei . . ."

"Yes. Of course." He looked back to Kress. "If you've nothing better to do after dinner, I should be delighted if you . . . you and Miss Brown . . . would care to join us. For a nightcap."

Kress made no attempt to hide his deliberation. He sees us, thought Roff, as a couple of trippers passing through. It's only curiosity at seeing me here at all that stops him turning us down out of hand.

"Where are you staying?" The lack of enthusiasm was confirmation. Shapland's point was made. If he'd only been able to offer an hotel, that would have been the end of it.

"We're on a yacht that's lying in the Pompano Beach marina," Roff said.

"It's a big marina." There was interest now.

"She's called *Fair Lady*. You shouldn't have any difficulty in picking her out. She's at the next slip to one yacht of about the same size flying a Japanese flag. Shall we say . . . eleven?"

Kress paused, his instincts advising him against the promptings of curiosity. Curiosity triumphed.

"We shall be delighted."

Everything would have been very different—if instinct had been followed.

2

"Who *was* that man?" asked Kelly.

"That man," said Kress, staring after the departing Sergei Roff, "was a nonentity I once used as a catspaw."

Kelly raised her heavy eyebrows. "And now he's got a yacht about as big as Minahero's?"

"He said he was *on* a yacht. But it's certainly very odd."

Kress pondered on how much to tell her and then decided to tell her very little. To tell her the full story would have been to tell her too much about himself—and to have to relive the crucifying half hour when, seated like a petty criminal in front of Shapland and his two assistants, he was told exactly what he had to do if he was to avoid prison for falsification of the minutes of one of his companies and the bankruptcy which would inevitably follow.

Kelly Brown waited patiently. Hers was a rare and splendid job which she had no intention of putting at risk. She admired her employer without fully understanding him and the thing she understood least of all was his indifference to her sexually. The demands he *did* make of her were very clear: scrupulous attention to detail, total dedication to her job and absolute confidentiality. He paid her handsomely (but not absurdly) and, having trained her in Bahamian Company Law and the essentials of property development, used her both as a sounding board and a check on the correspondence passing through Grand Bahama in his absence. She was not in love with him, nor even attracted by him, and, although had he suggested she become his mistress she would have agreed, was intelligent enough to be relieved he didn't do so.

"Who would be the person to tell us?"

She recognized the tone; he was not asking her, but himself.

"Yes," she heard him muse. "Whisky Gordon."

He called to a waiter. "Bring me a telephone." And when the man went off. "What's Whisky Gordon's telephone number?"

She told him and when the waiter had brought the telephone and plugged it in, she got him the number, checked she was through correctly and handed him the instrument.

"Gordon," she heard him say. "Laurence Kress. There's a yacht called *Fair Lady* lying in the slip next to Minahero's. Find out everything you can about it. Who owns it; how long it's been on Grand Bahama; the number of passengers on it and anything you can about them. I'm at El Morocco. Phone me back with everything you can get without fail within the next hour."

Within forty-five minutes the call was returned. When the instrument had again been removed, he said to Kelly Brown, "It's owned by Newport Marine of Half Moon Street, London. It left Miami about a week ago and made a circuitous trip round Bimini, Andros, Nassau and Eleuthera before docking here. It's been hired on an open-ended charter by a Mr. Sergei Roff who's accompanied by a girl friend posing half-heartedly as his wife. There are no immediate departure plans."

"You were right then," Kelly said. "He doesn't own it."

"No," Kress agreed, nodding thoughtfully. "He doesn't own it. But the normal charter fee is approaching thirty thousand dollars a day and the last time I saw Sergei Roff he was absolutely penniless."

3

The saloon of *Fair Lady* was opulently furnished and superbly equipped; the walls were panelled. Seating was, apart from one or two occasional chairs, of banquette style in the shape of an uneven *U*.

Petronella and Kelly, next to each other, were drinking liqueurs, Kress and Roff a '61 Hine Champagne Cognac.

"Superb," commented Kress. "Tremendous finesse."

"Yes," said Roff. "The cellar is magnificent."

"It's not your selection then?"

"No, Laurence. But you know it's better this way with it being so difficult to pick up decent wines in places like Miami Beach. How do you handle it?"

"Oh, I have mine shipped from London. Or direct from the chateaux."

These were the opening pawn moves of a game of chess between two probing opponents. Neither was anxious to disclose his strategy; indeed neither had yet decided what his strategy should be.

"You live here all the time? On Grand Bahama?"

"God, no! I'm just renting something."

"So where do you mainly live? Still on Jersey?"

Kress shook his head. "Jersey was a mistake. I have a house in New Providence—Lyford Cay. And a flat in Geneva. And you?"

"Tucson, mainly. And a New York apartment."

"Tucson?"

"The climate suits me." Roff smiled faintly. "Also it reminds me of Morocco."

"I must go to Morocco sometime. One of the places I've never visited. Do you like Morocco, Petronella?"

"I've never been, either. Nor likely to. Sergei, would you mind?" She waved an unlit cigarette.

"Allow me." Kress reached for the table lighter as near to Petronella as to himself.

"Thank you." She drew on the cigarette, crossed her trousered legs and regarded him deliberately. "Which hotel would you recommend on Grand Bahama?"

"I've told you," Roff said testily, "We are not going to stay in a hotel."

"Oh, for God's sake, Sergei!" She turned her head. "Well, Mr. Kress?"

"Horses for courses. But . . ." the pause held meaning, "for you, probably this one." He waved a hand.

"The Pompano Beach, you mean?"

He nodded. "You haven't used it?"

"Oh yes. Of course. Lunch. The odd drink."

"They have some excellent top-floor suites with terraces."

"I'd like to look at one, Sergei."

"Once and for all we are not moving into a hotel!"

"I was merely asking."

"I must say," rescued Kress, "I would rather live on this boat than in a Grand Bahamian hotel with all those trippers."

"You have a boat?"

Kress smiled. "Of course."

"Do you use it much?"

"Not all that often."

"You don't fish? I thought that was all that people did who came to the Bahamas. Fish. It's all Sergei seems to want to do."

"My dear Petronella, they do a lot of other things as well as fish. Yes, I fish occasionally. But I'm not all that keen and in any case my yacht isn't suitable."

"Where do you keep it?"

"By the house I'm renting. It has its own dock. If you aren't keen on slaughtering creatures far more beautiful than ourselves, when Sergei goes off fishing why not come and spend the day at Eagle Rock?"

"I might do that," Petronella said.

Roff got to his feet and crossed to the sideboard.

"No more for me," said Kress.

Roff poured himself another brandy. "Kelly?"

"Thank you, Mr. Roff." She had a pleasant, lilting, Bahamian voice.

"I'd like that," Petronella said. "Spending a day or two on dry land for a change."

"If you remember," Roff said icily, "it was your idea we should charter this damn yacht."

"It's a fine yacht," Kress said. "Very . . . elegant. What's it's history?"

Roff told him. Kress listened intently, asking the odd question to show his interest was maintained.

Kelly said, "What did you say her name was, Mr. Roff?"

"*Fair Lady.*"

"I don't think she's ever been here before."

"I believe she's been mostly in the Med since her refit."

"You haven't chartered her before?" Kress said.

"I've never chartered any yacht before. Except for fishing."

"Are you going to do any fishing while you're here?"

"That's why I came. Who should I see to organise it?"

"I might be able to arrange something. A business associate of mine has a seventy-foot Knight and Carver fishing cruiser."

"Really?" said Roff, managing to look impressed.

"In fact I might even join you. Providing Petronella comes, of course. Or we might combine the two things. Have a day's fishing and then dinner at Eagle Rock. Remind me to speak to Minahero, Kelly, will you?"

"Yes, Mr. Kress."

"Minahero?" said Petronella.

"A Japanese gentleman I'm involved in business with." He told them about Dragon Cay, and then, before Roff could question him, "And what have you been doing all these years, Sergei?"

"Taking your advice. No, seriously, I'm very grateful to you. But for you, I'd still be running a Bond Street travel agency."

"That still exists?"

"I doubt it."

"And the Morocco agency?"

"I doubt that too." He glanced at Kelly. "She doesn't know?" Kress shook his head. "And you wouldn't mind?"

"I would rely on your tact. Subject to that, no, I wouldn't mind." He spoke to Kelly. "That scar and that broken nose—I'm partly responsible. A little matter of plastic surgery. I was creating a new identity for Mr. Roff. He became . . ." He looked at the deck-beamed ceiling. "Michael Downley, as I recall . . . But you seem to have got over that little problem, Sergei."

"Yes."

"I'd be interested in knowing how."

"Did you know," said Roff, choosing his words carefully, "what lay behind it all?"

Kress paused. "In other words," he said, "you no longer take it at face value."

"I've often wondered," Roff replied, "exactly why you were persuaded."

"Please do go on. I'm very interested," Kress said.

"They wanted me out of the country so that they could have someone take my place."

"A spy!" put in Petronella.

"Yes," said Roff quietly. "A spy."

"Mr. Roff is half Russian," Kress explained to Kelly. "He had a travel business which specialized in travel to the Soviet Union. He used to go there frequently himself. So when the British Government . . . well MI5 . . ."

"Six," Roff corrected him.

"Really?" said Kress good-humouredly. "So when MI6 wanted to infiltrate one of their men with a first-class cover they hit on Mr. Roff who was not only accepted by the Soviet authorities but spoke Russian fluently into the bargain."

It was well done, mused Roff—considering that until only moments earlier Kress had obviously had only a sketchy idea as to why he had been suborned.

"But of course," Kress went on breezily, "I never knew the end of it." He shrugged. "I was very busy at the time with a development in Spain."

"Benevente."

"As you say, Benevente. But tell me. What *did* happen?"

"They faked his obituary in *The Daily Chronicle* and made sure he got a copy," said Petronella, looking at Roff.

"How absolutely fascinating," Kress said.

"Apparently the cover of the man who took my place was blown," Roff explained. "I suppose they wanted him for other work so they tricked me into coming back so that the KGB could liquidate me . . ."

"Leaving the spy with a nice clear run. What a clever idea. So what happened?"

"The KGB killed the wrong man thinking it was me and I'd managed to keep the faked copy of *The Daily Chronicle.*"

"Leaving you with a royal flush. Hm." Kress was impressed. "How much did you take them for?"

"A million sterling and a hundred thousand a year so long as the spy was still in business for them."

Kress was impressed. "A cool million! Needs courage to ask for as much as that. And tell me—are you still getting the hundred thousand a year?"

"No," Roff answered. "But it doesn't matter. It was enough to build on."

"Doing what?"

"What you taught me. Property development. I told you, Laurence, I'm very grateful."

"Where do you do your land development?"

"California mostly. And, do you know Arizona at all?" Kress shook his head, interested now, everything else, Kelly, Petronella, the yacht in which they sat, forgotten. "There's a place called Tombstone."

"You're doing something there?"

"Couple of thousand acres. Ranch. Retirement cottages. Two golf courses. Hotel. Apartments."

"Really," said Kress. "Really." And, after a moment, "You've come a long way, Sergei. I'm glad to think that I have been of help."

4

"Well what d'you make of all that?"

Kress was driving Kelly home.

"How do you mean, Mr. Kress?"

"You think that was coincidence? Roff and that girl being in the same restaurant?"

"Why shouldn't it be?"

He nodded. "Yes. Theoretically. Any man who makes himself rich is liable to have a look at the Bahamas sooner or later and as likely as not try El Morocco."

He was silent for a while.

"On the other hand," he said, "he may have come here for the specific purpose of finding me."

"Why?"

"Could be one of several things. Ego. Proving he's succeeded, too. I would."

"Would you?"

"If I were him, yes, I think I would. I don't think I could resist it."

Kelly wasn't surprised; he often used her as a sounding board. With anyone else she might have said that that was honest at any rate but if ever she'd made such a remark to Kress, he would never have expressed such a confidence to her again. So she said nothing.

"All those years in Casablanca," Kress mused. "Dwelling on it. Beginning to suspect you'd been set up. Then finally finding out you had been. It must have eaten into him." He stared at his headlights raking the sea, breaking on a distant reef, as the road curved sharply. "You wouldn't think, would you, Kelly, that he'd ever come to see me as a benefactor? Even if by a peculiar twist of circumstances it all resulted in him making a lot of money."

"No. You wouldn't."

"Do you know where he was when I last saw him? In a dreadful little room in an inn called the Auberge du Chat near a village called Ploermel. It didn't even have a washbasin. It didn't even have a wardrobe. Just a dreadful-looking lumpy bed covered by a dirty counterpane and a chest of drawers. I didn't spend ten minutes with him. Just threw him a few shirts and things and told him he'd have to stay there until I could arrange to have him sent somewhere to be cut about by a plastic surgeon. Could you ever forgive someone who did that to you, Kelly?"

"No."

"And if you suddenly found yourself very rich, what would you do?"

"I might kill the man who'd done it to me."

"Do you think it's possible he's come here to kill me?"

"It could be."

"And the girl?" And when she didn't answer. "If you'd come all the way to Grand Bahama to kill a man, would you complicate things by bringing a girl with you?"

"They're not getting on."

"Aren't they? Or is *that* pretence? I wonder. Here we are."

He drew the coupe to a halt in front of her neat little bungalow. It was a warm, still night. The sky was filled with stars.

"Do you think he has come here to kill you? Or have you killed?" she said.

He shook his head. "Not really. It's too melodramatic altogether."

"I think you should be very careful?"

He nodded. "That's right."

"And I think," she said, "you ought to let him know that you've thought about it. Told me you've thought about it. Then he wouldn't dare do it."

"That's not good thinking, Kelly," he said.

"Why not?"

"Because if he's come here for some purpose, by telling him I suspect him I'll be putting him on his guard. And then I'd never find out. Until too late maybe."

"So what are you going to do?"

"Invite him to take a look at Dragon Cay. Invite both of them. Listen to what they say. Watch how they are towards each other when they think no one's looking at them. And have them checked out. When you go in, I want you to do two things. Phone Whisky Gordon and have him run a full check on them. And tell Jim Woolgar to keep one of the Aztecs free for Friday."

"What time is it?"

He looked at the car clock. "Half past twelve. Yes, I know. Gordon will be in bed and Woolgar at the Casino or some damn nightclub. Never mind.

Wake up Gordon and try every place in town until you track down Woolgar. But get hold of both of them somehow. All right?"

"Yes, Mr. Kress. Goodnight."

"Goodnight, Kelly."

She opened the door and got out, then paused. "Mr. Kress?" she said.

"Yes, Kelly?"

"If he had come here to kill you, would you be very frightened?"

He shook his head. "No, Kelly, I wouldn't be frightened." But that was a lie.

SIX

Woolgar was a young man in his prime living precisely the life which millions of young men throughout the world would love to live. A rangy, blue-eyed Australian whose curly hair had been streaked blonde by half a dozen years swanning round the Bahamas and the Caribbean, he was currently engaged by Oceanfront to ferry its directors and would-be land or cottage buyers from Grand Bahama to Dragon Cay in one of the two Piper Aztecs the company owned.

Kress, with impressive agility, was pulling himself aboard, ducking through the open doorway. Roff, following, took the seat beside him.

Woolgar slipped into his seat on the port side ahead of Kress and Petronella slipped in beside him ahead of Roff and pulled shut the cockpit door.

"Seat belts on," he ordered. He started up the engines and began to taxi out, busy getting his clearances sorted out with the West End auxiliary airfield control on the intercom as he did so. He turned his head momentarily to Petronella seated so close their shoulders all but touched. "Take her off with me," he suggested. "Get the feel of her."

Kress's thoughts, meanwhile, were elsewhere. Staring down at the brilliant sea, dazzling emerald over the pure white sand of the Little Bahama Bank, trying to still the trepidation which no amount of flying in smaller aircraft could ever quite remove, he tried to concentrate on the matters immediately to hand. The puzzle of Roff's sudden materialization was in no way solved.

His first enquiries had checked out the assertions made by the man beside him. And, remarkable though it might be, a man he had last known penniless, a mere travel agent, had in a mere five years become wealthy, even possibly wealthier than himself.

So, as he stared down at a sea so clear that the shadow of his own aircraft could be seen chasing across the white coral sand beneath it, he was wondering about Roff's attitude. Incapable of forgiveness himself, he simply could not believe a man could be so used as he had used Sergei Roff and not nurse dreams of vengeance. And then the girl? Petronella. Is she his mistress or some actress hired to play the part? He concentrated on what he recollected had passed between them. Her brittleness to Roff? Not unusual—he had seen rich men enough who would never accept an insult from contemporaries but would tolerate ill-humor, public slights, even humiliation from their mistresses; it was, after all, one of the reasons why he had always rejected advances made to him by such women. And then again, if this woman who called herself Petronella, was only playing the part of mistress to a wealthy man twice her age, then wouldn't it be that much *more* convincing if she publicly complained, made unreasonable demands, showed uninterest and generally needled him?

Already half-persuaded by his own reasoning, Kress glanced at the girl seated in the co-pilot's seat diagonally just a few feet from him and was convinced. Petronella was flying the Aztec, her hands on the yoke control, the skirt of her dress recklessly hauled up above her knees, her head slightly bent towards Woolgar to catch above the sound of the two Lycoming engines something he was whispering to her. They might or might not be man and mistress, but they were certainly accomplices. Their coming to Grand Bahama was part of a carefully planned operation, their meeting him in his favourite restaurant no accident.

Woolgar tapped the let-down plate strapped to his left knee. "Like to try and find Dragon Cay from this yourself or shall I give you the instructions?"

"Give me the instructions."

"Will do." He stared over the aircraft's nose at the distant long, low island of Abaco which stretched out ahead of them in a series of dazzling white sand beaches caressed by reef-protected water of amazing turquoise.

For the moment she had forgotten everything but piloting the aircraft. Forgotten the two men behind her, forgotten the mission which had brought her out to the Bahamas, forgotten her doubts, her fears, her anger, her grim determination at all costs to do what she had volunteered to do. All she was conscious of was the ribbed lines of the rudder pedals through the thin soles of her sandals, the vibration of the aircraft through the control yoke in her hands, the steady engines' note, the glory of the beautiful scenery around her, the hot sun, the blue sky, the emerald and turquoise sea, the joy of living, the challenge of the immediate task ahead.

She heard ground control come in and advise the wind speed and direction on Dragon Cay and Woolgar's response.

As the Aztec banked the mainplane slid from sight and looking down to her right Petronella could see stretching into the hazy distance southwards the greater area of Abaco, an endless forest bordered on either hand with cays, beaches, white reefs, green, turquoise, blue and violet sea. She could pick out the harbour below her now, the small white specks of boats at anchor, the creaming wake of a trio of fishing cruisers heading out to the deep water, the swiftly seen and gone sun flash reflection from a roof . . .

"See that lighthouse on your right?" Petronella saw it, tall, circular, candy striped in red and white. "That's on Hope Town. Island next to it is Man-O-War Cay. Okay. Now you turn on three one five. Good girl! Fine, fine. Take it off now. Right. That's Treasure Cay down there."

Roff was stretching his neck to try to look down over Kress's shoulder. But with the window curtains and Kress's head blocking the view, he could see very little. But from his own window he could see on the eastern side a passing line of islets, each seemingly with its glittering white settlements amongst casuarinas and coconut palms, its little groups of yachts, its hotels, dazzling beaches, its amazing multicoloured sea.

"How far are we from Dragon Cay?" he asked.

" 'bout ten minutes' flying. Say twenty-five miles, Mr. Roff. Shall we circle it when we get there, Mr. Kress? Give Mr. Roff a bird's-eye view of what is going on?"

"Yes," said Kress.

Suddenly he heard the Australian's nasal twang: "There she is! Dragon Cay! We'll be circling anti-clockwise, Mr. Roff," Woolgar was going on. "Why don't you go to the back behind Mr. Kress?"

Roff did so, manoeuvering himself onto the port side of the rear bench seat served by its own window. For a while he could see no more than a continuation of the coastline of Abaco but then with an "Okay, I'll take her for the circuit," Woolgar abruptly put the Aztec into a sudden steep turn to starboard and as he did so, Roff saw the whitening of the knuckles of Kress's hand as he gripped the armrest fiercely, and learnt something he hadn't known before—that however unafraid Laurence Kress might be in business, he was terrified of personal hurt.

Completing the turn which took him away from Abaco and round to the seaward side of Dragon Cay, Woolgar reversed direction. Now the whole of Dragon Cay could be taken in at a single glance. Of roughly dumbell shape it was perhaps two miles in length and at its widest rather more than half a mile across. On the Atlantic side an almost continuous reef, over which the surf was breaking gently, protected a whole series of white sand beaches and seawards from the reef a wandering swath of brilliant blue through greener water showed the line of a deep channel leading towards the real depths.

Down they went to perhaps a thousand feet, the Australian treating the Aztec as if it were a fighter aircraft rather than a twin-engined passenger plane and for the first time, from his new vantage point, Roff could see the eyes of the girl with whom he had fallen in love and they were thrilled, sparkling, filled with excited fire—and nothing to do with him at all. And in that instant he made a resolution: to accept what had been given to him over the last few days and nights and not to make a fool of himself by trying to continue it.

"It's the whole island you own?"

"Yes."

They were flying northwards now, just out from the island, leaving the developed part behind them. Here, it was virgin land, land which for countless centuries would have seen little if anything of humans, would have been home for lizards, land crabs, birds and insects and maybe turtles coming ashore to lay their eggs. And now it was to be ravaged, utterly and finally changed to meet the currently fashionable whims of men and women fleeing from colder climes.

The land started to broaden out as they approached the island's northern end.

"Is this where you're going to have the golf course?"

Kress nodded yes.

Roff tried to picture it—the close-clipped Bahama grass, the glaring white blots of bunkers, the carefully planted casuarinas, palmettos, shrubs, the eighteen fluttering flags, the little knots of men and women, brightly clad, the sun flashing on their swinging clubs, the attendant broad-wheeled buggies with garish golf bags sticking from the back compartment, the artificial ponds cunningly placed to catch the errant shot, and, peeping out here and there, not so ostentatiously as to spoil the meticulously manicured and very private tranquillity, the houses of the truly rich who could afford these extra-costly sites. It would all be gone: and the silence, broken only by the heavy trade winds through the trees, the steady, regular break of surf upon the reef and the call of birds, would be replaced by laughter and chiacking, by curses and commiserations in foreign tongues.

Well, he had been responsible for the same sort of thing in other places and was hardly fitted to feel a pang at this rape of innocence. Yet, briefly, it was what he felt. But he had come with a mission to accomplish and perhaps now was as good a time as any to show his personal interest.

"Looking for finance?" he asked.

Kress, who had taken off his glasses, paused in his cleaning operations. "Why?"

"I might be interested."

"Well," said Kress, as if giving it thought. "I suppose it's not impossible. Depends on how interested you were." He had half turned in his seat. "Mind you, I don't know if there's room. You could come in on the golf course. That's a separate thing."

"Are you in that? The golf course?"

"No."

"Then I wouldn't be interested."

"It'll be a sound investment."

"Maybe."

"Well I should think that's the only way in. I don't think there's any room otherwise. I had to buy at over the odds to get control."

"Do you think this Japanese fellow you were telling me about he might be willing to unload . . ."

"I should think it's very unlikely. There are one or two minor stockholders who might be. If you like, I'll make enquiries."

"If you would."

"All right." Kress had had all he was prepared to take of circling. He replaced his glasses and called out, "That's enough, Woolgar. Put her down."

SEVEN

Petronella, standing beside the glittering white aircraft with the silver stripe along its sides underlining the blue-painted OCEANFRONT LIMITED lettering, watched the three men descend. Kress followed Roff and then Woolgar, who was grinning at her as he passed, snapped open a door on the low part of the fuselage and began to haul out crates of beer. The breeze was welcoming, for all the sweetly rotten tang of mangroves and the soft white airstrip dust it carried.

"What's still to be done?" Roff asked.

"The second half of the marina. Roads. Cottages. And the hotel, of course."

"Has it got a pool?" asked Petronella "The one that's nearly ready?"

She was succeeding in irritating Kress.

"Not yet," he answered shortly. "But if you want to swim . . ." He broke off as a large Cadillac in the same silver as the Piper Aztec and also lettered with the company's name swept up to a halt as near to them as the road permitted.

"If you want to swim," he told her ironically, "they tell me the sea is very pleasant."

"Careful you don't overdo it," Roff said quietly as Kress went across the grass to talk to the driver. "He's no one's fool."

"There's not much point in my tagging around with you all day."

"What's the matter?"

"Nothing's the matter."

"Well there damn well is. Am *I* supposed to believe this too?"

"I thought we agreed I was supposed to be as hard as nails."

"And sentiment is out?"

"If you want to know, it's bloody difficult to put over."

He nodded. "Yes, I suppose it is. But you still haven't answered me."

"Sergei," Petronella said. "We swanned around the Bahamas and we didn't even land anywhere and that was good."

"But, yesterday."

"Yes. It *was* yesterday." She stopped looking at him. "If you want to know I hate it but I'm doing the best I can."

Kress was heading back towards them, calling, "Ready, Sergei?"

"Come on," Roff said to Petronella.

When they got up to him, Kress said, "Petronella, if you really want to swim, I tell you what we do. We drop you off at the club-house and they can fix you up with towels and so on and Woolgar can take you somewhere."

They got into the Cadillac. Kress in the front beside the driver, Roff and Petronella in the back. The air-conditioning struck ice cool after the mid-morning heat.

"Mr. and Mrs. Roff," Kress told him.

The man turned his head. There was something about him which convinced Roff he was employed by the construction company. "Hallo," he said. "Name's Boon. Nice day."

"When isn't it out here?" said Petronella.

"You'd be surprised." Boon somehow looked too workmanlike to be acting as chauffeur. He wore blue denims and a lemon-yellow shirt with buttoned patch pockets.

They were on their way. Chuck and Woolgar were following in the Toyota.
"I see the other Piper's here as well," said Kress.
"Yeah. Warbeck and the Jap got in an hour back."
"Warbeck's our architect," Kress explained to Roff. "And the man Boon refers to as the Jap . . ."
"I don't like Japs," Boon said. "My dad was on Corregidor."
"The Jap," Kress said dangerously quietly, "is Mr. Minahero. And whether or not you like it, Boon, Mr. Minahero is, after myself, easily the largest stockholder in Oceanfront. Now take us round by way of the Minatour, will you?"

2

They met the transverse road at the point where huge scars indicated the location of the hotel buildings and their service roads and bulldozers were busy carving out pits and trenches. The salty air was sullied by the stink of oil, petrol and burning wood and the quiet peace of Dragon Cay by the clatter of standby generators and the thumping of compressors.

Boon halted the Cadillac on a little mound short of the security gate in the high wire fence, which entirely enclosed the hotel site, the mound's extra height providing them with a fair view of the operations. "Want to go and take a look-see, Mr. Kress?" he asked.

"No," Kress said. "I don't think Mrs. Roff's shoes would be quite up to it."
"There's the Jap," said Boon. "Just coming out of C."

"C" was the architect's hut—a sizable building in which several draughtsmen and subcontractors' representatives worked. Warbeck, holding a rolled drawing, followed Minahero.

Now what's *he* doing here? Kress asked himself. Tramping round in all this mess? And what's that drawing? And at once he remembered Minahero's enthusiasm for mounting fish, guessed what the plans were and was furious. Seething with silent anger, he watched the Japanese carefully picking his way, taking not the slightest interest in the work going on around him, heading for his car.

"All right, Boon," he said. "That's good enough. Take us to the marina now."

An artificial finger into the lagoon, which provided access to a small island, had been extended by reclamation for the development of the smaller hotel, the club-house, a restaurant and bar, a self-service store and a number of shops. These buildings, together with some planted gardens, a car park and a few gaily painted cottages, occupied a piece of land manicured to form half a hexagon, the angled sides of which provided (or would when completed provide) moorings for perhaps two hundred craft. The westerly half of the marina was by now in service and, for all that the hotel was not, a fair number of fishing cruisers of greatly varying sizes together with some sailing yachts and motor boats were already occupying moorings in the slips and no doubt others would be filled when their owners returned at nightfall.

The road connecting the east and west marinas was set back sufficiently inland to allow space on its lagoon side for the hotel, a good-mannered two-storied building with a shingle roof. For a few moments Kress engaged the attention of Roff and Petronella by describing the functions of the various buildings, only to bring his explanations abruptly to a close when Warbeck and Minahero drew up outside a one-storied building near the slipway and went inside it.

"If you'll excuse me, Sergei," he said unhurriedly. "I want to have a word with Minahero. Why don't you have a look round and I'll join you both in half an hour or so in the club-house bar. Woolgar will look after you and then he can take Petronella off swimming somewhere and we can all meet up again for lunch."

And with no more ado, he got out of the Cadillac and left them.

Roff watched him drive off.

"All right," he said, "that's one you've convinced at any rate, so let's go and get you kitted out." He made a pace towards the club-house but she didn't move. "What's it now?" he snapped. "Changed your mind?"

She nodded. "Yes." She wasn't looking at him but at Laurence Kress just entering the building near the slipway.

"What exactly *do* you want to do?"

"Don't be unreasonable, Sergei."

"I'm trying not to be."

"I've got a job to do. You know that. For God's sake don't make it more difficult than you have to."

"So what do you want to do?"

"Meet Minahero."

"Which means *he's* something to do with this business too."

"Yes."

"And the Woolgar angle?"

"You understood that perfectly well."

"So did Kress. You don't imagine for a moment that you fooled him, do you?"

She looked at him, her eyes regretful.

"I'm doing the best I can," she said. "But perhaps I've got a lot to learn." They walked out along one of the pontoons. There were cruisers moored both sides, sterns inwards, outriggers smartly inboard to the flying bridges.

"I can't see," Roff said, "what the hurry is in your trying to meet Minahero as Kress has already said he's going to fix it up for us to go fishing on his boat."

"There's no guarantee he'll come himself."

"His yacht's just along from us."

"That would be too obvious."

"You've got to be obvious but getting to know him mustn't be. That's about it?"

"Yes."

"What a stroke of luck him being here today."

"Yes."

"An opportunity just too good to miss."

"Oh, don't go on so!" She was very angry with him. Not for what he was saying but because he was so cheapening himself.

"How far do you take it?" he said. "All the way to the bedroom?"

"Shut up!" she said.

They had reached the end of the pontoon. There were no boats on either side. She stared miserably at the gaily coloured fish which swam around the end piles.

"I asked you a question," he insisted. "And I want an answer to it. You may think that's unreasonable. And maybe it is. But I don't mind admitting it. When I saw you flirting with that Australian, I was jealous." He grasped her wrist, turning her towards him. "So answer me. Does it go as far as sleeping with him?"

She felt the pain of his fingers digging in her flesh. Her lips were tight; her eyes were moist. Somehow the sun-hat she still held in the other hand, and which was to do with fun and holidays, looked terribly out of place.

"Yes," she said. "It does. And now for God's sake, Sergei, don't torture me any more."

3

"*O-hayo,*" called Kress.

Minahero, who was bent looking at the drawing, stiffened—but he turned unhurriedly. "*Konnichi-wa,*" he said.

Kress glanced at his watch on its over-heavy gold strap. "Ah yes," he said. "Eleven-fifteen. I stand corrected. Good morning, Warbeck."

There was a third man with them. Kress raised his eyebrows enquiringly. "Sam Spaull," said Warbeck. "Shopfitting sub. Sam, this is Mr. Kress." They shook hands.

"You did next door?" said Kress very pleasantly.

Next door was the deep-sea-fishing gear shop.

"Sure did," said Spaull.

"And a very nice job too." Kress didn't hurry. There was no way they could hide the drawing. "And I speak both as client and one-time architect. Did you do any of the other shops?"

"I did 'em all."

"And in here?" Kress said easily, coming to the point. "What are you doing in here? I thought this was just for stock. May I see?"

He walked up to the trestle table. Sure of what would be shown, he needed to do little more than glance. But he made some business of it. "Uhm." And again. "Uhm." And, turning to Minahero, "Yes. That oughtn't to cost too much. But, Yasuo, I thought we'd agreed to abandon the mounting shop?"

Minahero smiled—but not with his eyes. His small mouth, turned down at the corners, was very tight.

"Let us not talk about it now," he suggested.

"But, my dear chap, when you've come all this way especially to discuss it."

Minahero went on smiling—but he didn't speak.

"Look," said Kress most reasonably. "I tell you what. Don't let me interrupt your confabulations." He had chosen the word advisedly. "Why don't I leave you all to sort out the detail now, and you and I, Yasuo, can discuss the principle later? How long do you think you'll need, Warbeck?"

"Oh, not long," the architect, exquisitely embarrassed, replied. "Ten minutes, say."

"Oh, don't hurry. Please. Look, Yasuo, when you've finished, why don't you come and join me in the club-house? There's an old friend of mine I've brought over to show what we're doing I'd very much like you to meet." And, encouragingly, "The man who's chartered the yacht *Fair Lady* lying along from yours."

4

The Deep Water Bar had been designed specifically to appeal to fishing enthusiasts, its dark panelling an excellent foil for the many mounted fish upon its walls. It boasted a long bar directly facing the broad balcony where full lunches were served and on the walls at either end of this bar were a white marlin and a sailfish and central over it a blue marlin of prodigious size.

Elsewhere were mounted fish of almost every type which could be caught in the locality.

When Kress came into the bar he found it sparsely occupied. Outside, on the terrace two or three couples were drinking. In the centre of the bar the only person Kress knew by sight, Jim Woolgar, was chatting to a stranger.

Kress went up to them.

"Mr. Kress," said Woolgar, nodding, but not getting off his stool. "Meet Senator Dillard. Mr. Dillard, Mr. Kress."

"Hi!" said Dillard, un-senator-like, thrusting out a beefy hand. "First name's Rodney. What's yours?"

"Laurence."

"Care to join us, Laurence. What you having?"

Kress nodded briefly to the bartender.

"Mr. Kress only drinks champagne this time of day," the barman said.

"Well then champagne it is," said Dillard. "Why don't we all drink champagne?"

"I'm expecting several friends," Kress pointed out, loath to miss out on a connection with a real live senator but sensing that some sort of drinking party might develop.

"Better fetch out a magnum, Wilberforce," said Dillard cheerfully. "You got magnums?"

"We got magnums, sir," said Wilberforce. "What kind you want, sir?"

"Dom Pérignon," said Kress.

"Soon come, sir," said Wilberforce, going off to fetch it from somewhere.

"Come for the fishing?" Dillard asked.

Woolgar explained Kress's connection with Dragon Cay.

"Well seems a nice place you're putting together," Dillard commented. "You've just arrived?"

"Sailed in this morning."

"Your own boat?"

"Sure. Brought her over from Fort Lauderdale."

"Will you be staying long?"

"Depends. Want one of those for my New York apartment." He pointed to the marlin above the bar.

"That's quite a fish, senator."

"It's Rodney when I'm fishing. Yeah, that sure is quite a fish. What would you say, Jim? About seven-fifty?"

"Eight twenty-two, sir," advised the barman, who had just returned with a magnum of Dom Pérignon.

"Eight twenty-two! You don't say? Well that would be great but I'd settle for . . . Six hundred?"

"You've got a chance," said Woolgar. "Numbers start building up in spring."

There was much fishing talk. Kress took little part but sat quietly, working things out, sipping his champagne, waiting for Minahero and hoping he'd arrive before Roff and Petronella.

He was disappointed. He heard Dillard whistle softly and say, "Who's *that* lady?"

"Mr. and Mrs. Roff," said Kress.

"And who's Mr. Roff that he should be so lucky?"

"He's an old friend of mine. In the same line of business."

"Looks like a good business to be in."

Dillard hadn't for a moment taken his eyes off Petronella, who, with the hat which had proved such a nuisance deposited somewhere, had paused by the doorway accustoming herself to the gloom of the Deep Water Bar.

"Mrs. Roff wants to go swimming," Kress told Woolgar. "I told her you'd fix her up and run her somewhere."

"Sure," said the Australian quitting his bar stool with alacrity. "I'll run her to Slipper's Cove."

"Did you say Strippers Cove?" asked the senator bawdily. "Can I come too?" And to the barman. "Set up a couple more glasses, Wilberforce."

Roff came over with Petronella.

Kress made the introductions. Dillard organised the pouring of two glasses of champagne and personally handed them to Roff and Petronella.

"I've told Woolgar to take you somewhere you can have a swim," Kress said. And to an attractive, efficient-looking woman who had just come in, "Good morning, Mrs. Butler, I wonder if you could fix Mrs. Roff . . ." he indicated Petronella . . . "with something to go swimming in."

"Good morning, Mr. Kress," said Mrs. Butler, who was the club's hostess. "Yes, of course."

"Don't bother," said Petronella. "I've changed my mind."

"It's one helluva of a beach," pressed Woolgar. "Pinkest sand you ever saw."

"We don't have the time," said Roff shortly.

"What time do you want to go back, Mr. Kress?" asked Woolgar hopefully.

"I must be back by four."

"Why not use the pool?" said Mrs. Butler.

Kress had forgotten the club pool; Woolgar had hoped it would not be mentioned.

"You've got a pool?" said Petronella.

"We have a beautiful pool. Do you want to borrow some trunks, Mr. Roff?"

He shook his head. There were more useful ways of spending the day.

"Why don't we all go swimming? When we've cracked this bottle?" suggested Dillard, who had drunk a trifle too much already. "Another glass for Mrs. Butler, Wilberforce."

"No, thank you, senator," Mrs. Butler said. "Later perhaps. *Would* you like me to find you something, Mrs. Roff? We've got quite a selection?"

Petronella was uncertain.

"What are your plans?" she asked of Kress.

"I have to sort out a couple of things with Minahero who'll be coming over shortly. Shouldn't take very long. Why don't you go and have your swim?"

"Like I said, why don't we all go and have a swim?" interjected Dillard.

"Yes, why not?" Kress agreed pleasantly. "And then we can all have lunch."

"All right," said Petronella.

"Wilberforce," said Dillard. "Take that bottle and glasses down to the pool."

"I'll see it's brought down," said Mrs. Butler.

Petronella went off with her and Dillard, with a "See you, Laurence," and a nod to Roff, followed them—as did Woolgar. Kress realised this was the first time he had been actually alone with Roff since the Auberge du Chat.

"Well, Sergei," he said, wondering how best to get rid of him quickly, "what do you think of Dragon Cay?"

"I'm impressed."

"Still feeling you might like to invest in it?"

"Yes."

"Well, look. I've got Minahero coming across to see me any minute. Give me ten minutes alone with him and I'll see what I can do."

"Didn't you say you thought he wouldn't unload any of his holding?"

"I did. And I don't. But it's worth a try. You might make it a condition of investing in the golf club. There's finance wanted there."

"But you're not in that?"

"No. I told you."

"Me neither then." Curious, he told himself. Wants me to believe he can get me in even though he knows he can't. Might as well bring it to a head.

"Are there any circumstances under which you'd cut me in on your share of it, Laurence?" he demanded bluntly.

Kress looked at him very hard.

"None," he said. "I told you when I cut you in on the Benevente business that I never involved myself in any business where others had control."

"I wouldn't have control."

"You might if you teamed up with Minahero."

"Why should I?"

"It's a long way to come. Arizona to Grand Bahama." Kress decided to start building his stockade against the worst eventuality. He took off his spectacles and started cleaning them. "You know, Sergei," he said, "there aren't all that many people who'd turn the other cheek as you are doing." He examined his spectacles. "I wouldn't, for one. If you had done to me what I did to you five years ago . . . Well . . ." He smiled, but there was a warning in the smile. "I think I'd be far more likely to hire someone to kill you. And that wouldn't be very difficult here in the Bahamas."

It was as if a mist had been blown away and all that in one direction had been indistinct was of a sudden sharp and clear. The mist, Roff told himself, had been the spell cast by Petronella; if he hadn't been so enchanted by her he would have realised long ago that Shapland's meticulous researchers would have informed him that there was no question of Laurence Kress ever letting slip control in any of his projects. Whatever he had been sent here for it was not to buy shares in Dragon Cay! That had been subterfuge, pretext, blind. Yes, but it was all he had to go on—he must use it. And use Kress's fear.

"You shouldn't have said that, Laurence," he answered quietly. "Because by doing so you have probably set in train a series of events which neither of us have the power of reversing. You were working it out on the flight over, weren't you? Why I'm here in the Bahamas. You don't believe it was just a coincidence I happened to end up dining in the same restaurant as you were. And of course you're quite right. Five years ago for motives no one will ever know you agreed to become part of a conspiracy aimed at taking away my liberty to run my life the way I'd chosen to. You turned a reasonably successful and contented man into a fugitive with a scarred face in an alien country. And having done so, no doubt forgot all about it. But I didn't, Laurence. Once I came up for air and began to put all the pieces into place, I made a resolution. That one day you would pay, and pay heavily, for what you'd done to me."

"My dear chap," Kress endeavoured to interject, "only yesterday . . ."

"Only yesterday, I told you I was grateful to you. Yes. And in a way that's true. You taught me a great deal, Laurence. You taught me that without money a man is powerless. You taught me that making money was nothing like as difficult as most people think it is—that it is, above all, the belief that making money is a difficult thing to do which prevents people making it. Well I've made my money. I don't know how rich you are by now but I'd hazard that if I'm not even richer, I'm certainly not far behind. So far as power goes we're more or less on a par."

He picked up his glass of champagne and turned it slowly in his fingers, watching the bubbles appear from nowhere, rise, and vanish into nothingness again.

"You threatened me just now," he said, still looking into the glass. "That was unwise. Threatened men live longest."

"I did not threaten you."

Roff put down the glass again, untasted. "Perhaps you didn't mean to, Laurence," he said, looking at him now, at the hard, dark eyes behind the heavy spectacles, hard eyes which held a glint of fear, which gave him pleasure. "But nevertheless you did. For in effect you said that you suspected I had come here to kill you, or have you killed but that was a game which two could play." He nodded. "And it is. Think of it, Laurence. You and me, both rich, both powerful, both uncompromising. You terrified . . ."

"Of you?" The laugh was harsh.

"Not of me particularly. Just terrified. Of being hurt. Of being killed. And me . . . unforgiving, vindictive, thirsting for revenge. In a minute or two your Japanese chum will come in and we'll chat about Dragon Cay. And then my girl friend will come in with that slob of a senator and that randy Australian leering all over her and we'll sit down to a splendid lunch and you'll order the best wine this damn place can offer. And to anyone passing by we'll look a jolly international party of rich people having themselves a ball. But you won't enjoy your wine, you won't enjoy your lunch, you won't enjoy being the expansive host, the great success, the high panjandrum—not this time, Laurence, because all the time you'll be wondering exactly what I have in mind and how you can best counter whatever that may be and how much time you've got to do it in. And after we break up, you'll brood on it. It'll never be out of your mind. And it'll build, won't it, Laurence? Suspicion will turn to certainty. Self-preservation will start to call the tune. And if you have the courage, which you may not have, you'll end up hiring some thug to kill me. But, Laurence, I'll be aware of the way you're thinking and I won't be sitting idly by waiting for someone to take a pot shot at me or cut my throat with a machete. So, as I said just now you shouldn't have said what you did because in saying it you have started a chain of events which are all but irreversible. Which unless it can he halted here and now must lead, inevitably, to one of us killing the other if only to protect ourselves."

"Do you imagine," said Kress (who was indeed frightened but whose agile mind in spite of fear could still work clearly) "that after this conversation I won't take intelligent precautions to see that if I should be killed there will be ample evidence pointing towards you?"

Roff smiled. "A note dictated to pretty Kelly? A chat with your Japanese friend? No, of course you'll see to that. You'll see to it immediately, whatever the end of this conversation. But there's a difference between us, Laurence. I have a positive motive for killing you; yours would be negative. You'll never know how strong my motive is. You'll never know whether the knowledge I might pay the penalty would be a sufficient deterrent to my risking it. And there's another difference between us—I'm not a coward."

"Well," said Kress, with all the aplomb he could contrive, "it's all very interesting and all very melodramatic but even so I don't see why we have to descend to levelling insults. And I take it that at least I'm no longer required to try to persuade Minahero to cut you in on Dragon Cay?"

He took off his glasses and went through the usual performance. Roff waited patiently for him to finish. When he had, when the glasses were back in place, he said, "No, Laurence, there's no need for that. Because I never did intend to buy shares in Dragon Cay. I intended to have them given to me. By you. As repayment for three years of living with a scarred face in a wilderness. You will make over to me exactly half your holding. For nothing. I shall then have exactly the same control as you have and that will be crucifying for you. And I shall regard it as honour satisfied. And this must be done immediately. There can't, as I'm sure you'll agree, be any question of this dribbling on between us. So, I tell you what to do. When your Japanese chum comes in, fix for all of us to go fishing on his boat tomorrow and bring with you the necessary documentation which we can both sign with Petronella as our witness."

"I very much doubt if Minahero . . ."

"Yes, he will," Roff cut in sharply. "Petronella has winning ways."

"And if I agree?" asked Kress, who needed time to plan a course of action.

"Minahero," Roff answered, "can deliver us back to *Fair Lady* and we'll continue with our little trip."

He saw the Japanese man entering. "Here's your Far Eastern friend," he said. "I'll leave you to it."

5

"Shall we sit outside?" Minahero suggested.

Kress, unusually ruffled, his mind bedevilled by awareness that the matter which had caused him such extreme irritation had suddenly become of absolute unimportance, nodded.

"A pleasant spot to sit and view the little world we are creating, do you not think?" observed Minahero, selecting a table from which the swimming pool could be seen.

"Very pleasant." Kress sat with him.

"Who is that girl with Woolgar?"

"Her name is Petronella."

"I have seen her before. She is, as we would say *utsukushii*. Beautiful. She is with a man on that fine old yacht near to mine. The man you want me to meet, I think. Where is he? This man?"

"He'll be along shortly. His name is Sergei Roff. He's half Russian but you'd never guess it."

Minahero nodded. The Panama was strictly level on his forehead, hiding his soft grey hair.

"I hope, Laurence," he suggested, "you understand why I asked Mr. Warbeck to prepare me drawings for a mounting factory. It was . . . precautionary. To save us time if I can finally persuade you."

"It's very important to you, Yasuo?" said Kress.

"I would not say that. But it makes things very neat. And, you know, we Japanese, we like things neat. It is also very efficient."

"And you Japanese like things efficient?"

Minahero smiled.

"I have a problem," Kress told him. "One you can help me on. This man Roff. I knew him some years ago. He was in a small way of business as a travel agent and I cut him in on one of my schemes. In Spain."

"The one you called Benevente?"

"Yes. Benevente. I set up a Cayman holding company of which Roff became a director. The funds were cleverly embezzled by the two resident directors who made it appear that Roff was responsible. There seemed to be only one sensible thing to do, which was to get Roff out of the country and provide him with a new identity. It required some plastic surgery. That scar he has on his face and that broken nose. He looks quite different now. He sat only a couple of tables away from me in El Morocco and I didn't recognize him."

"But he recognized you?"

"He came here to seek me out. You see for more than five years Roff's been dwelling on an injury he's convinced was my fault . . ."

"When in fact all you were doing was trying to help him. How very ungrateful."

Kress's hard eyes met those of the Japanese behind their gold-framed spectacles—and found them sympathetic.

"Yes," Kress said. "Ungrateful in the extreme. And yet you can understand it."

"And he has come here, you think, Laurence, to repay that injury."

"Yes."

Minahero put his stubby fingertips together. "That you can understand."

"Just now," said Kress, "not ten minutes back, he tried to blackmail me."

"How so?"

"By threatening that unless I give him a substantial part of my holding in Dragon Cay he will kill me."

"He said so?"

"In as many words."

"And you believe him."

"Yes."

"How can I help you, Laurence?" Minahero spoke almost offhandedly—he was looking at Petronella who had just climbed out of the pool and was talking to Woolgar and Dillard.

"He has asked me," Kress told him, "to arrange for the three of us to go out fishing on your boat tomorrow and stipulated that during the day a contract, to be witnessed by his girl friend"—he nodded towards Petronella —"be drawn up to give him what he's after."

"The girl being . . . ?"

"His mistress? Yes." Kress paused, then said deliberately. "But she is getting tired of him."

Minahero's eyes followed every movement of Petronella but displayed no lust.

"She was not here when he made this threat?" he suggested.

"No."

Minahero turned towards him, blinking his eyes.

"Are you willing to sign such a contract?"

"No. I will sign a contract. But it will be flawed. It will not meet with Bahamian legal requirements."

"To what purpose?"

"To the purpose of gaining time."

"To do what?"

Kress did not answer.

"Laurence," said the Japanese. "Is there not a solution much more simple? You have told me that this man has threatened to kill you."

"Or have me killed."

"It is the same. If you write a letter stating that and put it with someone. Your lawyer perhaps. Your bank. Or your secretary, who is most efficient. And tell this man what you have done, I do not think you will need to be more concerned."

Kress shook his head.

"You are not prepared to risk your life on such precaution?"

"No."

"*Hai.* Perhaps you are right. Men who are angry do strange things. But it would be a good precaution."

"Yes," said Kress. "I shall take it, naturally."

"You must do it before the fishing."

"Of course."

"And the other thing. The contract that is flawed. That must be prepared before the fishing."

"You are agreeable?"

Minahero raised a single finger. "Understand me, Laurence. I do not read contracts which I witness. I do not know what they contain. I only witness signatures. Now the other thing . . ."

"At the next board meeting," Kress said, "I will withdraw my objection to your fish-mounting factory."

"A letter now will be sufficient."

"Of course. I will have my secretary type it out."

"And I may tell Roff that tomorrow we are going fishing? All of us?"

Minahero nodded. "All of us." He glanced towards the men busy farther along the verandah, three men, busy constructing a masterpiece of a cold buffet. "You will not want to be too late going back with so much to do. I too have things to arrange. I suggest we have lunch as soon as they are ready. And perhaps you will ask Mr. Roff and the others if they would care to join us."

EIGHT

They were far enough out to have lost the land smells and for the southern coastline of Grand Bahama to be visible only on the rise to the long, slow swell which left the ocean's surface oily enough for the drips of water off flying fish to puddle it. Already they were over the deep blue water. The sky was scarcely clouded overhead, although on the western horizon there were clouds, drawn parallel to the ocean, which rose to towering cauliflowers and anvils.

Roff and Petronella were in the stern of the *Dai Nichi,* which was equipped with a fighting and two fishing chairs. Kress and Minahero were both up on the bridge with the Japanese captain, and another Japanese was on station in the flying bridge. The crew, which numbered five, was dressed identically in half-sleeved slate-blue tunics over slate-blue trousers, excepting only that the captain (whose name was Fujita) wore a naval-style peaked cap as against the army-styled peaked caps of the other three—of whom Roff had so far seen only the one whose duty it was to rig the billfish baits and generally stand by to give assistance as required.

Petronella was in the fighting chair and Roff—just in shade—diagonally a little behind her on her right-hand side while the Japanese, a squat but powerful-looking fellow, stood patiently, arms folded across his chest, on the other side, as far back, which was quite a distance far back, as the commodious stern cockpit permitted. Whether or not he had enough English outside the basic requirements for carrying out instructions to do with fishing had not been made clear but to a very considerable degree his presence inhibited conversation. Had he been elsewhere, it would have been otherwise, for the vision forward from the cockpit (which was in any event half shaded by the projecting deck above) was effectively cut off by a sportsfishing boat with a massive outboard engine which was carried piggyback athwartship on it so that only the flying bridge could be seen above it, and that only from the very stern.

Both of them were trolling long with silver spoons, rod butts in central chair gimbals, drags light on the reels, with only Petronella wearing a harness as it had been unanimously agreed that hers should be the first strike on the pair of matched eighty-pound test-line rigs arranged in the outer sockets beyond the armrests of her chair. She was leaning back relaxed, her feet on the footrest of the fighting chair, her elbows just touching its armrests, her hands lightly round the rod. She wore white slacks, Plimsolls and short socks and a loose pink shirt under a sort of navy waistcoat. Her hair was ponytailed.

Roff leaned forward. "Peta."

She swivelled her chair so that now he could see her profiled against the deep blue of the sea. "Yes?"

"Why?"

"What?"

"Are we being left by ourselves?" He was speaking as quietly as he could—just loud enough for her to hear him.

"Could be the gunwale."

"The gunwale?"

"Not very high, is it?"

It was quite true; a man could so easily be tipped over.

"With Fido here?" he scoffed.

She didn't answer, thinking about it, watching the port side marlin bait skipping and jumping over the boat's white wash. She saw the problems from a different angle, knowing the things she knew. But even so could take his questions seriously. He had recounted his pre-lunchtime discussion with Kress and she had lain awake for a long time the previous night, reflecting. It was the second night in succession they had not had sex and she knew they would not have sex again. She had worked out precisely, and correctly, how he would have analysed the situation between them and she was sad because he was so wrong and there was nothing she could do to put him right. So she came back to Laurence Kress. What was he thinking, up there on the bridge with Minahero? Or planning? Watching the Pompano Beach Hotel shrink rapidly as they motored out from its marina, it had occurred to her how simple it would be to catch a man, or woman, off balance and push him over the *Dai Nichi*'s coaming, designed especially low at the stern to facilitate the hauling aboard of huge fish.

"Perhaps it's as well we do have a guard dog," she agreed.

"No. He hasn't the guts."

Sergei would have the guts, she thought. He was a fine man whom circumstances had treated unkindly and yet had not been broken. He was blessed with an optimistic nature. That was a weakness. She remembered a bit of doggerel she had once heard to the effect that optimists believed we lived in the best of all worlds and pessimists knew this was true. That neatly summed up the difference between him and Laurence Kress. Sergei was by nature kind; Kress vicious. With Sergei suspicion followed trust; with Kress it was the other way around.

"When are you going to sort it out with him?" she asked.

"There isn't any hurry. And it can hardly be a complicated document."

"You really think he'll sign it?"

"He's arranged all this. Why bother?"

It was only lip service she was paying. Lip service to an idea of so little account. She wondered gloomily how it would be when it all came out.

The Japanese interrupted her ruminations and she was glad. He came beside her, said "Excuse," and taking the starboard-side rod out of the socket began to wind in the massive Penn reel. When the line had come in close he put the rod back, went to the gunwale and, pulling the bait in by the wire leader, examined it, grunted dissatisfaction, snipped with pliers the leader just ahead of the fish and threw it hook and all disgustedly into the sea. "Excuse," he said again, unnecessarily, and going to a locker behind her fetched from its ice chest another balao. She watched in silence, still slightly sickened by the process but much impressed as he rebaited the leader, which he did with extraordinary dexterity and speed.

"Mother's training always tells," murmured Roff. He broke off, fancying a change in the tug-tugging of his spoon. But it was nothing—or perhaps a piece of seaweed momentarily caught and then broken free again. "I wonder what it means," he said. *"Dai Nichi."*

"Great Day. Roughly."

"How do you know?"

"His nibs translated when I asked him. Over lunch yesterday."

He did not pursue the fact she hadn't mentioned this. She had known his thoughts. Emotions. He saw her now in the borrowed bikini and see-through cover-up which made her nakeder. A too-tight scarlet bikini bra. The bikini she had been wearing that first time he had seen her, posed by that Tucson pool, had been chaste by comparison. Or was that himself? Seeing her differently. Seeing her beside that bloody Jap through lunch. Smiling up at him. Ignoring the rest of them. Even ignoring the senator! And him fuming—like a jealous schoolboy! Within half an hour of a discussion on life and death!

"There was another *Dai Nichi,"* he heard her saying quietly.

"Eh?" It seemed an extraordinary non sequitur.

"It was a prison ship. Or rather it carried a lot of prisoners. About a thousand. From Java to Japan."

He stared at her, confounded. "How do you know all this? Is there a connection?"

"Not so far as I know." But she pursued it. "A lot died on the voyage. And a lot more afterwards. About a third in all."

"Who told you?"

"Shapland," she said simply.

"Look . . ." he began.

She shook her head, interrupting him. "It's not part of it," she told him. "At least, not really." And after a pause, "It's a strange coincidence though." But she might have been speaking to the sea.

2

It was hotter now. There were cool drinks in the armrest sinkings. But the ice was melting in them and their outsides were dewed. The deckhand who had served them had spectacles, a moon face and teeth edged with gold like the framing to a picture still to be painted. He had smiled incessantly. His name was Ota. It was no clearer if he had good English than had the fishing hand to whom he had spoken in staccato Japanese. Minahero had not been down; nor Kress. The sea was endless, vaguely heaving oil all about them, blue oil but for the white wake streak. They were weaving a bit, apparently following a frigate bird.

"Strange they haven't been down," said Petronella.

She was no longer even bothering to hold the rod. She was not exactly bored. It was pleasant enough, even, in spite of Fido, intimate, here in the stern cockpit. She had boarded with a presentiment of danger. But the heat and the oily sea and only the occasional sight of other fishing cruisers or an aircraft on a straight-line course overhead to break the sameness, had lulled her fears.

"Face, I suppose," said Roff.

She nodded. "A sea reputedly teeming with fish and in an hour we haven't had a strike."

He chuckled. "And after that crash course in Miami."

She smiled and swivelled round almost to face him liking what she saw. His scarred face, so full of character, his iron-grey hair, his grey-green eyes. The feeling he gave that whatever he said could be relied upon, that the decisions he took would not be taken for effect, or out of impatience, but on the basis of a proper judgement of the facts available to him. That under any normal circumstances she could have left decisions to him.

"Sergei . . ." she began, but the sudden screaming of a reel cut off his name. She swivelled back, confused, looking from one to the other of the three reels on the rods with butt ends in her chair cups. But it was none of these. The scream came from the other reel. She swivelled back. And as she did so the huge bull dolphin which had felt the pain of the hooks on Roff's spoon leapt from the sea like the launch of an underwater missile. Full eight, ten feet, perhaps even more, it must have risen, magnificent, body vivid gold and green blue-spotted, forked tail chrome yellow, dorsal fin a purple-blue as brilliant as the sea itself, the most beautiful fish designed by nature and pound for pound one of the most powerful of them all.

Now everything was happening. The Japanese man they had christened Fido was leaning out far to starboard over the gunwale, his head twisted up to the flying bridge, shouting, *"Sakana! Sakana! Sakana!"* then hurrying round to reel in the marlin lines to avoid a tangle. Petronella, remembering the instructions of her Floridian mentor, was reeling in her troll. Kress and Minahero, unable, because of the athwartships sportsboat, to follow the action from the bridge deck, leaving the Jap in the tower to steer the boat with his topside controls, were hurrying along the upper deck and down the port side companionway. And Roff was fighting a dolphin of a length and depth of body which made the two or three they had caught off Miami mere spindles by comparison.

The fish kept jumping, twisting and turning in the air, crashing, turning the oily sea into a mass of spray and poppled water; Roff was winding one-handed furiously, without a harness taking the strain, while the line sped out against the drag; the rod bowed to a half circle, the tight-strung segments of line between the roller guides, the line itself taut as a bowspring, all testifying to the power of the splendid creature.

He did not hear the clattering of feet down the stairs behind him, he did not think of the reason why he was aboard at all, he had forgotten Petronella —he was lost entirely in the struggle. Life was in instants reduced to a trial of strength, a test of endurance, a tussle in which experience and instinct, patience and expedience must each play their part set against a canvas of blue sea, blue sky, hot sun, and a leaping, twisting fish. He knew that if the hooks held in the soft mouth, the contest would be long. Had the dolphin taken either of the balaos on the marlin rigs with their eighty-pound test lines, the struggle would have been brief but on the twenty-pound-class tackle of the trolling lines it would be another matter.

The fish sped suddenly to starboard of the boat, the line twanging round as if to scythe off Petronella's head as she reeled in her own last few yards, but the man on the flying bridge was equal to the situation and brought the *Dai Nichi* hard over to port to equalise the situation. Minahero, in jerks of speech, was unhurriedly calling to the girl to quit the fighting chair and out of the corner of his eye he saw her rise. Sergei made no move to take the chair, waiting for the dolphin's first desperate rush to ease but hauled back on the rod to lift the line a trifle higher, winding all the time. Then, suddenly, although the tension seemed no less, he noticed that he was recovering line, that it was wet where before it had been dry and, not without risk, he lifted the rod upwards, taking the butt end from the gimbal, and, holding hard against the strain, quit his own fishing chair and made the few paces necessary, slipped into the fighting chair and with huge relief dropped the rod butt into the other cup.

The line was coming in faster now, building on the drum. He waited for another run but it failed to come. The line built steadily and, of a sudden, the fish was close behind the boat, then tacking sharply to the side and rising to the surface. He swivelled his chair to keep straight on it and now he could see the small silver spoon low down in the dolphin's mouth and the powerful blue-green back and the brilliant yellow tail and the strange, flat head which seemed to bore through the water. The fish was huge for its type; even in Minahero's words heard dimly, hardly translated into sense, he picked out the nuance of surprise. Then as quickly the fish was gone again, sounding out of sight—but the sun, shining through the pellucid water bathed the great body and reflected back so that there was a huge shifting pool of iridescent colour on the surface just behind the boat. The colour was amazing. It was as though the sea were lit from underneath by an unreal yellow-green phosphorescence. Then this, in turn, died back to blue as the fish dived deeper, drawing the line to a steep and uncomfortable angle and he had a mental picture of a whirling propellor slicing through it. But Minahero shouted something in Japanese and the engine note changed as the man on the flying bridge increased its speed and the line began both to straighten and to tear off again at speed. He wound fast against the pull, hauling the rod back high, pressing against the footrest, but the line still ran out, first all the wet and then he was back to dry again and losing this.

And so it continued. Line was lost, then gained. Periodically the fish would come close to the boat, seeming not to be struggling, seeming in fact to swim with it and then, suddenly, unexpectedly, it would turn and run again. His fingers around the rod grew numb, those winding sore. But he was gaining experience fast, learning how to use the fighting chair, swinging his body so that the Jap up in the tower had less to do, pumping the fish, pulling back the rod then lowering it, gaining line that way.

And gradually he was able to relax, realising that so long as he kept his wits about him, he would win. The fish was firmly hooked, it must be tiring. Only by an error or inattention on his part could it escape. And with this realisation, the other things came back to focus: those around him—Kress, Minahero, Petronella and the man waiting with the gaff; the reason for his being here at all.

"Could someone bring me a beer?" he called.

"I'll see to it," said Petronella.

"Thanks," he said, not looking up at her, keeping the fish in line. "How big d'you guess it goes, Laurence?" This to check that Kress was still with them.

"What do you think, Yasuo?"

"Maybe fifty. Maybe even fifty-five."

"Uh huh." He remembered something he'd been told. "Odd there aren't any more."

"More?" said Kress.

"More dolphin. When you hook one, you often get a whole shoal of others following. Didn't you know that, Laurence?"

"No. No, I didn't."

" 's a fact. Can be quite fun. Especially when it's a school of smaller fish. You know, eight, ten pounders. You can troll several lines at once. Of course you risk tangling. Well, sooner or later you do. But it's exciting."

He considered he'd said enough on that. It could be overdone. Anyway Petronella was back.

"I've organised your beer," she told him.

Her voice was cold, detached. He understood. For a while, taken over by the excitement, she had almost forgotten why she was on the boat, why she was in this part of the world at all.

He tightened the drag a trifle and transferred right hand from reel to rod and eased the fingers of his left hand, opening and closing his fist, stretching the fingers out.

Minahero, smartly but efficiently clad in a neat long-sleeved check shirt worn outside his trousers, came into view for the first time.

"If you have cramp, Mr. Roff . . ." he suggested pointedly.

Roff grinned. "I have. But it's not *that* bad." He knew that was just excuse; that Minahero did not for a moment imagine he would hand over the rod for someone else to play and maybe boat the fish because of a little cramp; that the reason Minahero had come to the stern was nothing to do with the fish at all—it was to be nearer Petronella. Just for a moment Sergei looked away from the line to glance at the Japanese and sure enough he was eyeing her. But it was impossible to read his thoughts, the small mouth pursed down, the unblinking eyes, the high-boned immobile face told him absolutely nothing.

The scream on the reel brought him back to the task in hand.

3

It took Roff just over an hour to boat the dolphin which weighed nearly sixty pounds. Quite suddenly it was ended. The fine, beautiful fish seemed at the finish to understand it was defeated and to swim quietly to the stern and sacrifice itself to the point of the shining gaff. With a single twist of his massive shoulders the Japanese man swung it inboard and picking up the club laid ready struck it once, efficiently, on the head and killed it. And at once it seemed as if all the dolphin's life was in its colour for as it lay there, bleeding, wave after wave of different colours, each less brilliant than the last with an astonishing rapidity changed it from glorious gold and chrome and blue and emerald to lead.

They put it in one of two coffinlike receptacles which lay fore and aft and could be exposed by lifting cockpit deck flush hatches. Minahero was evidently proud of these for he called Kress over to examine them.

"You see, Laurence? Each big enough to take even a black marlin of one thousand pounds or more. And both refrigerated. Do you want to have yours mounted, Mr. Roff?" said Minahero. "It can now be arranged."

"I don't know," said Roff, looking at the leaden dolphin. "It wouldn't look all that attractive."

Minahero smiled. "The taxidermist restores the colour. It is a remarkable fish. Perhaps you will accept it as my gift. As a reward for playing it so skillfully. It was very well done, Laurence, was it not?"

Kress nodded grudgingly. "Very well done."

"But I am sure with the same opportunity you would do as well."

"I daresay, but . . ."

"Come now, Laurence, I am sure you can. Let us have a contest. One hour each in the fighting chair. First you, Laurence. And then we lunch and you can settle your business with your friend. And then after lunch . . . first Mrs. Roff. And finally myself. There will be a prize. I will have them make a silver cup . . . no, a gold cup to remind us of its colour, with the name of the winner on it. For the largest dolphin caught today."

"There may not be any more about . . ."

"Oh yes. If we fish especially for them." He climbed halfway up the companionway to the upper deck and gave clipped instructions to the Jap on the flying bridge. When he came down again, he said, "I have instructed O'Kana that we fish especially for dolphin and he is to look for things that float. Weed. Driftwood. Where these things are there are dolphin usually. We were not fishing especially for dolphin but for billfish. If we do not put the marlin rigs out and each competitor has two rods trolling . . . You do not mind, Mr. Roff? You only had one rod. But then, you have caught a fish. A big fish. A fish that will be hard to beat."

"No, I don't mind," said Roff.

"Good, then it is settled. Now, Mr. Roff, if you will go up on the bridge and help look for debris and Laurence if you will take the fighting chair and Mrs. Roff, if you would not mind, there are the lunch preparations and a woman's touch . . ." He smiled expansively and enquiringly.

"Of course," said Petronella. "Anything I can do."

"That is very kind. I will come with you and show you where everything is kept. Miyako!" He gave instructions to the man Roff had nicknamed Fido. "I have told him what we are doing, Laurence." He smiled. "And remember it must be dolphin. No other fish will count."

It was of course quite patently obvious what he was about—organising his guests in such a way as to have Petronella to himself. But there was nothing Roff could do about it and clearly she was not going to object. He climbed the port side companionway, made his way along the upper deck and, nodding to the captain, Fujita, took the luxurious chair beside him and, from what was now a most impressive height, began to scan the oily sea through which the *Dai Nichi* ploughed a steady course at about six knots. Kress, meanwhile, no more enthusiastically, occupied the fighting chair in the side sockets of which Miyako arranged two rods with twenty-pound test lines, each trolling identical spoons to that on which Roff had hooked his fish.

Within the ship itself, the fifth member of the crew, the cook, was busy in the galley, from which a straight companionway led to the main bridge above, while Ota was setting out a table in the dining-room.

For all of Minahero's interest in deep-sea fishing, the *Dai Nichi* was not a boat specifically designed for such a purpose. While equipped with all the latest electronic navigating, communicating and fish-finding equipment it was, if on a smaller scale than *Tsuki No Hikari*, in essence a fibreglass-built luxury cruising yacht whose original design had been cunningly modified to permit fishing to be done from it efficiently and in comfort yet without impinging on what might be happening elsewhere. Thus whereas in smaller game-fishing craft the sport and what is happening elsewhere on the boat can rarely be separated, on the *Dai Nichi* it would have been perfectly feasible for an owner to invite two sets of guests with differing interests each scarcely aware of the presence of the other. And, as well, entrance to the yacht was from the side with the only access to the cockpit either down the port companionway to the upper deck or via a small doorway in the rear starboard corner of the main saloon.

Thus Minahero could assure himself of Petronella's uninterrupted company. "Please," he said, with a movement of his hand.

Petronella sat where directed. On a small table a bottle of champagne in an ice bucket and just two glasses testified that all of this had been most carefully planned. While Laurence Kress and Sergei each did their hour-long stint of fishing and looking out for debris, Minahero would have her to himself. Meanwhile he rang for Ota who came through and took instructions, all of which were given to him in Japanese, and when he had withdrawn, Minahero explained, rather pointedly, "I have instructed Ota to see that anything your husband and Laurence may require is provided to them." And then, blandly, "But, of course, he is not your husband, is he?"

Petronella felt the sudden quickening of her heart. This was the important moment. If she failed to handle it correctly, it would all have been for nothing. Partly to plan what to say, partly to give her pulse time to settle, she raised her head and for quite some moments regarded him in silence. This was a very dangerous man, she told herself—a far more dangerous man than Kress, for example, could ever be. She remembered Shapland's briefing: "He is clever, thorough and utterly self-controlled. So far as we are aware his only weakness is for women and even that is carefully masked. When you are talking to him, you must remember he will be weighing and remembering every word you say. If you interest him, then he will make exhaustive enquiries about you. Which is, of course, why we are establishing Roff's phoney background, and your own, so thoroughly. You much watch very carefully for the first sign he is suspicious about you because once that happens you will be of no use whatsoever to us and in considerable personal danger. If he thought you constituted the slightest threat, he would have you killed without a second thought."

Seated here in this light, airy saloon, almost feminine in style with its light wood panelling and pastel colours, seated here with a man whose inscrutability was allied to an unemphatic manner and complete composure, she felt the first prick of fear.

"You don't really expect me to answer such a question, do you?" she said.

He smiled. "A little champagne?" And without waiting for a response he poured two glasses from the already uncorked bottle.

"Your husband," he said, "has come all this way to fish. But he has done very little fishing."

"We aren't in any hurry."

"You are staying with us long?" And at her shrug, "They are all much the same, the islands of the Bahamas."

"So I've found out."

"You aren't enjoying your visit?"

"I'd enjoy it better off the boat."

"You could move into the hotel."

"I've already suggested that."

"And . . . your husband cannot be persuaded?"

"Oh all right." She spoke irritably. "He isn't my husband."

"But you've known him for a long time?"

"Yes."

"Please! People interest me, you see. And the reasons why they do things. Laurence, for example. He is out there fishing now. He has never come fishing with me before."

"It's meeting Sergei. After all these years."

"Yes. That is quite a coincidence." He paused. "But Laurence does not think it is?"

"Not a coincidence?"

"You do not sound sure yourself, Mrs. Roff. Or should I call you Petronella now?"

"What exactly do you mean?"

"About not being sure? It was the way you spoke. Not as if you didn't know yourself. But as if you had not decided whether you should agree with me or not. But Laurence and I are in business together. Oh. I am so sorry. No, please." He pressed a hidden bell-push. Almost at once Ota presented himself. *"Makitabako nai,"* Minahero admonished him mildly. Ota bowed and fetched a gold and silver cigarette box and matching lighter from across the saloon, placed them in front of his employer, bowed and withdrew. Petronella took a cigarette from the box and accepted a light.

"You don't smoke?" she said.

Smiling, he shook his head. "My vices are otherwise." He closed the box. "They have some business to do?" His look was enquiring.

"Yes."

"Oh, he has told you of it?"

"Of course. He wants to invest in your development."

"So Laurence tells me. That is another coincidence?" Petronella frowned at this. "That we are all in the same kind of business?"

"Not really."

"No." He reached out a hand and placed it momentarily on her knee, the first time he had touched her. "Do you not think we should be friends?"

"Of course."

"Then let us speak frankly." He removed his hand. "Mr. Roff has not come here to catch fish. He has come for another purpose."

"Why do you think that?"

"Well to begin he does not like catching fish."

"But that's absurd. Just now . . ."

"Just now, he was excited. But that is not the same. I watched his eyes as that dolphin died. He was sorry for the fish. A confirmed game fisherman is not. He has caught too many to be sorry for them. That was just an excuse for coming here. To catch fish."

Petronella shrugged. "Well of course the whole thing's stupid."

"Yes."

"You know about it?"

"Benevente? Yes. He is worried. Laurence."

"Worried?"

"He thinks that Roff may try to kill him."

"Kill him? Nonsense!"

"Nonsense?" He chuckled. "No. It is not nonsense." He lifted a hand to check her. "It is not nonsense Laurence thinks that; it may be nonsense that is what Mr. Roff has in mind. So."

Petronella drew on her cigarette. This was very dangerous ground. It had to be clarified.

"Well the whole thing's stupid," she said. "Childish."

"Revenge?" He shook his head. "We Japanese do not think that revenge is stupid. When the law cannot help you it is the only form of justice which is available."

"Where does it get you?"

"Where does life? Tell me, have you known your Sergei long?"

"I think that's my business, isn't it?"

"He has a wife."

"How do you know?"

"Laurence is very thorough. He has a wife and he lives with her in San Francisco. She is a lady he met in Morocco where Laurence arranged for him to go . . ."

She interrupted. "Why does this so interest you?"

"People interest me." For a moment his guard was down. His eyes flickered over her body; she saw the slight tightening of his mouth. A frisson of cold ran through her. She faced up to it.

"What are you saying, Mr. Minahero?"

"That you interest me." And when she did not respond, "There is something I do not understand. Roff has been living for some years—since he returned from Morocco—in San Francisco with this lady who is his wife . . ."

"In fact she is not his wife."

She had not surprised him. "No. Laurence discovered that as well," he said.

"But he'll never leave her." And after a manufactured pause. "He's too damn soft!"

"So Laurence is worried over nothing?"

"Of course he is. I never heard anything more ridiculous."

"He will be glad to be reassured. Do you know the purpose of this fishing trip?"

"Yes. But, look!" She put her hand on him now. "Please don't tell Kress he isn't really in any danger. Let Sergei have his way. Get his document. Then he'll be satisfied."

"And then you will leave Grand Bahama?"

"Yes."

"I would rather you stayed. I do not mind if Mr. Roff leaves but I would rather that you stayed." He paused.

"Are you by any chance propositioning me?"

"My dear Petronella," Minahero said imperturbably. "The relationship between yourself and Mr. Roff is coming to an end . . ."

"It is not!"

"Some more champagne?" He had barely touched his own. She had noticed over the lunch on Dragon Cay that he had scarcely drunk.

She shoved her glass across. "Yes. All right."

He poured the wine very slowly, as if it interested him to watch the glass filling.

"I am still not clear," he said. "It does not seem a big revenge to have a piece of paper signed. To kill a man, that is one thing. To add to your portfolio an investment in one more development . . . ?" He shook his head.

"What did Kress tell you?" she said. "About how it came about that Sergei ended up in Casablanca?"

"That the local directors of a Cayman Island's holding company had embezzled the funds . . ."

"And forged the papers to make it look as if Sergei had done it?" She laughed. "Do you believe that?" She was on safe ground. Kress would never dare to explain what lay behind it all.

"I see," said Minahero. "And yet I do not see."

"It's apparently always been a boast of Kress's that he controls everything with which he is connected. And he controls Dragon Cay. In the long run, no one, not even you, can do anything unless Kress approves it first. That doesn't worry you?"

"Not at all. My interest in Dragon Cay is simply that of an investor."

"Well then you're very different people, you and Laurence Kress. According to Sergei, it'll make Kress squirm to be forced to make the controlling interest over to him."

Minahero thought about it. Nodded. "Yes. I think it would. And that would be sufficient revenge? Yes. Not with most men. But with Laurence. Yes. I see. But it is a dangerous thing your Sergei is risking."

"As soon as he's got control, we're leaving."

"That would be best for Mr. Roff, I think, but not necessarily the best for you. Where would you go? Back to Arizona?"

"He's only bought that to be near his development. Just as Kress has a house here to be near to his."

"So where would you go?"

She hesitated. "Back to England, I suppose. For the time being."

"And he would go back to San Francisco? For the time being? Do you not find it . . . unsatisfactory?"

"Are you offering me anything better?"

"I have offered you nothing," Minahero said, glancing at his watch. "I wonder if Laurence has caught his dolphin yet. He still has twenty minutes."

"Shall we go and see?" said Petronella, embarrassed by his sudden change of attitude. She got to her feet.

"No, please. Let us give him the full hour. If we go out to him now he will probably make that an excuse to stop and that will spoil our little contest. In the meantime let us talk about other things. About unimportant things . . ."

4

It was perfectly organised and superbly timed. With exactly fifteen minutes to run to complete Kress's stint, the attention of the man who had been dubbed Fido by Roff but whose name was Miyako, was apparently attracted by something he saw floating past the yacht. Keeping his eyes on this he made his way hurriedly to the stern at the same time calling *"O San! O San!"* excitedly to Kress who left the fighting chair to see what was going on. He found him pointing down with a jabbing finger into the water a yard or so astern and the better to see what the excitement was all about Kress leant over himself, whereupon Miyako, taking hold of the club used for dispatching fish, brought it down with great force on the back of Kress's head at least knocking him unconscious, if not possibly killing him outright. He then dropped the club and, leaving Kress slumped over the transom, went to the locker from which he extracted one of the lumps of lead, which it was cheaper to risk than anchors where the bottom was rocky and to which had already been attached two short lengths of wire terminating in large treble hooks. Taking this device he unhurriedly hooked it in behind Kress's belt and in his trousers and then simply upended the whole consignment into the sea. Kress actually went in head first but the weights having less resistance accelerated so that for the briefest of moments the bloodied head, most strangely with its heavy spectacles still in place, popped up out of the water only then to be drawn swiftly down and out of sight.

Miyako then hosed down the cockpit, although in truth there was little blood except on the transom itself and even here there was not very much and what there was, like the black hairs matted with blood on the fish club, was soon disposed of. Miyako took a final look round to make sure that everything was in order and then, quitting the cockpit by the port companionway, made his way to the bridge, muttered *"Benjo"* to the captain and descended by the forward companionway to the galley and thence the head. While all of this was occurring not once had O'Kano on the fly bridge allowed his attention to wander from searching the sea ahead for flotsam.

Exactly on the hour, which was only two or three minutes after Miyako had gone down, Ota's head appeared from the galley calling in Japanese to Fujita, who dismissed him, and then Ota said courteously to Roff, "Mr. Minahero say the hour is finished and will you please join him for a drink and lunch. Please do not go by galley way." Much relieved, Roff, who, with his mind still alert to the contract yet to be signed, had found it difficult to concentrate on floating debris, made his way along the upper deck and down the companionway to the fishing cockpit. He was not particularly surprised at finding it deserted, having assumed that Kress would have been called in also and so he made his way without delay into the saloon via the door in the starboard quarter. This too was empty but at once Ota came in with a tray of dry martinis.

"Mr. Minahero showing lady round below. He say, please to wait. Will not be long." And with a bow, he put the martinis down and silently withdrew, closing the saloon door behind him. Roff took one of the martinis and found it well made and, with it in his hand, ambled round the saloon enjoying the delightful Japanese prints with which the walls were decorated. After perhaps seven or eight minutes, Minahero and Petronella came in to join him.

"Ah," said Minahero, "Mr. Roff. You have a drink. Good. Petronella?" He reached for one and handed it to her. Roff did not miss the first usage of her name nor the pale tightness of her face.

Minahero, however, was totally at ease.

"You are admiring the pictures?" he suggested.

"Yes," said Roff.

"They are only prints of course. We call them *ukiyo-ye.*"

"What does that mean?" asked Petronella.

"It means 'floating world.' I do not know that I can explain. It is a feeling perhaps. A contemplation of the world. Not this one but many are very misty, no?" She nodded. "There is always more than we can see. In Western paintings you look and that is what there is. But with the Chinese and Japanese . . ." He spread his hands.

"I think I understand," said Petronella.

"And you like these prints?"

"Yes."

"I have others and better. And *kakemonos,* scrolls."

"No."

"You must dine with me in my apartment. I have had it made to look as if it was in a Japanese house. You must come to dinner. We will have a Japanese evening. We will wear kimonos and sandals which I will lend you. And we will drink warm sake and we will eat sukiyaki. Or maybe we will have tempura. I remember last time Laurence came we had sukiyaki." He glanced benignly round. "But where is Laurence?" He looked at his watch. *"Ju-ni han,"* he muttered. "He has had too long. Twelve minutes." He crossed the saloon and opening the door to the cockpit, looked into it and came back immediately.

"He is not there," he said.

"On the bridge perhaps?" suggested Petronella.

"No," Roff said, "he can't be on the bridge. The captain asked me not to come down via the galley. I came in through that door." He nodded. "And Kress wasn't there. No one was there."

"Miyako should have been there," said Minahero. "Those were my orders."

Roff smiled. "I gather he had to go where Laurence has most probably gone."

Minahero said nothing, but left them in unusual haste.

"He had better be in the lavatory," said Petronella.

NINE

"Mr. Noel Baker?"

"Speaking." The voice was deadpan.

"My name is Roff. I need to speak urgently to George Le Clerc."

"What telephone number are you ringing from?"

Roff gave the number.

"Put down the receiver but wait by the telephone."

Roff did so. Almost immediately the telephone rang. He picked up the receiver. "Yes?"

"Who is that speaking?"

"You know who it is. Sergei Roff."

"*Where* are you speaking from?"

"From the telephone in the card room on *Fair Lady* in the Pompano marina."

"Have you ever been to the Freeport Inn?"

"Yes. For lunch."

"The Windward Palms Hotel?"

"No."

"Go there. Go by taxi and be there by eleven-thirty tomorrow morning . . ."

"Tomorrow! This is urgent!"

The urgency was ignored. The voice continued deadpan. It was not a recording but it was curiously like a recording.

"By eleven-thirty tomorrow morning. Ask at the reception if there has been a call for Brian Maitland. You will be told that there has been and that the caller has said he will ring again. Go and sit by the pool and order yourself a drink. Take no one with you. Now will you repeat that, please?"

Roff was becoming angry.

"Now listen to me, Noel Baker, or whoever you are. We're passed 1984 and I am not waiting until tomorrow to see Le Clerc. Something very serious has happened . . ."

"We know exactly what has happened and it is quite impossible for you to speak to the party you want to speak to as he isn't on the island. Now will you please repeat the instructions?"

Roff shot a helpless glance at Petronella in one of the two armchairs ranged either side of the writing desk at which he was sitting, then did as he was instructed.

"Correct," the voice confirmed. And the line went dead.

"You got that?" said Roff, putting the receiver angrily down.

"Most of it."

"Le Clerc's not on the island. Or so that . . . that jerk makes out!" Frustration forced the expression unusual for him. "And they know exactly what has happened. *His* words!"

"Do you think they do?" said Petronella.

"How the hell can they when we don't even know for sure ourselves."

It was early evening. They had been back aboard *Fair Lady* for several hours through most of which Roff had been vainly trying to contact Noel Baker. Petronella had just come from her bath. She wore a white cotton towelling robe. Her hair was freed and lay loosely over her back and shoulders. Her legs and feet were bare.

"But we do," said Petronella quietly, putting up a hand to shift some of her hair from falling across one eye. "One of those Japs pushed him over." She raised her head. "Unless you did."

He looked at her levelly. "Do you think I did?"

"You had the best reason. You had the time."

"It was meant to look like that."

"It would always have looked as if it was meant to look like that."

"Yes. Because it's a damn funny yacht. Fancy not being able to get to the stern cockpit except directly from the saloon or bridge. In most of them you simply walk along a side deck. And fancy not being able to *see* what's happening from the bridge because a runabout just happens to have been put across the line of sight."

"I doubt if Minahero had it designed so that he could push people off the end whenever he felt inclined."

"He had it designed." And when she did not reply, he went on, not without satisfaction. "Surprised you, hasn't it? Wasn't in the script someone should push Kress overboard."

"It *could* have been what Minahero suggests . . ."

"Scenario! Kress is a man who knows it all. Ignores the advice he's given.

Tightens the drag on both reels because he thinks that way he's more likely to hook his dolphin. Has to excuse his guard dog who's got a call of nature and, worried in case I suddenly catch him by himself, takes one of the rods out of the cup and goes and sits on the aft coaming so he can both go on with fishing and see anyone coming into the cockpit. And, would you believe it, gets a marlin strike, loses his balance and, whoops, over he goes. Rod and all!"

"It has happened."

"Sure it's happened. But not this time. And you no more believe it than I do."

She got out of the chair. "I've got to go."

"Go? Where?"

"I'm having dinner with Minahero."

She would have said no more but as she made to pass him he shot out a hand to seize her wrist. Biting her lip she looked down at him, her hair tumbling across his arm. "Let me go, Sergei," she told him quietly. "I know what I'm doing."

He released her wrist. She rubbed it slowly with her other hand. "You might as well know. He's got a letter Kress wrote yesterday saying you'd threatened to kill him which Kress apparently was going to tell you he'd written before you went through with that contract."

Roff got to his feet and poured himself a drink. It was quiet on *Fair Lady* but music from a nearby boat came faintly to his ears.

"Sit down," he said. And, irritably, when she hesitated, "It won't do your cause any harm to keep him on tenterhooks."

She went back to her chair.

"So this particular scenario," he said, "is that Minahero has a letter written by Kress which, allied to the fact that Kress has disappeared and that, apart from a Jap without an axe to grind, I was the only one who could have pushed him overboard, would give the Bahamian police sufficient grounds for arresting me . . ."

"Sergei . . ."

"Let me finish." His voice was grating. "On the other hand, from Minahero's point of view, quite apart from it being far less bothersome to have an accident rather than a murder on his boat, there could be a spin off. He might be able to do a trade. And you're willing to do that trade. That's what you're saying, isn't it? Only there's one thing you aren't taking into account." He tapped his chest. "Me. The man you're making this great sacrifice for." He shook his head. "No, Petronella. Go and sleep with him. After all it's something you talked about doing long before you knew anything about this letter. And long before it even occurred to you Kress might be got out of the way. Go and become his mistress." All the time his voice was rising. "But don't try and make out you're doing it on my account! And as for that letter, if it does exist, tell him to send it to the bloody Secret Service or any one he damn well likes!" And in a sudden outburst of quite uncontrollable anger he hurled the still half-full glass with all his strength across the room, and, not even glancing at where it smashed, stormed out.

2

She sat pale and trembling, staring at the scratched and dented panelling, at the star of liquid dripping down the wall, at the glittering glass splinters on the chartreuse carpet. She reached for a cigarette from an open box on the writing desk beside her. She smoked it greedily, spoiling its end so that she had to pick bits of tobacco from her mouth. Kress's death, if dead he was, was startling, disconcerting, puzzling even, but, she told herself, it in no way affected what she had come to do. Kress, alive or dead, was an irrelevance. Even who had killed him was irrelevant. She did not believe it had been Sergei but she had to accept the possibility. For the first time with her he had lost control. He could have lost control over Kress, in a sudden rush of blood to the head seen the perfect opportunity of revenging himself for the humiliation, the lost years of life, the disfigurement the man had caused him. He could have.

But she didn't believe it.

Then it must have been engineered by Minahero. After all, the pieces fitted. The rather childish competition. Sergei sent to the bridge to be out of the way and, as he'd said, that sportsboat blocking his line of sight. The establishment of an alibi by keeping close to her. Yes, it certainly could have been engineered by Minahero. But if he had a reason for ridding himself of Kress, surely he could have found a better place for doing it than on his boat; and in all the months they had been working together on Dragon Cay a better time than now? The fact that Minahero might have, in fact almost certainly *had* planned Kress's execution, was not difficult to accept— Minahero, she knew from Shapland, would have had as little compunction in killing man or woman who had become a nuisance as most men or women would in killing a wasp which threatened to sting them. But she came back to the same questions: the time; the place.

Unless . . .

Unless it was not really Kress he wanted to be rid of but Sergei!

She sat quite still, the cigarette, forgotten, sending a tiny coil of smoke to the ceiling of the charming, opulent, silent little room.

Because he felt threatened by Sergei?

Why should he? Sergei knew nothing of his affairs. Had given not the slightest reason for Minahero to suspect he could pose a threat.

Then the other reason. Herself?

Would a man kill another in such a way as to throw suspicion on a third merely to open the path to a possible satisfaction of his lusts?

But she was merely trying to argue against her own conviction.

She remembered her cigarette and smoked it thoughtfully, not liking her thoughts at all. If that analysis was right, then she was personally responsible not merely for Kress's death—which wasn't all that important—but for putting a decent man . . .

A decent man! She laughed inwardly, scornfully, at herself.

Sergei Roff wasn't a decent man. He was the man because of whom the impossible had happened; because of whom she had discovered love was possible again.

She ground out the cigarette and got quickly to her feet. This wasn't any good. If she allowed herself to wallow in such sentiments, purpose would be lost, the months of planning, the sacrifices utterly wasted. She had been groomed, at her own request, to carry out a task. And the time had come to start carrying it out.

She went quickly from the card room and down the stairway to their stateroom. She threw off the robe and went to the wardrobe, trying to decide.

There was very little time.

Sergei must go, he had served his purpose anyway.

If he went now, back to his Anita, Shapland would give the clearance for her promised.

If he didn't go?

If he didn't go, Minahero would give that letter to the police.

Or there would maybe be an accident.

3

Minahero had not exaggerated. The entire internal structure of his penthouse suite had been removed to allow its total refurbishment as a Japanese home of consequence. Panels of *tatami*—corn-coloured straw in oblongs edged in black—had replaced the carpets. *Fusuma* doors—lightly framed doors covered both sides with paper—which could be slid the width of a complete wall or, if required, removed entirely, took the place of partitions. *Shoji*—large sliding screens of translucent paper—served as windows. The ceiling was of narrow *sugi* wood panels supported by thin, clean battens. There remained nothing which could give the slightest indication this was not the interior of a dwelling found somewhere in Japan.

In the reception room into which Petronella was directed, with the exception of a pair of large velvet-covered cushions, the room was devoid of furnishings and this emptiness combining with the quiet, mild colouring of paper and tatami and the soft, subdued light filtered through the translucent paper instead of glass in the window walls, produced a feeling of airiness and peace. Any sense that this was merely an apartment on the top floor of a modern Western hotel was entirely banished.

She stood transfixed and in the instant of her entry (at the behest of a Japanese servant garbed in a plain kimono, who had admitted her into a simple hall where she had changed her shoes for silk slippers) all the complex thoughts which had occupied her mind from leaving *Fair Lady*, through the sumptuous lobby of the Pompano Hotel and in its utramodern lift which, conveying her silently, swiftly, upwards, ill-prepared her for the shock which lay ahead. And she had still not shaken off the sense of vulnerability when another screen slid back and through it walked Yasuo Minahero.

He was wearing a silk kimono of a little above ankle length worn over some sort of linen undergarment decorated in red and black silk at the neck and tied around the waist with a soft silk sash. Over all of this he wore a dark-coloured, huge-sleeved, loose, hip-length cloak which hung open down the front. His feet were encased in black cotton socks, *tabis*, with a special shaping for the big toe which separated it from the others.

He stood in the opening, quite still, observing her and at once she felt embarrassingly out of place. On an impulse and to make a point, rather than some provocative dress she had chosen washed denim slacks and a powder-blue cashmere pullover. Her only jewellery was two huge circles of silver earrings; her hair was loose about her shoulders. Nothing she could have selected could, it seemed to her in that baffling moment, have been more inappropriate in a room of such delicacy and taste and faced with a host so correctly attired for it.

Yet to judge by Minahero's reaction this was not so.

He nodded, as if approvingly, and smiled. "You have chosen simply," he told her. "I am very pleased."

"Are you?" said Petronella, coolly, rediscovering her role.

"Yes," he answered. "I will show you why. Come."

He turned his back on her and went into a further room. She hesitated, then followed him. The room she found herself in appeared to be an inner hall, for the walls were all undecorated translucent screens which clearly led to other rooms. In this hall was a stand and carefully hung upon it what she took to be a kimono. On a small low table was a tiny handbell. There was nothing else at all. The kimono was exquisite in buffs and, coincidentally, powder blue, with motifs of flying swallows.

"It is beautiful, is it not?" he suggested.

She nodded. "That kimono? Yes."

"It is properly called an *uchikake* not a kimono," he corrected her, "but to call it a kimono is not entirely wrong. You will remember the prints your Mr. Roff was admiring on my boat? Some of the artists of the school preferred to paint actors and"—and there was the slightest pause—"and courtesans. I commissioned this *uchikake* to be created after a particularly famous painting. I invite you to wear it. You may feel more . . . at home."

She understood the remark precisely as she was intended to. She could, if she chose, take it as an insult—in which case he would bother with her no further. Or she could accept it and in doing so, while not committing herself, signify willingness to be propositioned.

And the decision must be swift.

She nodded. "I'll wear it. Why not?" She could not have been more offhand.

"It is not that simple," he told her. "That is the overgarment. There is formality to these things."

"It's all right," she said.

"Good." He paused—but the pause was not hesitation. "You understand it would not be appropriate for you to wear modern underclothes."

"Of course."

He nodded as if they had reached an understanding. "If you will ring that bell," he said, nodding to it, "someone will come to help you dress and to arrange your hair."

He bowed very slightly, in fact more an unhurried nod of the head than a formal bow and withdrew, sliding the screen closed behind him. Petronella took a step towards the *uchikake* to examine it and found it to be of heavy silk, beautifully worked. She shook her head in silent disbelief, hesitated and then quickly picked up the bell and rang it.

At once a stout but gentle-looking Japanese woman in a brightly coloured kimono and stiff formal obi entered, hands clasped together over her stomach, bowing.

"Hallo," Petronella said, absurdly.

The woman smiled and, her eyes not for a moment leaving Petronella's, backed with tiny steps. It was clear she was to follow. She did so and passing through a further barely furnished room found herself in another with wooden walls and a floor of wooden slats, clearly a bathroom for in its centre was a tall rectangular tub of some beautifully fragant wood filled with steaming water heated by a kind of stove within the bath itself.

She understood. Before donning the priceless *uchikake* she was to bathe, and bathe in Japanese style—not for reasons of cleanliness but to signify her willingness totally to accept a role. Before he was prepared to proposition her,

Minahero required tacit confirmation that if she did accept, then any future behests, however unusual, would be agreed to without question.

And so she bathed, discovering with help from the servant the Japanese method of first soaking herself in a crouching position in the intensely hot, perfumed water, then washing herself beside the bath with water ladled out with a wooden box, sluicing off soap and lather, and only then getting back into the bath for a final soak. And for all the strangeness of the operation and the even greater strangeness that she could allow herself to take part in it, she admitted the extraordinarily relaxing effect it had upon her body.

After the bath her hair was unhurriedly arranged, tied at the nape of her neck and fitted into a kind of snood to the end of which was attached gauzy pieces of material to pick up the colours of the *uchikake* while to the crown of her head a butterfly was pinned. And then she was dressed. The woman either knew no English or had been forbidden to use any that she had, but through the complicated business with a word here and there she gave names to the varied articles. At first, against her flesh, the *kosode*, a short-sleeved kimono of white silk and then *hakama*, a strange garment of red silk, a sort of skirt-trousers held up at the waist with a silken sash and so long as to trail along the floor, then over the *kosode* other kimonos, each of different shades, each of heavy silk, each lower in the neck and slightly higher in the hem to show a margin of the one beneath. And finally the superb *uchikake*. And it seemed to Petronella that with each new layer she was losing not only a little of her Western reality but also her independence.

Made ready at last, she entered the room where Minahero awaited her, conscious of the weight of the layers of heavy silk, hearing the swish of them across the soft tatami, restricted by them in her movements but made more graceful too, only too well aware that the combination of these garments and her sandals were obliging her to walk in a manner more fitted to her costume than to her normal self, that all these things were conspiring to reduce her confidence, addle her mind and make her the pliant tool intended.

His back was to her; he was kneeling on the right hand of the velvet cushions, his legs tucked under him, his haunches resting upon his calves and inner sides of his heels, his toes turned inwards so that the upper and outer part of his instep bore down upon the cushion. He made no attempt to turn towards her and his not doing so was as clear an instruction as any spoken. She was required to take, without demur, the second cushion and kneel beside him. And the curious thing was that it seemed to her far, far easier to do this than protest. It required all her self-control and courage to object: "Mr. Minahero, don't you think you're carrying this too far?"

At this he rose, easily, and, turning to face her, said with a smile, "Would it be too much for an Englishman to ask a Japanese lady to sit beside him in an armchair?"

"We're not back two hundred years in time."

"No," he agreed. "But in Japan, I dress like a Westerner when I am at business. When I go home I discard my Western clothes and wear a kimono and sit in the Japanese manner. One cannot compromise."

"I will show you something," he told her. "Come with me."

He led her through one of the openings in a screen, through another simple room with its own tokonoma its own chigai-dana but this one containing a few exquisite pieces clearly placed with a studied concern for spacing, then sliding back a further screen, exposed a door. This he threw open.

"I own also this apartment," he told her—and she was looking at a modern sitting-room with fitted carpet, floor-to-ceiling drapes, furnished in excellent, comfortable, contemporary taste. "We would look absurd, would we not, if we spent the evening here dressed as we are?" And, when she did not reply, repeated his earlier words. "One cannot compromise." He shut the Western world out again. "Now I will show you something else." He led her back and, sliding wide a shoji, preceded her out onto the balcony. And here, perhaps, the surprise was an even greater one for, out of what would originally have been no more than a wide, spacious, paved concrete terrace, beyond a narrowish strip of flooring (so polished as to have the appearance of being lacquered) and more than overhung by a projecting roof, a Japanese garden, mutedly lit by ishi-doros, strangely shaped stone lanterns placed strategically here and there, had been created, and cleverly created so that beyond it only the sky could be seen. There was nothing to suggest this was the subtropics. There were no flowers—there were simply rocks, water, sand and stepping stones, and the stone lanterns which seemed to possess an eery living quality. In a way it was a curious reminder of the yard to the house in Tucson where she had met Sergei for the first time; in a way it could hardly have been more different. For whereas that had been uninspired and functional, the garden here, created on a balcony cantilevered out above the twelve floors of the hotel below, small of space, exquisitely designed, exemplified the artistic feeling of Minahero's race in its purest form; simplicity, honesty, naturalness, beauty, space, all were contained in a few square yards echoing, integrated with and completing the ambience within.

She walked behind him, using the stepping stones for all the complexity of their placing, to the edge of a small pool with boulders seemingly casually arranged. In the pool swam golden and cream-coloured carp.

She shook her head. "It's incredible," she admitted.

His look held triumph, his smile contempt. "There is nothing which cannot be achieved when one decides. And nothing which cannot be replaced. Except tradition."

"If you have the money."

"Yes. And the determination."

"You never wear Western clothes here?"

"Never."

"Never entertain people wearing Western clothes here?"

"No. In any case the Japanese do not often entertain people in their homes. If it is necessary to entertain, I entertain on my yacht, in a restaurant or, occasionally, in the other apartment."

"Even when you offer them the tempura you mentioned this morning?"

He smiled. "This morning I did not quite tell the truth. To be polite one lies occasionally. The late Mr. Kress has never dined with me in this apartment. Nor would I have invited him to do so for I do not believe, however great the advantage to be gained from it, he would have been willing to co-operate as you have done."

In other words, she realised, he has created here a small piece of Japan which isn't to be sullied. And she wondered about the motives which lay behind his doing this. If they were as straightforward as simply feeling more comfortable in the clothes and surroundings in which he had been raised. Or if they were out of sentiment or nostalgia. And then she wondered if there was room in the ethos of this formidable Japanese for such affections. Or if something altogether different lay behind it, something deeper, something menacing.

"You have to be very rich," she said, "to be able to indulge such inclinations."

"The word is not appropriate," he answered. But he did not explain. "I am very rich," he went on. "Richer, even, I think, than you imagine."

"As rich as Kress?"

He laughed quietly. "You Westerners," he said, "do not understand what real riches are. I could build this whole hotel out of contents of this apartment. Come, I show you."

He led her inside again and, taking her round the apartment, showed her various scrolls, vases, plates, incense and writing boxes, screens, perfume bottles, jades and the like, the great majority of which were not even on display but hidden away in sets of built-in wall cupboards and drawers, screen boxes and the like. Gradually it was driven home to her that, without exception, each item was of its kind a classic and of enormous value, that here in effect was a collection of priceless artefacts which would have made any museum curator swoon with envy.

"But why on earth don't you show these lovely things when you've got them?" she protested. "It's a sin for them to be shut away in drawers and things."

"You do not understand Japanese philosophy. Joy can only exist in simple and artistic surroundings. You Westerners clutter your homes with ornaments, you have paintings on every wall, different patterns wherever you look. Your eye can never settle on contemplation of the beauty and form of a single item. And always the same. Summer, winter, autumn, spring what you look at, except perhaps a changed vase of flowers, is always the same. In a Japanese home proper regard is given to the different seasons. Whole walls can be removed and put away, sets of painted doors replaced with others. And perhaps two or three of many rare and beautiful things can be displayed in carefully chosen locations and be, for a little while, a source of artistic contemplation."

"Is this how it is all over Japan?" Petronella asked.

For the first time he showed anger, although not at her. "No. It has become chaotic."

He did not explain but Petronella thought she understood.

They came back to the first room.

"Please," he said, "sit down."

There was nothing for it but to squat as he did on the velvet cushion. To do so was both difficult and painful and she felt slightly absurd, considerably reduced and curiously exposed seated near the centre of this graceful yet all but unfurnished room. He took his place beside her on his own cushion, then clapped his hands. Almost at once the woman who had helped her dress entered carrying two low tables which she placed in front of them. She then withdrew to return almost at once carrying a small lacquered tray on which were a pair of tiny porcelain cups two-thirds filled with Japanese green tea. She placed these, one each, on the tables in front of her, bowed deeply and silently withdrew.

"You take the cup with right hand," Minahero ordered, "and support it with left."

She did as instructed. The tea had a flavour subtle yet at the same time pure. When they had replaced their cups, he said, without solicitude, "You do not find it too uncomfortable?"

"It's very uncomfortable," she answered.

"You are young and supple," he said, quite without sympathy. "You would soon get used to it. Now may we talk about Mr. Roff? I asked on the boat, before that most unfortunate incident took place, how long you had known him. You did not tell me."

"I've known him a couple of years or so," she replied offhandedly. "On and off."

"Not all the time? No. Of course. He has this other woman who is not his wife."

"Yes."

"I am surprised one as beautiful as you is prepared share with another woman."

She took an enormous risk. "Hasn't your wife had to share you with other women?"

He was not annoyed. "Firstly she is Japanese. Secondly she is my wife. A wife can accept a mistress, so can a mistress a wife; but not, so easily, a rival."

"You realise he cannot stay on Grand Bahama?"

She decided to ignore this. "Kress," she said, "was . . ."

He interrupted her. "Kress was a small-minded and stupid man."

"You really think a fish pulled him overboard?"

"Is that important?"

"It is to Sergei."

"Perhaps we should ask those whose business it is to specialise in such things what they think."

"The police? But you must know, Mr. Minahero. You spent long enough with them this afternoon."

"The Bahamian police are very nice. And very understanding when you lose a friend and business associate. Particularly one who has a substantial investment in their country."

"You mean you didn't tell them about that letter?"

"They would not like me if I did."

"They prefer an accident to murder."

"Of course."

"Well it's all very well, Mr. Minahero . . ." She wondered if the contrived indignation was convincing. "Look! I simply have to know. I can't go on living with a man who . . ." She broke off.

"What are you going to do?"

"I'm damned if I know."

"If, let us say, I was to give that letter to the police, how would you be placed?"

"What d'you mean, 'How would you be placed?' "

"Has he made ample provision for you?"

"If you want to know he's made no damn provision."

"Did you tell him about the letter?"

"No."

"Why not?"

"Because I wanted to think it over. To give myself time to decide *what* to do. Anyway, how do I know there is a letter?"

He regarded her mildly through his gold-framed glasses. "I have it here." She looked at him angrily.

"You're playing with me, aren't you? What do you want?"

He moved his head. "That other apartment. The one which connects with this one. It could be yours."

"For as long as I was of interest to you?"

"How long you were of interest to me would depend on yourself."

"But at the end?"

"You would in your terms be a rich woman. The longer the time, the richer you would be."

"So much a week? Is that what you're saying?"

"That is not what I am saying. I have said what I have had to say."

She realised she had nearly blown it. Nearly. *Had* she blown it, he would have risen to his feet and had her shown out. She wondered if she agreed whether she would be expected to have sex with him at once.

He seemed to read her mind. "You may have time to consider it. In any case I would find it embarrassing for anything to begin before Roff has left."

He rose to his feet.

"Let us say no more about it for the present. By now dinner will have been prepared. Come."

He stood above her, looking down. A man with soft grey hair and enigmatic eyes behind gold-rimmed spectacles, with a small mouth and a high-boned, immobile face. He looked anything but a caricature of the Japanese; he looked very real. And, because what she knew of him enabled her to see through the mask, very dangerous.

TEN

The Windward Palms Hotel proved to be a comparatively modest establishment set in the centre of the island and near the International Bazaar and the Princess Casino. Roff found himself a chair by an empty table sheltered by a group of palm trees and well back from the bar and the L-shaped swimming pool, ordered a beer and impatiently awaited events. He had carried out his instructions, enquired at the reception desk as to whether there had been a call for Brian Maitland, was advised there had been and that the caller would ring again.

A full hour passed with no developments and to begin with the time had passed quickly enough as he pondered on his conversation that morning with Petronella. After storming out from *Fair Lady*, he had spent the evening ridiculously, drinking heavily, gambling recklessly in the casino and finally trudging up and down an empty beach in the starlight trying to work things out. Returning to the yacht (much to his surprise, and rather to his discomfort considering what he had been imagining through the evening), he had found her asleep in bed. He had taken a bottle of whisky and sat out with it on the forward deck, a prey to conflicting emotions, trying to decide upon a plan and failing hopelessly. When the bottle was half empty he had taken himself off to one of the spare staterooms. In the morning he had woken to a foul-tasting mouth, a splitting headache and anger at his own futility. By contrast Petronella, fresh as a daisy, in the same pullover and jeans, had seemed quite at ease.

"I've ordered breakfast on the upper stern deck," she had informed him. "Is that all right?"

He had looked at her gloomily from his bed.

"And before you ask," she had gone on, "I didn't. And you look terrible. Why don't you have a swim or something?"

Twenty minutes later, showered and shaved, he had joined her.

She poured him a cup of coffee. "Are you having any breakfast?"

He looked with distaste at the various possibilities. "Orange juice."

She poured the orange juice; ice tinkled deliciously in the jug. The breeze was fresh, making a little chop upon the sea. From where he sat he could look across an area of grass to the tennis courts of the Pompano Beach Hotel and beyond them to the hotel itself. He wondered which of the top-floor suites, which together formed a kind of lid to the squarely built hotel, was owned by Minahero. He drank off the orange juice.

"Which one of those up there is his then?" he demanded.

"He's got two."

"What's the spare one for? His mistresses?"

"Yes. Apparently it is."

"And he's offered it to you?"

"Yes."

"And you're going to take it?"

"Yes."

"Then why did you come back?"

"Because it's only on offer when you've left the island."

"So I stay."

"Then that letter goes to the police and you'll be arrested for killing Kress."

"Which I didn't do."

"Which you didn't do."

"Oh. So you *do* believe that."

"I believe it but what I believe doesn't matter a twopenny damn."

"What the hell is this all about?"

"You've done what you came to do . . ."

"Done what I've . . . Oh! You mean delivered you. That's what it was all about, wasn't it? That's what I was conned to do. The whole crazy business. Being lured to Tucson. Taught to fish. This floating gin palace. Kress!" He could not stay sitting. "Theoretically my mission was to see that Kress lost control of Dragon Cay . . ."

"Which he has."

"Because some Jap pushed him over the side. But that wasn't in the blueprint, was it? And what's it signify anyway? Kress being out of orbit? No. My job wasn't to see that Kress lost control of Dragon Cay. That's maybe what my job was supposed to look like. And did look like. And in fact I damn near pulled it off. Is that why Minahero had him killed? To stop me pulling it off?"

She watched him pacing up and down in the confined space of the after deck.

"No. And for the same reason. Minahero's got no more control now than he had this time yesterday. Anyway he's not interested in control. If he had been he could probably have done the whole thing on his head."

"Easily," said Petronella. "You're talking about real money now."

"Not the sort of money I've got? Or Kress had?"

"No."

"And now you're trying to make me think the reason you're going in with Minahero is because he *is* that rich! Don't waste your time. What you're interested in is getting close to him. Becoming his mistress because that way you can find things out that otherwise you couldn't. Right?"

She did not reply.

"This whole set-up was targeted to that end, wasn't it? He had to be persuaded to believe that you were here for the taking. That you were the current baggage of a man you were getting tired of—or getting worried might give you the push. You arrive with Sergei Roff who's got a perfectly good reason for being here—to get even with a bastard who set him up as a fall guy years ago. That makes sense. I've made myself rich. Put myself in the position to get my own back. So I'm rich and on the warpath. That all hangs together. No reason for Minahero to think anything else. And it all works out. Just the way it's been planned. He falls for it hook, line and sinker. In fact he's so bloody keen to have you he even arranges to rub out poor old Laurence. So what's it feel like Peta, having a death on your hands?"

"I've thought of that," Petronella answered quietly. "And I didn't like it." She came across to him and looked him in the eyes. "There's a lot of things I could say to you, Sergei," she told him. "A lot of things, I'd like to say. But I can't say them and nothing you say to me is going to *make* me say them. You're not far off. The thing between you and Kress was, as you say, a smokescreen. And it's worked. In the process Kress got killed. And probably for just the reason that you've given. And I don't like it. But I'm not going to lose any sleep about it because what he did to you was unforgiveable and it's only rough justice what's happened to him. You probably feel you've been treated like a . . . I don't know. Like an old dishcloth which can be discarded when it's served its purpose. And so you have. But you were the only person Shapland could find who would fit the bill with Kress and at least . . ."

"He'll give me a clearance on Anita!"

"That wasn't what I was going to say. But he will."

"I didn't need one."

"I know."

"But you went along with it. Let me fall in love with you."

"I couldn't help that. And in any case . . ."

"It's all right," he interrupted harshly. "That's over."

She turned away and, gripping the handrail, stared down at the sea lapping against *Fair Lady's* side.

"Sergei," she said. "I can't tell you what this is all about but you must believe me that it is because of something that has to be done. And you must believe me when I tell you that if you don't leave Grand Bahama now— you've succeeded, whether you like it or not, in what you were sent here to do —you'll ruin everything. And anyway you'll be arrested for the murder of Laurence Kress."

"What's the form? Do you move in pronto to his spare apartment or transship on to his gin palace?"

"Please," said Petronella, "be kind."

"I've lost my kindness."

She sighed. "All right. I move into the spare apartment as a base. Meanwhile as soon as the police give a clearance on the *Dai Nichi* she's shifting to the marina on Dragon Cay. Apparently Dillard . . . that senator we met in the Deep Water Bar . . ."

He nodded grimly. "I remember. The one who couldn't keep his fish eyes off you."

"Apparently he wants to charter her now and again while he's staying on Dragon Cay. She's better equipped than his own boat is."

"Minnie needs the money?"

"No. Dillard's a big noise in game fishing because of who he is and with the right exposure can drum up the right publicity."

"You certainly got to cases, didn't you?"

"I made a good start on what I've come to do."

"Go on."

"When Minahero takes the *Tsuki* over to Dragon Cay, I go with him."

"Travelling harem."

"If you like."

She drew away from the handrail and faced him again "I wish you'd have faith in me, Sergei," she said quietly. "It's possible one day I may be able to explain. Then maybe you'll not think so badly of me."

"But you won't be the same, will you, Petronella?" He grasped hold of her and kissed her hard, without feeling, held her body tight against him. The action called for no response and she did not respond.

He pushed her from him still holding her by the arms.

"I can still do that now," he said. "It may not mean too much but at least it doesn't make me sick."

She tore herself from his grasp. "Don't spoil *everything*, Sergei," she said. "Please."

And she turned away to hide her tears.

2

It was close on one o'clock when Le Clerc showed up. The pool was still and the tables around it mostly empty with the hotel guests gone within or having chosen the shaded and more distant areas for lunch.

As usual he was immaculately dressed, although his formal suit struck a discordant note in this holiday atmosphere. He carried a heavy leather briefcase. He looked too successful to be a commercial traveller. He might have been taken for a potential buyer of the hotel.

Roff wasted no time on small talk. "You might as well know," he opened, "I'm not leaving Grand Bahama. Shapland's started something that's not going to be so easily finished."

"My dear fellow . . ."

"You can cut that out."

Le Clerc shrugged his massive shoulders and opening the briefcase took out a fat envelope. "Before you make too much a fool of yourself, you'd better look at what's in there," he suggested. "Only for your own sake, don't make it too public."

Roff held the small eyes in the great fat face and read the triumph in them.

"What now?" he said.

Le Clerc chuckled. "A surprise." And he laughed, not loudly, from deep within his belly. "We're full of surprises."

Roff put his hand into the capacious envelope and his fingers closed on something stiff. He pulled it out. It was a British passport. In the name of Karl Sodek. He stared at it unbelievingly, flicking through the pages, noting the visas, the small oil stain made by a dirty-fingered Mexican customs inspector more than a year before.

"So you didn't destroy it after all," he said.

"One never knows when something may come in useful," said Le Clerc, putting his podgy fingertips together like a bishop.

Roff took out other items: driving licence, credit cards, chequebook. He made no attempt to hide them, laying them one by one on the table in front of him.

"And my stock certificates?" he enquired. "The ones you had transferred into the name of Sergei Roff?"

"They're still in the name of Sergei Roff." He gestured. "These things are purely to get you out."

"So you did make all the changes."

"Of course. How else would Mr. Kress . . ." Le Clerc paused meaningly, immensely enjoying the moment, "the late Mr. Kress have been able to check up on you?"

"You're bloody proud of yourselves, aren't you? But you make *me* sick!" And in a sudden spasm of quite uncontrollable anger, Roff swept his arm across the table, scattering the documents to the terrace, where they lay, some with their pages opened, fluttering in the breeze.

Le Clerc remained imperturbable, a man self-coached for this very moment.

"You risk harm to no one but yourself," he observed.

"No!" responded Roff fiercely. "If that were so you wouldn't be here."

Le Clerc looked at him for a moment or two, then nodded. *"Touché,"* he agreed cheerfully. "But I had to make special flights to do it. My dear fellow you should be grateful."

"I'm supposed to become Karl Sodek again just to get out of here?" The double chins bunched at the other's nod. "Because I'm half suspected of

pushing Kress overboard. Is that what Petronella told you? Well she must
have, mustn't she? That bloody Jap or any of his gang wouldn't have told
you. Nor would the police. They don't even know you're here, Le Clerc, do
they? At least not as Le Clerc. Not up to the games you're up to. All right. So
you know Kress is dead. And so you know Minahero's got a letter from him
saying I threatened to kill Kress . . ."

He broke off. A sudden fixity in Le Clerc's smile, brief, soon camouflaged,
but in that instant unmistakable, advised him of his own and possibly serious
mistake. Le Clerc hadn't known about that letter. Whatever Peta might have
told him, she hadn't told him that.

"How do you know that Kress is dead?" Roff asked, in quite another tone.

"Because his body has been recovered."

"What!"

"By a fishing cruiser on its way back to Bimini." And evenly, as if explaining a quite unimportant point, "With his head smashed in. So you see, my
dear Sergei, your position is . . . somewhat delicate." He put his hand into
his pocket and withdrew something from it which he laid down on the table
—an airline ticket.

"There is," he said, "a flight booked for you in the name of Karl Sodek on
a plane to Miami which leaves in . . ." he consulted his watch. "Which
leaves in precisely seventy minutes' time. Down there," he waved a fat hand,
"are documents enabling you to catch it. You will exchange them at Miami
Airport for the document you required as a quid pro quo for helping us in this
little matter with a man who will meet you on arrival. If, on the other hand,
you are so foolish as to attempt to stay on Grand Bahama, before the day is
out you will most certainly have been arrested for the murder of Laurence
Kress and what with motive, opportunity and this letter of which you have
just informed me, I would hazard your chances of acquittal are slight indeed."

He closed his briefcase and rose to his feet. "And now if you will excuse
me, I have things to do."

He held out a podgy hand, which Roff ignored.

Le Clerc shrugged. "Oh and by the way, you will I am afraid have to travel
exactly as you are. *Fair Lady* is already on her way back to Miami. I am sorry
about the inconvenience but at twenty-six thousand dollars a day, she has
been an expensive prop. Good-bye."

And he turned and, unhurriedly, went into the hotel.

3

Roff caught the Miami flight. What else was there to do when it was quite certain that if he missed it, Le Clerc would have laid before the local authorities sufficient evidence to ensure he would be arrested?

He left, knowing there were many points unanswered but knowing too that it had all been carefully contrived so that he would be denied the time to find the answers to them. He left without making any attempt to contact Petronella, without even knowing where he could have contacted her except perhaps through Minahero. He left without the least idea what the whole, extraordinarily complicated scenario was all about, except that it was to do with a mild-mannered Japanese of fantastic wealth who was at that moment almost certainly welcoming a girl who had turned his attitude to life on its head on board his yacht or in one of his two apartments. He left bitter, frustrated and very angry. He left outmanoeuvred, discomfited, empty-handed. But he did not leave defeated. Something had been started which must be seen through to its end.

ELEVEN

"Who wishes to speak to him?"

"Miss Petronella Harrington."

"I do not know . . ."

"It's urgent! Very urgent!"

"Please wait."

While she did so, Petronella began to re-analyse the reflections which would occupy the agile mind of Yasuo Minahero. Sergei's sudden departure from Grand Bahama would surely not surprise him. The man had come, he would reason, with a specific purpose: in some way to triumph over Kress. But Kress was dead. What purpose was there in remaining merely to be arrested for his murder?

"Good afternoon."

Minahero's swiftness in answering caught her off balance—which perhaps was no bad thing.

"Yes?"

"He's gone!"

"Roff?"

"Yes. And the boat. I came back from having my hair done and the . . . the . . . the swine's sailed off and left me!"

"No."

"What d'you mean, no? I tell you . . ."

"Fair Lady sailed two hours ago. Roff was not aboard. But it is correct he has left the island. He caught the two-twenty flight for Miami."

"He what! How d'you know?"

"When I was advised *Fair Lady* had sailed, I made it my business to find out. Where are you?"

"Downstairs. Surrounded by my bloody luggage."

"I will come down."

The phone went dead.

With her heart beating uncomfortably fast, Petronella quit the booth and, crossing the lobby, chose the corner of a settee. The lobby, heavy with dark woods, cool, was, apart from hotel staff, empty at this off-peak hour of the afternoon. She lit a cigarette and waited. She had finished it before Minahero arrived.

He sat in a leather armchair placed at right angles to her settee, studying her for a few moments before speaking. She had chosen carefully: a simple dress with thin straps which left her arms and shoulders bare; a casual straw bag with some obvious shopping in it. Her knees were hard against each other; her hands clenched on her lap.

"So," Minahero said. "You are on your own?" She nodded, letting her tongue briefly touch her lips.

"There was no message left?"

"We had a blistering row when I got back last night. He called me . . ." She broke off, and reaching for the bag, scrabbled in it for cigarettes.

"You told him subject of our conversation?"

"Of course not! What do you . . . ?" Again she broke off, cigarette packet in hand. "I told him about that letter. Well, it came out. Who the hell does *he* . . . ?" She took a cigarette from the packet and put it in her mouth. A waiter passing by swooped with matches. When he had gone, she said, through smoke, "Is that offer still open?"

"What did he say? When you told him about that letter?"

"That he didn't give a damn about it. That if Kress hadn't been pulled over by a fish, you must have organised it."

"Organised it?"

"Organised someone to push him over. One of your crew."

"How absurd. Why should I do that?"

"That's what I said to him."

"And this morning?"

"He was like a bear with a sore head. But I never thought . . . Look. Is that offer still open, or isn't it?"

He examined her. Quite deliberately. Allowing his eyes to wander over her. Eventually he said, "You understand exactly what I expect of you?"

"Of course."

"I am Japanese. The Japanese have a different attitude to women."

She did not speak.

"And I have . . ." he paused deliberately, "my little foibles."

She felt the sudden race of her pulse. "Don't most men?" she managed.

He nodded briefly. "Very well. You may have the apartment. You will have five thousand American dollars a week paid into an account you may open in any bank you choose, here, in England, America, anywhere you like. That for your future. When our relationship has reached its end. Meanwhile I will meet expenses you incur if they are not absurd. Is that agreed?"

"Yes."

"Good." He rose to his feet. "I have a meeting to attend. Wait here, please."

He crossed to the reception desk and shortly afterwards the hotel manager came out from a room close by and spoke to him. He came back.

"I have explained. The porter will take your luggage up to the apartment. Please join me on my yacht at seven this evening."

He nodded and left her. She watched him walk out into the brilliant sunshine beyond the lobby doors.

2

She had expected that he would make sexual demands on her that evening but to her surprise when she joined him on his yacht she found two other couples with him: an Italian film director and his wife and an American art dealer and his. Minahero's attitude towards her was quite other than it had been the previous evening or in the lobby. He treated her with courtesy and respect equal to that he showed towards the other women and his guests, who had evidently known him for several years and knew better than to enquire into her background. It was clear she was accepted as their host's latest mistress and, she thought probable, was on trial by Minahero for the role of companion for such occasions.

The next two weeks were largely taken up by a visit of several days by Minahero to Japan but on those on which she saw him, before he left, she was treated to a style of life to which few women, and certainly no courtesans, could have objected. The financial arrangements promised were put in hand and she was encouraged to buy anything she felt like having. He did not intrude in her apartment; he made no demands on her. She dined with him on evenings when he had no business commitments, usually in the hotel or one of the island's restaurants, occasionally on the yacht, but never in either of the apartments. On one occasion they flew over to Dragon Cay and accompanied Senator Dillard deep-sea fishing on his so far unsuccessful quest for a mountable marlin. For the rest, she was left more or less to herself free to lounge by the hotel pool or explore the island.

It was a curious, frustrating, even baffling fortnight. And quite wasted. At the end of it she was not one inch further forward. Before leaving Minahero had held several meetings, always on his yacht and from which she was excluded—but in any case there was nothing secret about these meetings and amongst those attending were Warbeck and Boon and, she gathered, some of the minor Dragon Cay stockholders. In a word, ostensibly, Minahero was no more and no less than what he presented himself to be: an extremely rich tycoon involved in a major property development who could afford to indulge his fancies, which included beautiful women, priceless Far Eastern artefacts and deep-sea fishing. Thus far all the careful planning and vast expense which had successfully resulted in her ingratiating herself with him seemed utterly fruitless.

3

On his return from Japan, Minahero sent for her. She had been sunbathing by the pool and had no knowledge he was back. The summons was in the form of a note. Her heart beating furiously, she went up to her own apartment in accordance with his instructions.

He was waiting for her.

"You will come to my apartment tonight and be dressed by Yo-oko. We will dine in Japanese fashion. After that you submit to anything I wish of you. Is that agreed?"

She nodded, numbed.

"Good," he said. And he turned and, opening the connecting door to his own apartment, left her.

4

Perhaps the worst aspect of that first astonishing and degrading night was not the pain, nor even the degradation itself, but Minahero's attitude. His sexual powers, stimulated she suspected by drugs, were quite remarkable; his caprices aberrant and multifarious. Yet he displayed little lust. It was almost as if he was carrying out a series of strange rites either from some inner compulsion or in accordance with orders given to him. If there was pleasure in it, none was shown. There was not an atom of respect for her, there were no compliments on her beauty and she was made to feel an object of utter worthlessness.

The locale of this, the first of many such nights, was the simplest room of all—a tatami floor, three walls of undecorated screens or sliding doors, the fourth a range of cupboards in which were kept the necessary articles and contraptions which made possible the curious passions of this mysterious man. Many thoughts passed through Petronella's mind as she submitted one by one to his commands: the knowledge that with only papered screens and doors dividing room from room, she was either entirely alone with him and thus completely at his mercy should his lusts, apparently in control, over-whelm him—or else that there were listening witnesses to her humiliation; the presumption that she was merely the latest in a train of women he had degraded; the possibility that it was the process of degradation more than sexual appetite which drove him to these extremes. And, and this above all, that when this ordeal was over, whether through it she had failed or suc-ceeded in her endeavour, she would discover herself permanently defiled.

And she thought too of Sergei Roff to whose desires, she would have submitted without this feeling of debasement but whose demands she knew instinctively would have been kept within the bounds of what could not be hurtful to her; and of two other men, one bearing the name of Livesey, the other that of Harrington, both now dead. And it was only by thinking of these three men and what had happened to them, and of the breed of men who had been the cause of these happenings, that she found the courage and determination to continue.

5

Petronella spent most of the time, when Minahero was not actually engaged in business matters, with him. He was always at pains to explain the Japanese way of life as he saw it and to coach her in appropriate behaviour. She learnt that under no circumstances was she to enter the recess of the *tokonoma*, that it held for the Japanese both moral and spiritual significance, that it was the most sacred place in any home. He had her coached in the first basic principles of the art of *ikebana*, insisting that of all the many schools the only one worthy of her study was the ancient and austere school of *ikenobo*. He made it clear that she was at liberty to import any plants suitable to this style from anywhere in the world with the proviso that they must always be appro-priate to the season of the year. He explained the workings of a Japanese household, the thinking behind its architecture, its strengths, its weaknesses, its history and beliefs. The food served in his apartment was invariably Japa-nese and she was taught to assist in its preparation. After the initial occasion he never shared a Japanese meal with her—on the contrary she was required to bring to him in succession the most beautifully prepared dishes, kneel down to serve them, to speak only to enquire if the food was satisfactory or whether more was wanted. When she objected that while she might have become his mistress, she had not become his slave, he explained mildly that his wife was not his slave but this was how she was expected to behave and did.

Gradually she came to understand his credo. The only country of merit in the world was Japan and that was flawed by the creeping poison of Western influence. The only sex of significance was the male sex, the only children of importance boy children, the purpose of a wife purely domestic. Only courtesans were entitled to share man's thinking and that only to a limited degree. The duty of a modern-day Japanese man was to take advantage of Western experience and the opportunities it offered and use these for the benefit of Nippon. He was ashamed and fearful of the country he saw his beloved Japan becoming and would have been far happier born centuries earlier in the days when the warrior caste constituted the ruling class.

She learnt, quite quickly, that there was absolutely no purpose in trying to delve deeper into his motives or commercial affairs when in her Eastern role —then, except insofar as she helped provide the background which when away from Japan he missed or was there at night for the satisfaction of his lusts, she scarcely existed. But away from his apartment, dressed in Western clothes, playing the part of hostess to the men and women she met on his yacht, on his fishing cruiser, in the hotels and restaurants of Grand Bahama, or while over on Dragon Cay, it was another matter. In those surroundings, serving a different purpose, she became again worthy of respect and he treated her very much as he treated all other European women. It was, she soon realised, only on such occasions there was any hope of progress.

6

What was to lead towards the breakthrough occurred about a week after Minahero's return from Japan. She was in her own apartment, resting, when he walked in.

"We will be leaving in two hours' time for Dragon Cay," he told her.

She looked at him from the bed on which she was lying, half undressed. "Flying?"

"No. On my yacht. We shall be staying there for a week, so pack enough clothes."

"What sort of clothes?"

"You remember Dillard?"

"That American senator? Yes."

"I wish you to encourage him to stay. He is important to me."

"Why's he so important?"

"He is president of one of the most active deep-sea fishing clubs in North America. He has come down to catch a marlin big enough to mount in his New York apartment and he has not succeeded. In three days he is due to go home. I would like you to help me persuade him to stay long enough to catch his marlin."

"Why?"

"Is it not obvious?"

Petronella shook her head. Her hair was spread about the pillow. She wore a slip and her long legs were stretched out above the counterpane. She knew that here, in her own apartment, he would not touch her. Yet she fancied he was tempted and felt able to take a risk or two.

"What isn't obvious to me is why you bother with Dragon Cay at all."

"Please," he said, "do not enquire into my business."

She shrugged, putting her hand up to a shoulder strap as if to straighten it as an excuse for shifting her body temptingly.

"As I'm not to talk about your business, unless I'm to persuade Dillard to stay on longer by hinting maybe I'll let him sleep with me or something, I really don't see . . ." She broke off, intentionally. "Will we be taking any of your gear with us?" she asked pointedly.

"No." His eyes were masked.

"I'm having a holiday?"

"If you care to put it that way, yes."

She sat up, putting her hands between her head and the bedhead and leaning back against it. "I'll try to persuade Dillard to stay on. But I've got to have some reason for doing so."

"Listen," Minahero said. "I want Dillard to catch that marlin. I want him to be photographed beside it. I want him to have it mounted with my compliments and take it back with him on his yacht. And when he gets off his yacht in Fort Lauderdale, I want more photographs. Television maybe. I want it put all over America that Senator Dillard came down to Dragon Cay with a purpose and fulfilled that purpose.

"From tomorrow, we will go out fishing on *Dai Nichi* every day. You. Me. Dillard. Apart from the crew, no one else. And we will catch that marlin . . ."

"If he hasn't so far . . ."

"He has caught one too small for mounting and raised two more and lost both."

"Maybe he'll lose a third."

"It's having that marlin that's important to him. Not catching it."

"Oh, I see. We catch it and give him the credit?"

"If necessary. I am told he is losing heart."

"I've got to put heart back into him."

"Exactly."

"How?"

"I do not think I need to tell you."

"Aren't I supposed to be your mistress?"

"I do not need to know what is happening off the boat. You must be discreet," he said. "But you must persuade Senator Dillard at all costs to stay and catch that marlin."

He went to the door, paused, turned. "You will do what I ask?" he said.

"On one condition."

"Which is?"

"If Dillard catches that marlin, or gets one with his name on it, I get a bonus for services rendered. Fifty thousand dollars."

Without hesitation, Minahero nodded. "Fifty thousand dollars." He glanced at his watch. "Please be on the yacht by five o'clock."

TWELVE

Having arrived in Miami, Roff killed the afternoon buying a few necessities, then telephoned Anita.

"Sergei," she said, "what the hell is going on? You go off for a couple of days in Arizona then disappear off the face of the earth and then that toad Le Clerc . . ."

"Look," he interrupted urgently. "I haven't time to explain anything now. I just want you to tell me what your movements are for the rest of the evening."

"But Sergei . . ."

"No! Do as I say, Anita! Trust me!"

There was a silence. He could imagine her in their comfortable Kent Woodlands home, sitting fuming at the telephone, trying to keep calm, to control her anger. He wondered how much she knew. "Sergei" and not

"Karl" said a great deal; mention of Le Clerc still more. He was filled with curiosity. But it would have to wait to be satisfied.

"Well if you want to know," she told him at length, "I'm having dinner at Bill and Myra's. But I can cancel it."

"No. Don't do that. What time do you expect to be back home?"

"About eleven."

"I'll phone you then. I'm sorry, but I've got a lot of things to do and very little time to do them in. 'Bye."

He put the phone down on her. He hated doing it but it was the only way. He booked in at the airport hotel under the name of Walter Shine, had a couple of drinks in the bar, toyed with a meal, then telephoned again.

"Hallo?" He was relieved to hear Myra's Southern drawl. Bill would have proved more difficult.

"Myra, it's Karl. Is Eva there?"

"Sure. But didn't you know, she's changed her name? It's Anita now." There was a rich chuckle. "I'll get her for you."

Anita came on. "Yes?" She was still furious and confused.

"Anita, I couldn't say anything before. Our phone's almost certainly tapped. And obviously it's difficult for you now from your end."

"That's about the understatement of the year."

"Yes, I'm sure it is. So I tell you what you do. Spend the evening with Bill and Myra and try to act as normal as you can. I don't know how difficult that's going to be, because I don't know how much you know. When you leave them get to a telephone, not ours, and telephone me collect here." He gave her the number. "I'm booked in under the name of Walter Shine. Have you got that?"

"Yes, I've got it."

"Good girl! It's a helluva business for you, I know. But I *will* explain. And don't worry. Everything's all right."

When he put the telephone down, he found his hand was trembling.

It was nearly midnight when she rang him.

"Where are you phoning from?" he asked.

"It's all right. It's a booth in the St. Francis lobby."

"Good. First, how are you?"

"I'm a rag. But I'm all right."

The relief he felt told him something—that putting Peta behind him wouldn't be as difficult as he'd feared.

"And the play?" he said.

"Never mind the play. What's this all about?"

"I gather Le Clerc came to see you."

"Yes."

"What did he tell you?"

"That you were doing something for them and that if you pulled it off he'd give you a clearance on me and that if you didn't I'd be in trouble. He explained how . . ."

"But nothing about what I was doing, where I was . . ."

"Nothing like that at all."

"Well, firstly I've got that clearance. In my pocket. You're all right now. Nothing to worry about."

"For God's sake, Sergei!"

"I know. I know. But it's difficult knowing where to start. He told you we're back to being who we really are? That the Sodeks don't exist any more?"

"Yes."

"You must have had quite a time explaining that."

"It wasn't that stopped me sleeping."

He liked the way she said it. The irony, the acceptance of a situation and a hint of forgiveness in advance.

"What I had to do," he told her, "was deliver to a Japanese tycoon in Grand Bahama an attractive girl named Petronella Harrington under the guise of going there to get my own back on Laurence Kress who rents a house there to cover a development he controls in a nearby island known as Dragon Cay."

"Say that again."

He did so. There was quite a pause, then Anita said, "Deliver?"

"She was pretending to be my mistress. And for three nights she was."

"Thank you for telling me. Laurence Kress, you said?"

"No," he said, "let's not run away from it."

"All right, let's not."

He was glad it was off his chest whatever the consequences might prove to be. He could not have continued to share his life with her without telling her. If she couldn't take it, then he knew what he would do. Yet, now that he was faced with it, he wanted her to take it. They had shared so much.

He gave her ample time to speak and when she didn't, said, "Do you want to know about her?"

"Yes."

"Twenty-two or three. And just about the loveliest woman I've ever seen."

"Is it all over now?"

"Yes." It was a white lie. Or perhaps not a lie.

"So what's she doing now?"

"Living with this Jap, I imagine. There's a reason behind it. I don't know what it is."

"All right. Go on. With the rest of it. What about Kress?"

"He's dead."

"Dead!"

"Yes. And I have the option of being arrested for murder if I don't do what I'm told or having the Bahamas police continue to believe he was pulled overboard by a fish. It happened on Minahero's boat. One of his boats. That's the Jap's name. Minahero."

"What did happen, Sergei?" Her voice was very quiet.

"I don't know exactly."

"It wasn't you?"

"No. It was Minahero. I don't mean personally."

"Do you know why?"

"Just to get rid of me, I think."

"And *he* gave you this option?"

"No. Le Clerc did. Apparently another fishing boat came on Kress's body and he'd had his head bashed in."

There was another long silence.

"It doesn't seem very likely, Sergei, does it? I mean it all fits too well together, doesn't it? When you say this Japanese fellow wanted to get rid of you, you mean so he could lay his hands on this girl friend of yours?"

"Yes."

"When in fact the object of the exercise was for you to deliver her to him. So he has Kress murdered and lo and behold another boat comes on the body and Le Clerc hears all about it. No, I don't believe it. I just don't believe it."

He was glad he had Anita to speak to. She was wafting fresh air over the whole extraordinary business.

"I agree," he said. "There's something very wrong somewhere."

"When are you coming home?"

"Do you want me home?"

There was another pause. "Yes, I think so," he heard her say. "Yes, I do. But why the hell did you have to sleep with her?"

There was no possible answer.

"What sort of flight do you think you'll catch?" she asked, eventually.

"I'm not coming back to San Francisco yet. I've got something to do. Someone to see."

"Who?"

"Shapland," he said grimly. "I'm flying to London tomorrow. I want to know what this is all about."

"He won't tell you," she said. "You don't know Shapland."

"I'm beginning to. And I think I know how to make him tell me."

"You're crazy," she said.

"I just can't spend the rest of my life wondering what's behind all this."

"You may not have all that much left of your life to spend. Sergei, for God's sake! We've both . . ."

"Got a clean bill of health? Yes, I know . . ."

"Then going back there! It *is* crazy!"

"That's why I have to see Shapland. To get a clearance. Anita, I've had time to think this over. I know the risks I'm taking. But they've got to be taken."

"Why? Why? Why?"

Her anguish was crucifying; he had to harden his heart.

"If you'd had the half hour I had with Le Clerc this morning, you'd understand."

He distinctly heard her take a breath. He knew what it meant. That she had come to terms with the fact she wasn't able to dissuade him. When she spoke again, her voice was practical.

"Why not come home and fly to London from here?"

"Because I wouldn't. I've worked that out too. I'd put it off. Day by day. You'd persuade me to. And then maybe it'd be too late . . ."

"Too late for what?"

"I don't know."

"I just don't understand what you're talking about . . ."

"No. I don't see how you could."

"We're getting nowhere. We could go on all night and we'd still get nowhere."

He knew what she wanted him to do. To ask her to fly down to Miami. But he knew that would be the same thing as going home. He had to bring this to an end.

"Anita," he said. "Listen. You may be right. I may *not* be able to get enough out of Shapland to make it worthwhile going back to Grand Bahama. And if I can't get a clearance from him, I certainly won't go back because if I do there'll probably be a policeman jingling a pair of handcuffs waiting for me. But if I get my clearance I don't see I'll be in any particular risk because the only reason why the Bahamian police would start suspecting me of killing Kress is because someone's told them I'd a reasonable motive for doing so. And that someone would have to be Le Clerc who'll be under orders not to."

It was a lie, of course. Quite apart from both Minahero and Peta knowing, Kress would have taken his precautions. Kelly Brown would have had her instructions what to do if he died suddenly. And that was a strange thing—that she had had her instructions and apparently done nothing about them.

But there was no point in getting into that with Anita; she had worries enough as it was.

"What about this Jap?" she said.

"What about him?"

"If it was worth his while having Kress killed to get rid of you, wouldn't it be just as worth his while killing you if you go back?"

"He'd have to know I was back."

"So what are you going to do? Have some more plastic surgery?"

"I know," he said. "It's a problem. It's something I've still got to work out somehow."

2

When he arrived in London, it was to be informed that Shapland was abroad. He had no idea whether or not this was true. The temptation to give the whole business up and fly back home was considerable but he resisted it and after two frustrating weeks of continually telephoning, he got his appointment.

He was shown into Shapland who, had he but known it, was seated behind the same enormous leather-topped table he had been seated behind when Kress had been shown into him five years before and the whole, complicated business had been put in train. In fact the only difference between the Kress and Shapland meeting, and his own was that Tablian and Pentelow weren't there as well.

"Sit down," said Shapland.

Roff took the hard chair across the table and stared at the powerfully built man across from him, an iron man of intimidating authority.

"Well?" said Shapland.

"I want to know what this is all about." And when Shapland did not respond, "I intend to find out what this is all about."

"You have been given Miss Fermor's clearance?" Shapland said.

"Yes."

"Then what interest is it of yours?"

"You have to ask that question? My God, what sort of people are you?" Shapland was silent. Quite unmoved.

"Your instructions were," said Roff, "to buy a sufficient shareholding in Dragon Cay for Kress to lose control. You knew perfectly well that that was asking the impossible." There was no reaction. The thick lips clamped hard together under the Roman nose might have been a statue's. "In other words," Roff went on, "that was nothing but a blind. The object of the exercise was for me to provide that girl with exactly the kind of background she needed to make an apparent switch from me to Minahero."

The hard eyes did not waver—and told him nothing of what was going on inside the big bald head.

"You know of course that it was Minahero who had Kress killed?" Roff said.

"Mr. Roff," Shapland replied, "there is something you should understand. It is quite immaterial to us whether Kress is alive or dead and if he is dead how he came to die."

"Le Clerc said his head had been smashed in." And, at Shapland's dismissive gesture, "His body wasn't found at all, was it? That was just another lie to hurry me out of Grand Bahama."

"You should be grateful to Le Clerc, Mr. Roff," Shapland said. "But for his intercession with the authorities you would certainly have been arrested."

"In other words you're working with them on this business. What is it, Shapland? Drugs? Is that what Minahero does? Uses all this deep-sea fishing set-up to smuggle drugs somehow. And you don't know how he does it? And that's what the Petronella business is all about? Infiltrating her into his organisation?"

Shapland rose, massive, commanding. "I don't think we have anything more to discuss, Mr. Roff," he said.

Roff stayed where he was. "We have a great deal more to discuss, Shapland," he said. "And we will discuss it. And I will tell you why. Because otherwise I will see that Minahero is informed that Miss Harrington has been planted on him. And don't try threatening me because it wouldn't work."

"Because you have taken the necessary precautions before coming here?" He paused, then added, "As you did last time?"

Roff nodded. "Yes. Unless stopped by me that message will get through to Minahero."

Shapland sat down again. Unhurriedly. "What exactly do you want to do?" he said.

"Help."

Shapland thought about it.

"Very well," he said. "Firstly you are correct in your assumption. We are aware that Minahero imports large quantities of cocaine from Colombia into the United States."

"Through his boats somehow?"

Shapland's head, sunk deep in the collar of his well-made suit, moved slightly, denying this.

"His boats are regularly searched. He is most co-operative."

"You mean he knows you suspect him?"

"Well, of course. With the amount of drug smuggling that goes on through the Bahamas, almost everyone who owns a boat there knows he is

under suspicion. As I say, Minahero is most co-operative. Even to the extent
of allowing us to take dogs aboard. We are quite satisfied neither of his boats
have ever carried as much as an ounce of heroin or cocaine."

"You're not telling me the whole thing, are you?" Roff challenged him.
"Why should it worry you who smuggles drugs from the Bahamas into the
States? There are probably a dozen large organisations doing it, to say noth-
ing of scores of small fry shipping it to Florida on speedboats. Why pick on
Minahero? It's not in MI6's bailiwick, is it? Looking for drug smugglers?"

"You are right, of course," said Shapland, unperturbed. "We are not interested in the drug smuggling. It is the use of the profits which interests us."
He stared at Roff in silence for quite some little time, obviously deciding,
then said, "You wish to help?"

"Yes."

"Why?"

"Pride. And the girl."

Shapland nodded—as if he understood. "Very well. Minahero is a Japanese
who holds fanatically, or perhaps I should say pathologically, chauvinistic
views in one way like those of Nazis who have never accepted Germany's
defeat but different in that, unlike many of them who refuse to believe that
Fascism is dead, he sees his own country doomed by Western influence. He is
not alone in thinking this way. There are many Japanese who feel as he does;
who see, under their very noses, the old traditions swept away. But the
difference between most of them and Minahero is that he has allowed resentment to become obsession and dedicated his life to revenging himself on
those who, as he sees it, have brought about this situation. In other words,
the West. But he is both a clever and a patient man. He is perfectly well
aware that there are others with both the experience and the organisation he
lacks who can achieve what he wishes to achieve much more efficiently, and
with less risk to himself. So what he does is subsidise various terrorist organisations—and we don't imagine he is very particular which, so long as
what they do is harmful to the West."

Roff thought of Minahero, quiet, thoughtful, mild. "You're quite sure of
your facts?" he said.

"Oh yes," said Shapland, as calmly as if discussing something of the least
importance. "Quite sure. He has financed at least two major air disasters in
which several hundred innocent men, women and children were killed and
quite a number of bomb outrages. We're not even sure he isn't behind more
than one Middle East kidnapping."

"It's incredible," said Roff.

"Surprising. Not incredible."

"Why don't you simply . . . what's the jargon? Liquidate him? You weren't all that fussy about Le Clerc intending to liquidate me."

"We have our reasons."

"All right," he said. "You have your reasons. But surely if it's that important, you can do something better than pimp a girl on him?"

"That is only one of the things we are doing," Shapland said. "And the others are no concern of yours. But, yes, we have sent Miss Harrington. We are fortunate in that Minahero has a weakness."

"Women."

"Well not women in general. They have to fit a certain . . . specification?"

"Be young and beautiful."

"And Western. It is all an extension of this hatred, Mr. Roff."

Sickened by the enormity of what this signified, Roff lost his temper. "What you're saying is that she isn't the first girl you've pimped!" he shouted.

But nothing, it seemed, could upset Shapland's equanimity. "In fact," he answered evenly, "she is. The operation you have helped us carry out is hardly one which would bear repetition."

With a great effort, Roff brought his feelings under control. Anger would lead him nowhere. "What is Petronella Harrington supposed to find out for you?" he asked.

"She has not necessarily to find out anything for us."

"She's just there to be . . . useful?"

Shapland nodded.

"So it could go on for months? What she's having to put up with now?"

"Or end in days if she, or someone else, could provide us with sufficient information to prove that Minahero was smuggling drugs. Or for that matter had murdered Laurence Kress."

"You can organise things so that if I go back to Grand Bahama, I won't be charged with that?"

"That would not be a problem."

"And will you?"

Shapland looked at him long and hard, then nodded. "Very well, Mr. Roff. But I must warn you that we take no responsibility. That the British Government would deny any connection with your being there. And that you cannot rely on us for assistance. And I must have an undertaking you will do nothing which will increase the risks that Miss Harrington is already taking. We cannot replace her."

"I would not be going if that were the case," Roff answered bitterly. "You said *rely*. Can I take it that until I embarrass you, I will have backing?"

"What backing do you want?"

"Well the first thing I have to do is get back into Grand Bahama."

"You would be wasting your time. Minahero and Miss Harrington are on Dragon Cay. Living on Minahero's yacht."

"Do you have contact with her?"

"Yes."

"So there is someone through whom I could contact her?"

"Yes. You have already met him. He goes by the name of Wilberforce."

"The barman in the Deep Water Bar?"

"Precisely."

"If I went in there I might be recognized."

"I am quite sure you would be. But a meeting elsewhere can be arranged. What else do you want?"

"I have to get on to Dragon Cay."

"Hardly difficult. You can fly straight into Abaco where you are not known and get across in a small boat. Is there anything else?"

"Yes," said Roff. "Just one question. How did you persuade Miss Harrington to undertake such a filthy business?"

Shapland stood. "We did not persuade her," he answered. "We did not even recruit her. She offered us her services."

THIRTEEN

"Sure! Sure!" said Rodney Dillard. "I know it's important. But it's not so important it can't wait."

"You were coming home Tuesday."

"Yeah, Clara, I was coming home Tuesday and we were flying up to New York Saturday. Now I'm flying direct to New York Saturday and I'll meet you there. What's the difference?"

"The difference is that I'm supposed to sit around making excuses while you're having yourself a ball in the Bahamas."

"I'm not having a ball, Clara, I'm just trying to catch my marlin."

"That's more important than your business? More important than your political career? More important than your wife? More important than your daughter getting married in three weeks' time?"

Dillard selected the last, as the easiest to deal with. "Where's the problem? So Janie's getting married. What am I supposed to do about it? Help her choose her trousseau?"

"There's a helluva lot of things to do. There's hiring the cars, there's arranging the insurance, there's . . ."

Clara Willard went on for a long time and Rodney Willard, taking the call in lemon yellow bathing trunks, his ample body nicely tanned after three weeks of Bahamian sunshine, let her have her head. Clara would have her say and in the end she'd work herself up into a sufficient state to slam the phone down on him having got nowhere. And he would stay on Dragon Cay until Friday by which time maybe he'd have caught his marlin and maybe, and this, by now, was of a sudden about as important, maybe he'd have made that girl.

From his vantage point on the terrace outside the Deep Water Bar where he'd made his phone call, he eyed her with lustful speculation. He always sought his extra-marital opportunities far from home, taking care that there was no one in St. Paul who could level any accusation that he was anything but what he professed to be: a good family man who liked to get off for a little harmless fishing when he could spare the time from selling his meat and performing his proper functions as a senator.

But was this one a sensible choice?—that was the question. She'd given him the old come-on—a glance with a nicely shaped lifted eyebrow, a sly calf touch under a table top, a hand holding yours to lift a match to a cigarette with eyes mocking through the smoke. These things said volumes—but they didn't say all. And they didn't answer questions. First time she'd been with that sullen-looking fellow with the scarred face and broken nose. And now she'd switched to Minahero. Well that figured. You could have cut it with a knife that she and Roff were about washed up and a girl must live. But at this level they didn't usually move house that quickly. I mean, two weeks for Chrissake wasn't long. Of course she'd got her own stateroom. Very nice too. With a bit of luck you could slip in there for a cosy hour or two and out again and no one the wiser. Like today with Minahero gone fishing in *Dai Nichi* and Pet claiming a headache. Soon come, soon gone, that headache. *Dai Nichi* hardly through the reef and there she comes off *Tsuki* heading for the pool.

"Morning, Rodney."

"Make it, Rod, honey."

"Okay, Rod."

"Not going out with Minahero today?"

"Headache. Anyway he's gone to Bimini and won't be coming back until tomorrow night and I've got things to do tomorrow. Are you going to join me swimming?"

"Sure. Sure. Why not?"

"Not fishing today?"

"My luck's right out. I guess I'm never going to catch that big one."

"Why don't you get Yasuo to take you out again? Maybe back on his boat the luck'll change. Besides he's just installed a new sounder he's just had delivered from Japan. He reckons it's accurate enough to tell you if it's a billfish or a shark that's underneath."

"That so?" said Dillard, interested. "Of course that's one hell of a fishing cruiser that he's got there. Makes mine look crummy in comparison. Maybe that's a good idea. Try *Dai Nichi* again. Try that new sounder. Will you come too?"

"Love to. Day after tomorrow. Or the one after that? Or both?"

"I'm due back Tuesday."

"But you can't go back without your marlin."

"Well I did get one . . ."

"Two-fifty pounds? What's that? Just a tiddler. Still, I suppose . . . Rod, what exactly does a senator do?"

It had been at this point she had slipped off the beach jacket which had conveyed an impression she was nude underneath. But she wasn't nude, she was wearing the black and white polka dotted bikini in which Roff had first seen her.

"Take a long time to tell you that," he answered.

"We've got all day."

"Okay, then I'll tell you what a senator does providing you stop me the moment you start getting bored. But first I've got to get into my trunks and make a phone call. Don't go away, Pet, will you?"

She had smiled and put both scarlet-tipped hands over the bows of her bikini at her hips and faced him, somehow not just with her eyes but with her whole body. "No, Rod," she had told him. "I won't go away."

And now he'd made his phone call and hell, he had no business staying on. He'd been away too long already. He eyed Petronella spreading sun oil over her flawless skin. "Wilberforce!" he shouted. Wilberforce came out "Mornin', senator. Nice day."

"Sure is. Bring me a cold beer, will you?" And when it had been brought. "Been thinking, Wilberforce. They can get together a good picnic, can't they?" "Yes, sir! You want me to tell them fix a picnic?"

"For two."

"Anything special, senator?"

"Bit of everything that's good. You know, lobster and stuff. Fruit. And an ice bucket with champagne. Two bottles."

He took his beer and went to join Petronella now lying, glistening, in a long mattress chair. He was as excited as a schoolboy.

"Say, I've got a swell idea."

Petronella opened a lazy eye. "What's that, Rod?"

"Why don't we have a picnic on that beach Woolgar talked about? Slipper's Cove. Get away from the mob."

There was hardly a mob around the pool. Dragon Cay had still a long way to go.

Petronella thought about it. Her current job was to persuade Dillard to stay on and catch his fish, not necessarily sleep with him. And there was a look in his eye which reminded her of a dog tracking a bitch in heat. She didn't like the look of it at all. And she didn't like the look of Dillard generally. There was too much flesh about him. As if he ate too much of the meat he sold. It hadn't quite turned to sagging fat but it would before too long. And she didn't like his smile; it was fixed as if he was having his photograph taken. And she remembered what he was like when he'd had a drink or two too many. The pawing type. Ugh! But she had a job to do and on the whole a beach where she could complain of sand seemed a safer bet than a luxurious yacht with a stateroom the crew would have been ordered not to approach while their master was away.

"What a lovely idea," she said. "Yes, why not? Would you like me to go and order it."

"Done already!" He was very proud of himself. There was no hurry now. He could enjoy watching her here for a bit. "How about a drink while that oil soaks in on you?" he said. "Then we'll have a swim to cool us off. And then I'll get myself a car . . ." (he said this in a very Anglicized manner) "while you get anything you need from the yacht. How's that?"

"That's fine," said Petronella brightly. "I'd like a soursop and soda with a lot of ice."

2

Wilberforce, with a carefully timed tray of drinks in his hands, passed by her on the way to collecting what she needed for the day; Dillard had gone off to organise their transport.

"Miss Harrington?"

"Yes?"

"Come in and ask me for some cigarettes?"

He carried on down to the pool. Petronella made a business of opening her

beach bag and rummaging in it. Then went into the Deep Water Bar, which
was quite empty.

Wilberforce came back and putting the tray down, reached for a packet of
cigarettes and placed them handily.

"Roff's back on the island," he told her.

Her eyes opened wide in amazement; her heart gave a sudden pound.
"You're sure?" she demanded.

"Yes."

"Have you told anyone?"

"It's approved," he said.

"I don't believe it. Where is he?"

Wilberforce nodded his head.

"You mean. Here? In *your* room?"

"Right."

"When did he get here?"

"About four this morning."

"What does he think he's doing?"

Superb teeth flashed brilliant white against black skin. "Lawd knows,
ma'am! Lawd knows!"

"I can't see him now." She spoke jerkily, thrown by this totally unexpected
development. "I can't see him here anytime. It's far too dangerous."

He pushed the cigarettes across to her.

"I don't smoke that brand!" she snapped, not angry with him but because
the whole business of cigarettes was an irrelevance.

"There's a map inside," Wilberforce said. "It's where he'll be from tonight."

"But how can I possibly get to him?"

Wilberforce shook a neat, tight-haired head.

Petronella stared at the packet lying on the counter as if it had life of its
own, which, indeed, it almost seemed to her it had. Then she picked it up
and put it in her bag.

"Tell him, I'll get there somehow," she said. "But I don't know when."

3

Woolgar hadn't lied about Slipper's Cove, which (except possibly to serious
swimmers) offered everything which could have been hoped for in a semitropical beach. The sand was pure pink, the sea was very shallow for quite
some distance out so that the water was a shimmering turquoise only gradually merging into blue and deeper blue. Encircled by low cliffs of coral rock
hardly higher than sea walls behind which massed creaking coconut palms
and feathery casuarinas, it had an air of privacy while at the same time one or

two rough wooden tables and benches strategically located explained the total lack of seaweed on a strand whose sand was rippled like the waves themselves. In a word Slipper's Cove was as much a part of Dragon Cay as its marinas, golf course and hotels, bought, desand-flied, manicured, improved to a state of perfection for the inordinately wealthy and demanding men and women who alone would be allowed to enjoy it.

Petronella had hoped against all hope that some of them might also have decided to disport themselves upon it and her heart sank on their arrival (in the jeep Dillard had acquired from somewhere) to find it entirely empty; empty and silent but for the quiet shuff of small wavelets on the sand, the sound of the breeze through palm fronds and the chipping sound of some unidentified birds amongst the sea-grape. More even than she did with Minahero, she now felt herself a whore; whether or not she did actually allow the American to have sex with her seemed so much beside the point that she felt she scarcely cared if he did or not. Her perceptions were confused, her capacity for selecting between good and bad was dulled. Besmirched by a week at Minahero's hands, and yet for all these sacrifices seemingly being not one whit forward in her search for information had started to crush her spirit. She had begun to understand how it came about that innocent girls forced into prostitution eventually came to accept it as a way of life.

And now there was the added complication of Sergei. What the hell had he come here for? How on earth did he imagine in this private island he could avoid detection? Hadn't she quite enough to put up with without this extra problem? Because she must protect him; she had no option. Shapland had obviously squared it with the Bahamian authorities—but not with Minahero. Once he got to know about it, Sergei's life wouldn't be worth a button. When was she to get to see him? It had to be today. She daren't leave it till tomorrow. She knew him too well. He just would not stay inactive, fuming, holed up in an old fisherman's hut, hungry, thirsty, plagued by sand flies through the day and mosquitos through the night. Yes, but there was a connection here, a connection between Dillard and Minahero's cocaine smuggling. God knows what it was, but there had to be one. It had to be more than Dillard having his photograph taken with his damn marlin!

Her head went round and round. She needed to be sure that Dillard stayed. He'd told her on the way that he had arranged to extend his trip, that now he'd be leaving Dragon Cay next Friday. So she had five days. Today and tomorrow—she couldn't learn anything then, not with Minahero away. Tuesday, Wednesday, Thursday. Those were the days which mattered. But to be sure of them, for Dillard not to have second thoughts, she'd have to keep him sweet. Somehow. And she'd have to get to that fisherman's hut today. Somehow.

She busied herself setting out the lunch things.

"Leave it, Pet," she heard Dillard call.

"Only the equipment," she called back as gaily as she could. "Pour me a drink."

"That's an idea."

He passed by her and gave her bottom a playful slap. She had put on a pair of white shorts and a striped shirt over her bikini. She looked over her shoulder up at him, managing a grin.

"You'll get hot in all that lot," he hinted.

It took as far as the big ice bucket for him to summon up the courage. "With an empty beach like this what say we go swimming in the raw?"

"Sorry, mate," she said, "but there are times when a girl just can't do that."

"Oh." His disappointment was comical.

"Topless'll be all right," she said, to cheer him up.

She saw his tongue touch his lips before he bent to take the lid off. Inside were two bottles of champagne lying on a bed of ice. Also some other drinks.

He aimed the bottle like a gun at the sea and twisted the cork which flew out like a bullet but still ended on the sand.

"Didn't make it," he informed her unnecessarily. "Should have shaken it first."

He poured two glasses, put them on the table and then sat himself on the back of the bench near to its end with his feet wide apart on the seat.

"Come here," he said. "Let me show you how we drink champagne in St. Paul."

She joined him.

"Now," he said, "sort of sit on that."

He pointed to the corner of the seat back in between his legs. She half sat, half leant against it, her feet on the sand, and he brought in his legs to grip her thighs on either side. He then put his arms around her middle folding them together and pulling on them so that her back was against his chest. It wasn't very comfortable but she put one hand on his folded palms and looked half over her shoulder, smiling up at him.

"I don't see how we can drink champagne this way," she said.

He unclasped his hands, leaving the left firmly holding her against him, picked up one of the glasses with the other and held it out for her to take with her left hand. He then picked up the other glass.

"Now," he said, "you put your glass to my lips and I put mine to yours and we drink to each other."

It was all very complicated and, under the circumstances, quite absurd, but they managed it. She could feel the sharp corner of the bench back digging into her, his hand on her stomach moving upwards. She deliberately spilt champagne to break things up. God, how many hours of this, she thought, how many hours? She pulled away from him and reaching for a paper serviette began to mop her legs.

"Don't worry about that," he said. "Let's go in. The sea will clean you up." He jumped off the bench, pulled off his shirt, kicked off his shoes and stood waiting, watching her. She pulled off her own shirt, shook out her hair, undid her shorts and stepped out of them.

"Topless, you said," he reminded her.

"Okay."

She took off the bra.

"All right?" she enquired.

"My God," he said. "I'll say."

In the end they didn't stay so vey long. Marvellous tropical beaches are wonderful places for the young at heart but roues exercising patience do better in more complicated surroundings such as bars and restaurants where they are not thrown quite so obviously on their own resources.

FOURTEEN

The hut was on the north tip of the island, a safe enough place. Once they got round to building the golf course it would be levelled because it would interfere with the view when you drove towards the ninth green or looked backwards from the tenth tee. But for the moment no one bothered with it.

It was rough enough, earth-floored, tin-roofed. When it was hot you sweltered inside; when it rained heavily you couldn't hear yourself speak for the drumming. There was only one room really, although there was a sort of kitchen stroke washroom at the back and uncleared scrub behind for everything else. The one room had an iron ex-army bed, a table covered with faded, red-checked American cloth split where it had been creased or folded and a couple of bamboo chairs with sprung fibres. The fisherman must have been a reader because there was an old bookcase, bamboo also, but the books were musty with damp and most of them were worm-eaten and in many cases served as coffins for worms which had found the covers beyond their abilities and crawled round, chewing a circle until they died. Outside you looked at a bit of beach which, being exposed more than most of the island and as yet untended, was littered with palm fronds, coconut husks and jetsam and punctuated with petrified palm trunks which had taken on the obscene look of yard-long, long-dead shrimps which had somehow dug themselves into the sand and defied even northers to shift them. By the day it was an eerie, depressing place; by night it was beautiful.

"How did you get here?" Roff asked.

"Wilberforce brought me in the jeep Dillard hired. He's waiting back there with it run in amongst the scrub."

"Dillard? Oh yes. That American. Won't Minnie miss you?"

"He's gone to Bimini. Won't be back until tomorrow. What the hell are you doing here?"

He looked at her—in dark slacks and shirt and a kind of woollen shawl against the cool night air.

"Why the hell d'you think?" he said. "Because of you."

"It isn't any good."

"D'you think I don't know that? D'you think anything will ever be really good for me again?"

"Then you're a fool. And a bloody nuisance."

"Have you got anywhere?" he said.

"No."

"How long can you put up with it?"

"I don't know."

"Why are you doing it?" And when she didn't answer, he grasped at her and held her by the shoulders. "You've got to tell me why you're doing it," he said. "I have to know. Is there any reason why you shouldn't tell me?"

She shook her head miserably. "Not really."

"Then tell me."

"All right."

She broke free and sat on the edge of the truckle bed. And told him. About her brother, Billy; about Victor, the man she'd married.

"What did he do? Victor?" Roff asked when she had finished.

"He was in the stock exchange. When I married him he was heading right for the top. He had it all: the Porsche, the private jet, the brilliant future."

"And you loved him?"

"Yes." She spoke very quietly.

"Tell me about him. What he was like?"

"When he walked into a room everyone knew he had arrived. I was never able to imagine spending my life with anyone else. Or spending it without him."

It was curious, with really no words of description, Roff could see them. The brilliant young stock exchange executive and his dazzlingly beautiful wife, a positive, dynamic, exciting, sought-after, envied pair who stood out from the crowd.

"But always the pressure?" he suggested. "Which is why he took to drugs."

"Yes. Always. The hours, the strain, the speed of everything. I used to wonder how he coped with it. Marvel how he could leave at six in the morning and meet me fourteen hours later all set for a party, or dinner and a theatre, night-club even, knowing what sort of day he'd had and that he'd be having it again tomorrow. Knowing what he had on his mind. The responsibility he carried. The way he was at risk. It was as if he knew there was a time span for us and we'd got to crowd all the experiences, excitements, challenges which life could offer into it. That's how I learnt to fly, of course. In our own aeroplane which we kept at a club. He taught Billy, too."

"What did Billy think of him?"

"That he was a prince among nonentities like himself."

"What did Billy do?"

"Billy? Not much. Maybe he'd have settled down to things when he'd gathered confidence. But I don't know. Not everyone matures. A lot of people go through life without maturing and yet seem to be happy enough. Not setting the world on fire but making their contribution all the same. You know—by kindness, decency, just being there doing no harm."

"And yet it was Victor who . . ."

"Got him hooked on heroin as well? Yes. His own brother-in-law." Her voice became bitter. "Put not your faith in princes."

"It's hardly believable," Roff said.

"Have you ever been involved with heroin addicts?"

He thought of Anita. "Not directly," he replied.

"Anything is believable."

"Tell me about it."

She shook her head. "Read a book." She got off the bed and finding her bag took out her cigarettes. The match flared brightly in the earth-floored, tin-roofed room with its cracked walls and its sense of a time gone past.

"So what happened?" Roff asked her.

"Victor took Billy up in his aeroplane and when they were over the sea and high enough . . ." She flipped her hand expressively down towards the floor, its shadow from the oil lamp suddenly seeming to vanish out of sight.

"What a ghastly business."

"Yes." And, after a pause, "Of course it was well worked out." Her tone had a cynical edge. "Couldn't be proved there hadn't just been an engine failure so I got enough insurance not to have to worry."

After a moment Roff said, "You don't connect Minahero directly with it?"

"Lord, no. As far as I know he isn't even into heroin."

"You know why he does it? Minahero? Shapland's told you?"

"Yes."

"Hasn't it occurred to you, you've got an almost identical attitude to his? Minahero's?" And when she did not reply. "Peta, listen to me. You can't build life on hatred. Hatred's as bad as drugs. Hatred destroys everyone who gets trapped by it."

"It's also the longest pleasure."

"Are you going to take on the world? When Minahero's put away, assuming he is, are you going along to Shapland to sign on for another mission? Has he got a list for you? For God's sake, Peta!"

"I don't know," she said. "I don't know how I'll feel. I just have to do this thing, that's all I know. And no one, nothing's, going to stop me."

He shook his head. "You're changed."

"No."

"Yes, you are. You don't think you are, but you are. Because it's one thing being all keyed up thirsting for revenge. Rubbing your hands at what you're going to do to the kind of people who're responsible. D'you think I didn't go through all that with Kress? But it's something else you've actually started doing something about it, started getting your hands dirty . . ."

"As I have. Only it's worse."

"What d'you mean it's worse?" There was anger in his voice.

"I'm now being pimped on Dillard."

"You realise what you're doing! Turning yourself into a bloody whore!"

She laughed. "Turning myself? I am a whore! The worst kind of whore. The kind of whore who offers her clients carte blanche. And you've no idea, Sergei, how imaginative Minahero can be . . ."

As if of its own volition his hand came up and struck her across the face with such force as to send her sprawling in the sand amongst the fallen palm fronds and bits of driftwood. He felt no regret but stood there shaking in fearful anger and dismay, choked out of speech.

She saw him standing above her, his face lit by moonlight, his eyes glittering with helpless rage.

She laughed up at him. Deliberately. "That's nothing, Sergei," she mocked. "Do you hear me? Nothing! Do you know how *he* punishes me? With a special kind of whip! It's called a *sakaki*. And that's a branch off some damn tree. He's got a cupboard full of them he has sent over from Japan especially. And while he's whipping me with one of them, he's intoning exhortations. He makes out it's all to do with some religious rite for correcting fallen women." She laughed mirthlessly. "But I've seen his face—and more than his face—when he's doing it. And it's much more simple, Sergei. He's enjoying himself. Enormously!"

"My God!" he said, sickened by the image. And he staggered away from her.

She waited. In falling she had lost her shawl and she didn't bother to look for it amongst the debris on the beach. She just stood, waiting, idly brushing sand from herself.

He came back at last. "I'm sorry."

Nothing could have been more crucifying than his tone, which was lifeless.

"We've got to work this out," he said.

"Us?"

"Not us. There's nothing to work out about us." And after a moment. "Let's go back inside. You're so beautiful here in the moonlight it breaks my heart."

They went in again and sat in the sprung bamboo chairs. She lit another cigarette.

"This business of Dillard," he said. "I just don't understand it."

"He's president of some deep-sea fishing . . ."

"Balls!" he said. "Minahero wouldn't pimp you just for that."

"What did you come here expecting to do?" she asked wearily.

"I didn't know," he said. "I just had to come to see if there *was* anything I could do." He paused. "This business of Dillard and his marlin. It makes no sense." And, after a moment, "No more sense than his having Kress killed so that I'd have to get out of Grand Bahama. After all he could have had me pushed over just as easily. No. He had a reason for getting rid of Kress. I wonder what it was?"

He came back to Dillard. "Of course," he said, "there's a very simple answer. He's got drugs stowed away somewhere on his boat. You go out fishing on it and catch a marlin. When no one's looking someone slits the marlin open and stuffs it full of cocaine. Dillard has it mounted and takes it back to Fort Lauderdale, then ships it to New York and it's hijacked *en route.*"

Petronella thought about it.

"It makes a certain amount of sense," she said. "Being a senator, Dillard's not likely to have anyone opening up his marlin."

"It makes no sense," Roff disagreed. "Because it's both too simple and too complicated. Even on a boat the size of his *Dai Nichi* you can't risk being spotted slitting marlins open and stuffing them with cocaine like turkeys. Anyway the moment you land, Dillard'll want his fish hauled up on the weighing gantry so that he can be photographed beside it and how do you repair the slit in time so it won't be noticed. And in any case if he did have drugs aboard it would be altogether safer for Minahero to have them slipped ashore somewhere like this. Using a fast speedboat, the chances of being caught are negligible."

"So that's out?"

"I don't know. It's puzzling. But I tell you what you do. When you go out, watch very carefully what everybody does, particularly if you catch that marlin. If I'm wrong, if they want to use it to get some drugs ashore, then you can bet your bottom dollar Minahero will dig up some excuse to get you and Dillard out of that cockpit. And not for five minutes either. So what you do is say you've got a headache and want the blow or something. Anything to *force* him to insist you don't stay there. Then the moment you dock . . ." He rubbed his chin. "Yes. The moment you dock, stop and light a cigarette . . . No, that's too obvious. Just put your left hand up to your hair like this." He showed her. "There'll be someone watching . . ."

"You?"

"No, not me. I may not even be on Dragon Cay. But there'll be someone who'll take a good look at that marlin there and then and if it's a cocaine sausage that'll be the end of Minahero for the next twenty years or so."

"And if it isn't, that'll probably be the end of me."

He shook his head. "No. Because you're only to give the signal if you're certain that's what's happening. If you're sure it's not, you just do nothing. Okay?"

"Yes, all right, Sergei," Petronella said. "What are you going to do?"

"I'm going to Grand Bahama. To see a girl about a dog. A dead dog."

"Who about who?"

"Kelly Brown about Laurence Kress."

2

"Tell Mr. Shapland to telephone me at that number I've just given you."

"Mr. Roff . . ."

"I know what you're going to say, Mr. Tablian, or whatever your name is. No one tells Mr. Shapland what's he's to do. Well I am. And you can tell him why. Because providing he can organise what I ask, I think that within forty-eight hours or so, I may be able to give him the answer he's hoping for. I'll wait till . . ." he looked at his watch. "Until five o'clock your time. If he hasn't contacted me by then, I'll try it on my own but I may not be so lucky."

"Roff!" Tablian's voice was quick, to stop him ringing off.

"Well?"

"You know how to contact Le Clerc . . ."

"Bugger, Le Clerc," said Roff with satisfaction. And hung up.

Within the hour, Shapland telephoned. "Where are you?"

"Come off it, Shapland," Roff said. " You know exactly where I am. At the Island Inn on Abaco."

"When did you get there?"

"I swam across this morning while the sharks were having their breakfast."

"What do you want?"

"That's better," Roff said. "What do I want? Firstly I want you to get your people out here to organise a permanent watch on Minahero's fishing cruiser . . ."

"There is already."

"Hear me out. A permanent watch on it when it docks on next Tuesday, Wednesday and Thursday nights. And not anyone who's been watching it up to now. Minahero's probably rumbled them already. Someone new. Or more than one. Send them out especially if you have to. They're to watch for Miss Harrington coming ashore. If, when she does, she puts her left hand up to the back of her head and smooths her hair they're to rip open any fish that come ashore or are still aboard."

"Do you think we haven't thought of that one already, Roff?" Shapland sounded tired.

"Maybe you have, but do as I say. But if she doesn't give that signal they must do nothing. Repeat—nothing!"

"Very well. Anything else?"

"I've got clearance into Grand Bahama?"

"Yes."

"Have you any knowledge as to whether or not Kress's son has arrived?"

"He hasn't. He's still in England."

"Good. I want a police car put at my disposal . . ."

"A what!"

It was a pleasure to shake even Shapland. "A police car. With a driver and an extra policeman in full fig, pith helmet and all, sitting in the front."

"What are they supposed to do?"

"Just drive me where I tell them. That's not difficult to organise, is it?"

There was a pause. "No."

"I shall catch Flight GB 322, which leaves Marsh Harbour International

for Freeport International at nine-ten hours tomorrow morning. I shall be
travelling as Sergei Roff. They're to meet me at the airport. They're to run
me wherever I tell them and not ask any questions because I'm not going to
give them any answers, which is what you'd want anyway. Okay?"

"Yes," said Shapland. And, after a moment, "It's only just gone ten where
you are . . ."

"You disappoint me, Shapland," Roff interrupted. "You've just proved,
you're human. What am I going to do all day in Abaco? Well, I'll tell you.
Take a lesson in taxidermy."

3

"May I come in, please?" Roff said.

"I don't know," Kelly Brown said.

She stood framed in the doorway of her attractive little white-painted
clapboarded bungalow, puzzled and disturbed.

"You remember who I am?"

"Of course. You're Mr. Roff."

"Then may I come in, please?"

She still hesitated.

"Have you had instructions from anyone not to speak to me?"

She made her mind up. "I'm afraid I can't answer that. In any case, I have
a lot to do this morning and . . ."

"Miss Brown!"

She stopped, startled by his tone.

"You see that police car?" He had had it park at just a little distance. "We
can either talk here, privately, or you can come down and be interviewed at
the station. Whichever you prefer."

She hesitated for a moment longer, then stood aside to let him pass.
"Come in, Mr. Roff."

She closed the door upon them and Roff found himself in a most pleasant
room, which occupied the entire front of the bungalow and was delightfully
furnished. A couple of chintz settees and matching armchairs found ample
room amongst some good pieces of furniture and there was plenty of green-
ery and a nice arrangement of anthurium lilies and wild banana.

"Please sit down, Mr. Roff." She indicated a chair. She was thinking fast.
Laurence Kress had given her certain instructions (which had included which
office files to destroy and which to keep) in the event he telephoned her an
investigation of his affairs was imminent. He had not advised her what to do
if the police suddenly dropped in at home. She was conscious that having
been privy to certain somewhat unusual arrangements Kress had entered
into, she was at risk as an accessory. Such a call was not entirely unexpected,

although Roff would have been the last person she would have imagined
would have made it.

"I want to put your mind at rest, Miss Brown," said Roff, who had given it
all much advance thought. "I was, as you know, in business with Kress some
years ago and I have a pretty clear idea on the way he operated. As you did.
And if you hadn't gone along with doing whatever he wanted you to do, even
if it was illegal, he wouldn't have kept you on. So I daresay with him disap-
pearing like that you've had plenty on your mind."

Perhaps her amber skin paled slightly but she stayed calm and silent.

"However, it is not in connection with anything of that sort I have come
to see you and, hopefully, if we get along well enough, no one else will either.
Please do sit down."

Kelly sat, trimly, her knees together, her back very straight. "What is it
you want to know, Mr. Roff?" she asked.

"I take it," he said, "that you have been apprised as to how your late
employer came to lose his life?"

"Pulled overboard by a fish."

"Did you think that likely?"

"No."

"And very possibly you thought that I had pushed him over because Kress
dictated a letter to you to the effect I'd threatened him and if anything
happened to him, the police should look for me."

She nodded.

"And you took that letter to the police, of course?"

"Yes."

"And they reassured you that it had been, in fact, no more than an accident?"

"Yes."

"Are you satisfied?"

She looked at him levelly with eyes like glinting black olives which must
have turned a dozen men's hearts to jelly.

"I have to be, Mr. Roff," she said, "don't I?"

"Well we shall see," he said. "Now, Mrs. Kress? Is she still at Eagle Rock?"

She shook her thick, black hair. "No. She's gone back to Nassau."

"To consult with lawyers."

"I imagine so."

"Because Peter Kress is only her stepson."

"Yes."

"He'll have been in touch with you?"

"Peter? Yes."

Peter, Roff thought. Well, a girl must live.

"Do you know him?"

"I've met him once or twice."

"Has he any plans for coming over?"

Her hesitation said a great deal.

"I see," he said, "he has. But perhaps he's waiting for you to let him have answers to one or two things. Such as when it's finally accepted his father's body won't be found? Or such as when you're satisfied there isn't going to be an enquiry into his father's affairs which might be embarrassing to him?" He paused. "You're hoping he'll keep you on, Miss Brown, aren't you?"

"I'm hoping he'll keep me on, yes," she agreed, putting both hands on her knees. Her hands were beautiful, with long, coral-coloured nails.

"Did you tell him about the letter we were just talking about?"

"No."

"Why not?"

"I should have thought you'd have known, Mr. Roff."

Uhm, thought Roff, that was a mistake.

"You might have thought it an occasion when you were going to ignore what the authorities told you not to do," he recovered.

"This is where I live, Mr. Roff."

"You're a wise girl," he said. "Keep being wise. You're very close to a lot of trouble. More trouble than perhaps you know. Now. Just one thing before I tell you why I've come. A purely personal thing. Mr. Kress had an agreement drawn up for signature on Minahero's fishing boat the day he died making over half his holding in Dragon Cay to me. You knew about that?"

"Yes."

"Any comment on it?"

Now she didn't hesitate. She had evidently decided which side her bread was buttered.

"Yes, Mr. Roff," she said. "It was a flawed agreement."

"Would it have fooled me?"

"Unless you happen to know the ins and outs of Bahamian law, yes I imagine it would."

"Yes," said Roff. "Of course he only had it prepared to buy time. You know what for?" She shook her pretty head. "Think about it," he said, "I'm sure you'll guess. Now! Why I've come. Neither you nor I believe it was a fish which pulled your late employer overboard. He was either pushed overboard or killed aboard *Dai Nichi* and thrown overboard. The only people who could have done that are myself or one of Minahero's crew because Minahero took care to have Miss Harrington—the lady introduced to you as my wife—with him through the whole period when it could have happened. And as it wasn't me, it must have been Minahero. Now why? Why should Minahero plan—

because it must have been carefully planned—to have Kress done away with? Have you any idea?"

"None at all."

"You've thought about it? As a possibility?"

"Of course."

"And come up with nothing?"

"Nothing at all."

"They got on well?"

"Very well."

"There was nothing in their business relationship where they were at odds?"

"Nothing of sufficient importance to lead to what you're talking about, Mr. Roff."

"And yet Laurence Kress wasn't always the easiest man to get along with in business."

"He was all right. As long as he got his way. And he always got his way because he always controlled every business he was involved in."

"And that didn't bother Minahero?"

She shook her head. "Not at all. In fact the only time they ever had a disagreement that I knew of was over whether they should have a shop for mounting fish or not. And Mr. Minahero gave way on that."

But Roff hardly heard the last of it. "Minahero wanted the mounting shop and Kress wouldn't agree?"

"That's right."

"Do you know why?"

"Oh, I don't think he had a real reason," Kelly said. "I think he'd given way on one or two points and wanted to remind Minahero, and everybody listening, that in the end he was the one who made the decisions."

"Pride goeth before destruction," Roff mused.

"What?"

Roff stood. "Nothing, Miss Brown," he told her briskly. "Nothing at all. Thank you very much. You have been very helpful and if you act sensibly, I don't think you'll have anything to worry about."

"If I act sensibly? What's that meant to mean, Mr. Roff?"

"It means," said Roff, "that if you take care not to touch young Peter Kress with a barge-pole, you'll have been well advised."

FIFTEEN

A promising-looking day, Minahero had pronounced, a nice chop on the water under a cloudless sky and there seemed to be a wealth of fish about. Wherever Petronella looked there were sea birds busy with schools of baitfish amongst which bonitos were busy feeding so that the surface was continually broken as they slashed about amongst them.

The *Dai Nichi* zigzagged out from Dragon Cay northwards to Green Turtle Cay, keeping within a few hundred yards or so of the white beaches of island after island, hugging the line where the ocean suddenly dropped, cliff-like, down into the greater depths and the sea's change in colour could be drawn like a contour line.

Minahero was on the bridge with Fujita checking the returning echoes of the pulsed beam of sound from his new electronic sounder which, to judge by their catch on the Bimini trip, had apparently been hugely successful. O'Kano was on the flying bridge and the squat, powerful Miyako, impassive, arms folded, keeping his usual station when inactive in the cockpit. Dillard, harnessed up, was in the fighting chair and Petronella nearby in a fishing chair.

It was bizarre to be sharing the cockpit with a man you knew to be a murderer. It was not a question of being afraid—the absence of the runabout which, stowed athwartships had cut off the line of sight, was somehow a statement that no one was at risk. It was not abhorrent—Kress had not been such a man as to stir in Petronella the slightest sympathy. It was not even hard to accept—the incredible had become the norm. It was simply . . . bizarre. One was part of a conspiracy, accepting that conspiracy, hoping to use it for personal aims. The man who had murdered Kress was now at hand to assist an American senator catch his marlin. Had become a confederate. These days one mixed wih strange bedfellows.

She eyed Dillard, pools of sweat under the armpits of his shirt, a long peaked cap, with a fish motif, hiding his head, his huge, hairy legs projecting from shorts striped like boxer underpants, his plimsolled feet against the footrest of his chair

He sickened her, sickened her even more than Minahero. She knew that come what may she could not endure having sex with him. And that was strange. If at the beginning she'd been asked to choose, she supposed she would have chosen Dillard. His demands, she believed, would be straightforward and quickly satisfied. Yet Minahero had become . . . acceptable. That was probably, she supposed, because she had run the gamut of his strange desires and henceforth there would be only repetition. But apart from his ogling, and his pawing, and his hauling her against him on a dance floor, she had thus far avoided contamination at Dillard's hands.

She turned her head away and stared instead at the dazzling sea creamed white by the powerful engines and at the marlin rigs skipping and jumping in unison over the wash. Her mind travelled back to her crash course off Miami. Their mentor had been a grizzled Floridian, a decent, delightful man, a man with a face burnt to parchment by the sun and salt of a lifetime's game fishing, always pleasant, always patient, always helpful. Once, she thought, the world had seemed filled with men like him. Where had they gone? Now there were only Minaheros, Dillards, Kresses, Shaplands and Le Clercs. According to how you spent your life, so you met with the kind of men who fitted it. When this was over, would there be a going back for her? Could she ever again be the person she had been? Or was Sergei right—once you let hatred drive you into strange paths, could you ever again find the ways you once had known?

She allowed her thoughts to encompass the whole world of men and, astonishingly, there were only two in it she could recall who seemed of value: the Floridian who had taught them fishing. And Sergei. What good days they had been, she mused. Days of sunshine and blue water. Days of purpose. Days of a growing intimacy.

And she knew that she loved Sergei Roff and that her love for him was big enough to kill the pain of Bill and Victor and that without pain hatred could not survive. But she needed hatred; needed hatred desperately. Because without hatred as the spur, how could she play the part she had set herself, how endure Minahero's diabolical lusts?

2

They were using 12/0 reels loaded with one hundred and sixty pound lines, three-hundred-pound monofilament leaders and trolling king-sized marlin lures. There were just the two lines out, one to each outrigger; no risk was being taken that perhaps an engaged wahoo or dolphin would prove an inteference. This was not fishing for the fun of it—this was fishing for a purpose.

It was at about one o'clock when Miyako's cry, *"Sakana! Sakana! Sakana!"*

rang out. Petronella, half comatose in the sun after drinks and early lunch, raised her head and briefly saw behind the starboard side the bill like the end of a lance above the water. Then it was gone. Dillard, against all advice, grabbed with both hands at the rod, then, hastily, as if remembering, let go of it but stayed with his fingers inches from the butt. Minahero barked an order to Fujita and then hurried back to stand at the top of the port side companionway from the upper deck where he was positioned both to watch what might be happening and shout orders to the captain. From the flying bridge, O'Kana scanned the sea to the stern of the *Dai Nichi*. Only Ota and the cook, both somewhere below, were not involved.

For a while there was nothing to see but the lures, skipping and bouncing, flashing the sun, frustrating in their freedom. And then, quite clearly, the marlin was seen, a fish of great size actually following one of the lures, seeming almost to nudge it then head away. Minahero shouted an order and Fujita swung the wheel to draw the baits across the marlin's nose. It seemed at first a useless ploy. The marlin merely straightening its course and following along behind the starboard lure, its blue-black body a menacing yet frustrating shadow broken by the choppy sea. Then, suddenly, it struck, turning firstly away from the line behind the boat then turning back again and striking, in a huge burst of spray, a massive torpedo glittering in the sun.

Thinking about it afterwards, Petronella was unable to separate the immediate happenings: the line coming away from the outrigger in a long slow loop; Minahero yelling to Miyako in Japanese, and then to Dillard in English to hold back on his strike; the American grabbing at the rod, Miyako hurrying round to wind in its fellow; the line screaming out against the drag; the *Dai Nichi* curving round to keep straight on the fish; Dillard striking, striking, striking, obeying Minahero's shouted instructions; the marlin, huge, beautiful, hurtling from the sea, leaping clear of the ocean vertically, the long blue bill, the wavy dorsal fin, the Y-shaped tail, shimmering in the brilliant sunshine; her own heart pounding; Dillard whooping in triumph as he sensed the hooks were driven home; the rod bent circular; the line a bowstring . . .

But after these first few hectic moments there was ample time. Time to watch the titanic struggle; to pray and pray and pray that Dillard would not lose the fish because his success might bring nearer her own release. Time to study Minahero and see, for once, the determined calm wilt under strain. Time to remember she was not spectator but had her part to play; that her business was to stay alert, to follow every move, to log the changes of expression and yet to act out her role, to encourage Dillard, to catch Minahero's eye and convey to him her satisfaction at what was happening, not because he had to believe her satisfaction but because an attempt at showing pleasure was expected of her. Time, above all, to bear in mind that now was not the important period; that that would follow the boating of the fish. That somehow, without giving herself away, she had to concentrate on what was done, note every detail, miss nothing which occurred.

3

It was just after three in the afternoon when the great fish gave up the struggle, fought to a standstill by the combination of heavy tackle, brilliant boatmanship and the experience of Minahero who latterly stood by Dillard's side advising and encouraging. The double line appeared, Fujita slowed the *Dai Nichi* to a crawl, Dillard pumped the brute slowly to the surface, O'Kano (called down an hour before from the flying brige) reached a gloved hand over for the leader, wrapped the wire once around his hand and then again, Miyako reached out the flying gaff, the big eye glared at them balefully, the cruel gaff sunk home deep in the marlin's shoulder, the fish was hauled alongside, Minahero himself reached over with the rope . . .

"How much you figure he goes?" Dillard, his shirt clinging wetly to his body, his legs oily with sweat, his fists clenching and unclenching to restore their circulation, his voice unsteady with his triumph, held court.

Minahero gazed calculatingly at the massive fish hauled in via the gin poles and lying now between the *Dai Nichi*'s transom and Dillard's feet, a thin trickle of orange blood, diluted by the hosing, leaking towards the scuppers. "Seven hundred? Maybe seven-fifty?" he suggested.

"You don't say!" cried Dillard. "As much as that! I can see it's big. But Jesus! Seven hundred pounds!"

Minahero said something in Japanese to Miyako, who replied, nodding his bullet head.

"About that," Minahero concurred. "My congratulations, Mr. Dillard." He looked at his watch. "Only two hours. Very good."

Dillard started undoing his harness, turning towards Petronella as he did so.

"Well, Pet," he crowed. "How about that? Look good up there on the wall, eh?"

"It'll look great, Rod."

"We'll have a party! A party to end all parties! And you've got to come. You've brought me luck." Then, remembering Minahero. "That okay with you, Yassy?"

"Well it depends," said Minahero. "I would like to come. Of course. But it depends."

"Depends on what?"

"On when you have it. And where."

"Well in New York. Naturally."

"I have to be in New York for two or three days of next week."

"Next week! That'll be swell."

"But the fish has to be mounted."

Dillard waved problems aside. "So how long does that take?"

"Well . . ." Minahero sounded doubtful.

"You can rush it through. You've got the equipment."

"After the mounting there is the packing, the dispatch . . ."

"I'll take it with me."

"But won't you be going back now?"

He grinned at Petronella. "Said I wouldn't get back till Saturday and Saturday it's gonna be."

"You hope to catch an even bigger one?" suggested Minahero, smiling.

"No," said Dillard conclusively. "No more fishing. It's hard work, you know. From now on it's vacation time. You'll keep me company, won't you, Pet? You can spare her, Yassy? Eh?"

Minahero smiled, but did not speak. Petronella wondered what he was thinking. Even, momentarily, felt something approaching sympathy. In the excitement of his triumph, Dillard had lost the judgement he must normally possess. Maybe Minahero would understand—but she doubted if he would forgive the American for treating him as of such small account.

But Dillard, on a high, seemed blissfully unaware.

"Well," he said. "That's a mighty fine fish." He got out of the fighting chair. "Do we go back now?"

"So soon?" said Minahero. "We have several hours. Perhaps," he said courteously, "Miss Harrington would like to catch a marlin."

From the glance he cast her, Petronella knew she was to support him.

"Two in a day?" chuckled Dillard.

"It has been known," said Minahero. "In fact I have known five in one day."

And, taking for granted Dillard's acceptance that the fishing should be continued, Minahero began issuing orders to his crew.

From the locker against the bulkhead behind the fighting chair Miyako fetched two slings which, with O'Kano helping, were manoeuvred, with exquisite care so as not to damage it, beneath the fish.

"Miss Harrington," said Minahero (who never adressed her otherwise in front of others—and never gave her any name at all in private), "if you will stand there. There is not so much room with a fish this size." Petronella stood back in the corner by the companionway to the upper deck. "Ota!" Minahero shouted. The moon-faced Ota at once materialized from the saloon. Minahero gave some instructions in Japanese, whereupon Minahero and each of the three members of his crew took hold of one of the sling straps and together they gently slid the marlin round so that it was no longer lying parallel to the transom but was now beside the starboard coaming, fore and aft to the direction of the *Dai Nichi*, its rapier bill towards the prow.

Dillard seized the opportunity to join Petronella and slipping a damp arm around her waist, started chatting to her. She answered automatically, hardly taking in what he was saying, trying all the while to concentrate on what was happening in the stern.

She saw Miyako lift out the three flush hatch covers to the starboard of the two coffinlike receptacles under the deck level in which, she remembered, Sergei's own dolphin had been stowed, and she remembered Minahero's words to Kress: "You see, Laurence? Big enough to take even a black marlin of one thousand pounds or more. And both refrigerated."

Miyako stepped over the chasm and picked up his strap and together the four Japanese, not without effort, lifted the fish and were about to lower it in when Minahero called out, *"Abekobe! Abekobe!"* and with considerable difficulty in the confined space available to them the four Japanese inched round, like pole bearers who have approached a grave from the wrong direction, until the bill of the marlin was pointing to the stern and then carefully lowered in the fish.

"You see!" called Minahero to Dillard who had quitted Petronella and come over to have a look. "We strap in the fish so that it cannot be damaged by sliding about."

And sure enough Miyako was on his knees drawing the free end of the first of the pair of straps attached to the locker base over the fish, through the buckle and gently tightening it.

"Gee," Dillard commented, impressed, "you sure go to one hell of a lot of trouble."

"One has to go to a lot of trouble to catch and boat a fish that size," smiled Minahero. "It would be a pity to damage it any more than necessary afterwards."

"What are those pipes for?" Dillard asked.

"To refrigerate it."

"Never seen that either. Except for bait fish."

"It is regular these days, Mr. Dillard. On the big boats. When it is dead a fish soon loses weight if you do not freeze it."

"That's quite a point. How much you figure that one might lose before we got it strung up?"

Minahero shrugged. "Maybe five, ten pounds."

Dillard stared down at his prize lying strapped firmly in its coffin. Petronella came to stand beside him. There was something very sad about the fish lying there, its eye already dull, its powerful tail never again to drive it through the limitless depth and breadth of the deep blue seas where it had lived, its bill never to stun another fish but instead to be fingered carefully by gawping friends in some New York apartment while Dillard for the hundredth time recounted his adventure. Already, she noted, its glorious colours had begun to fade, although not with the bewildering speed with which Sergei's dolphin had lost its colours. But it was, so far as Dillard was concerned, no matter—the taxidermist with his paints and sprays would bring those colours back, even improve on them. Man was a clever devil.

"I think we should put the hatches on," said Minahero. "The sun is not recommended."

"Oh, sure! Sure!" said Dillard and stood back.

And the hatches were replaced.

"Well," said Dillard, "I figure the next thing for me to do is go get myself a shower."

"No," said Minahero firmly. "The first thing we must do is drink to the achievement of ambition." He smiled. "We always have something ready for such an occasion."

He gave instructions to Ota, who went within.

"And we must not waste time," Minahero went on energetically. "We have two more hours in which we can maybe catch another marlin." He ordered O'Kano back to his station on the flying bridge and Miyako to run out the lines again. By the time this was all in hand and the *Dai Nichi* had growled up to her normal cruising speed, Ota had returned with a bottle of champagne and glasses.

Minahero removed the bottle from the ice bucket and read the label. It was a Bollinger. "I do not think poor Laurence would have approved," he remarked wryly; "he would drink nothing but Dom Pérignon. But we have none." He smiled. "We live not as we would but as we can. Is that not right, senator?"

"Sure is," said Dillard.

4

Petronella waited in vain for Minahero to find an excuse for dismissing them but, if anything, his efforts seemed more directed to ensuring the cockpit was never left untenanted by either herself or Dillard. While Dillard showered and changed, he insisted she take the fighting chair and be properly harnessed against the chance of a second strike. When Dillard came back, Miyako fixep up a trolling rig for him and before they returned to Dragon Cay he had added to his tally for the day two small dolphin and a fair-sized barracuda, which were stowed in the refrigerated second coffin. The first was never opened again. Its hatches had never been out of Petronella's sight. No member of the crew had left his station. It had been quite impossible for anyone to have packed drugs of any sort into Dillard's fish.

As she disembarked, she cast her eye around the few individuals who might be hopefully awaiting the signal she couldn't give. On a yacht two fingers distant a white man was painting the handrails of a companionway; on another a black man messing around with an outboard engine; two youngsters were fishing off a third. Ashore a couple of Bahamians, one leaning on his bike, were chatting; in a car a woman in the passenger seat was reading a glossy magazine.

Minahero came ashore with her and led the way directly to the weighing gantry while Fujita had *Dai Nichi* cast off again and manoeuvred her stern inwards towards the slipway. The covers were now off Dillard's marlin and he was standing over it as if guarding it against it being spirited away. He was never still, talking to Miyako as if they shared a common tongue, calling to Petronella and Minahero across the water as they made their way along.

Fujita backed in tight up against the jetty and, not without effort, Dillard stepped up and over the transom and came ashore. Minahero stood beside him ready to superintend the winching out.

"That sure is some fish!" Dillard confided proudly to Petronella, as if he had not mentioned it before. "I just had another good look at it and you know what, Pet, it looks even bigger!" He burst out laughing. "It's like those fish that got away, they get bigger all the time! Wonder if it'll go that seven hundred. That's a big fish, seven hundred. Not all that short of the record. Course it wouldn't count. Not on one hundred and sixty. Pity that. I figure hundred and twenty, even eighty . . . well maybe not eighty . . . might have been enough . . ."

He went on garrulous, good-humoured, grandiloquent through the hoisting up and weighing, organised by Minahero personally, whooping with delight as the scale ran round. "Seven thirty-seven! Y'see that, Pet, seven hundred and thirty-seven pounds! That'll make the boys sit up!" He personally chalked the weight upon it, the date, his name and had himself photographed beside it from every angle. Against the background of the *Dai Nichi;* holding the rod with which he'd caught it, with, just behind and over his head, a lifebelt lettered DEEP SEA CLUB—DRAGON CAY; holding it gingerly by the tip of its dorsal fin; patting it like a family pet. He insisted that Petronella should be photographed with him too because it was she who had brought him luck and made the odd wisecrack that this was a photograph not for the family album; and then he hauled in Minahero, and then the crew: Fujita, Ota, Miyako, O'Kano and even the unnamed cook; he stood amongst the five of them in their quasi-military outfits overtopping them by a head. And then, with a final regretful glance at the great fish still strung up by its tail, what must they do but head for the Deep Water Bar and wet their whistles while they planned the evening's celebration.

5

Following the completion of the weighing ceremony, Fujita had complained that one of *Dai Nichi*'s engines was behaving less than perfectly and he wanted to take it out again on a short test run and Minahero had gone out with him, leaving Petronella the problem of how to extricate herself from Dillard. Her spirits were very low. She had accomplished what she had set out to do and achieved precisely nothing; there was not the slightest possibility that drugs had been introduced into Dillard's fish and now, ahead of her, stretched the prospect of that evening and two more days of Dillard's pestering. She was sick at heart with the whole rotten business which, now that she stood away from it, now that she no longer had the stomach for it, struck her as only screamingly unreal. She thought of Sergei, yearning for him.

In the Deep Water Bar she caught the eye of Wilberforce but it was impossible to exchange so much as a private word with him. It had got around that Senator Dillard had done what he had come to do, had caught his fish and that drinks, dinner, what you will were on the house. There was shouting, laughter, ribaldry. Dillard held court, centre of an admiring throng but, with the second of his ambitions yet to be fulfilled, was keeping close to her. Maintaining her act was, minute by minute, becoming more implausible. For weeks she had been buoyed up by a determination which had suppressed all contra affections; now each of them: regret, sensibility, caution, pride, resentment and fear itself clamoured to be heard. Nerves, overcontrolled so long, threatened to snap. Stifled by the heat, deafened by the din, defeated by failure, purposeless and weary, she could feel the last dregs of self-confidence draining out of her. Meanwhile Dillard would not leave her alone. His hand was round her waist, squeezing it; on her buttocks, patting them; brushing her breasts at the least excuse. He was drinking whisky and its fumes mingled with his body sweat and sickened her. Any moment now, she told herself, I shall throw this glass of liquor into his beefy face; any minute now I shall ram this cigarette end into his mauling hand; any minute I shall scream!

And it was in that very instant of crisis that she saw him there, by the door —Sergei!

She could have wept for joy. A flood of relief, a huge almost overpowering wave of it, swept over her. All else dissolved: the men and women crowding round her, the jabber and the chatter, the laughter, the smoke, the smell of beer and whisky. "Here, hold this!" she said to Dillard, shoving her glass at him. And she was pushing him aside, elbowing her away through the throng and holding out her hands.

"Sergei!" she cried. "Sergei, how wonderful! For God's sake take me out of here!"

He didn't answer. He simply looked at her, reading her misery, knowing he couldn't help.

"Sergei!" she begged.

He dropped her hands and, with the briefest indication of his head for her to follow, turned.

For the third time she tried: "Sergei?"

"Wait," he said.

She followed him. He walked quickly and with purpose through the club-house lobby and out into the night. It was all she could manage to keep up with him. Only when they were well clear of the club-house did he stop and speak.

"I had no business doing this," he said, as if furious with himself. "But Wilberforce got me a message you were just about at breaking point."

"Where were you?" she said, amazed.

"I've got a speedboat," he said.

"Where is it?" she asked eagerly. "Where is it, darling?"

"You have to go back," he said. And his voice was cold.

"Back?" She did not believe it.

"Back," he said. "If you don't go back you may ruin everything."

"There's nothing to ruin."

"Dillard caught his fish, didn't he?"

She laughed. Hysterically. Not loudly, but in a kind of quiet agony. "Yes," she said. "Yes, Sergei. He caught his fish all right. But there aren't any drugs in it."

"There *have* to be! It makes no sense otherwise."

"I tell you there aren't! There aren't! There aren't!" Her voice became a screech.

"Shut up!" he called at her. "For Christ's sake, shut up!" For a moment he seemed indecisive. Then he said, "We'll have to risk it. Come on!"

He wheeled and strode away not towards the marina but to the jetty where Dillard's fish had been winched ashore. Beyond it was a small stone pier, quite low to the water, which was used for bumboats and the like. Moored to it, squeaking its fenders, was a speedboat with a powerful-looking outboard engine.

She followed him down a short flight of stone steps and he helped her into the boat.

"Sergei," she began, "I can't tell you . . ."

"Shut up," he said. "We don't have too much time. Now I want you to tell me everything that happened today."

"I'll tell you on the way. Oh, Sergei . . ."

"Don't you understand?" he said, "I'm not taking you anywhere. I just want to know what happened and then you've got to go back to Dillard. Or to Minahero if you've cooked your books with Dillard."

"I can't go back. I won't go back."

"You can and you will. Now, listen to me. Both of us got involved in this for different reasons. You think you got involved to revenge yourself on the kind of people who destroyed your husband and your brother. You didn't. You got involved because you were filled with hatred which you had to get out of your system. And I got involved to protect a woman who once protected me. We've both achieved what we set out to do. You want out now; and I've got my bit of paper. But there's more to it than what you and I wanted; there's what Shapland and the people behind Shapland want. To nail that bloody man so he can't go on running his drugs and causing all the misery that does and then using his profits to blow up innocent women and children to satisfy his crazy notions! And now we've got this far. And I've a hunch this far is almost as far as we've got to go because I'm damn certain that fish of Dillard's is stuffed with cocaine to its bloody gills!"

"And I know it isn't."

"It has to be. Listen. Do you know why Minahero had Kress killed? To get me out of the way so that he could have a free run at you? Not a bit of it. He had Kress killed because Kress controlled the Dragon Cay development and had put his foot down about building something vital for Minahero's plans; a shop for mounting fish. They had a row about it."

"How d'you know?"

"Kelly Brown."

"They were thick enough for Minahero to . . ." She broke off.

"To let us all go fishing on *Dai Nichi?* Exactly. No, he couldn't have Kress in his hair. Even if Kress agreed to let the mounting shop go on as a quid pro quo for something or other there was always the possibility he might change his mind. Minahero couldn't risk that. It's a devilish clever idea. What kind of people are they who can afford the sort of rates you have to pay to moor your boat on this marina? They're top crust people. Top crust in commerce; top crust in politics. And many of them above suspicion. So what do you do? You invite them for a day's fishing on your boat . . ."

Petronella interrupted, scornfully, "Then wait for them to catch a marlin?

Stuff it full of cocaine. Mount it. Send them off home with it and hijack it *en route?*" She shook her head at him. "Sergei it isn't any good! How do you know they're going to *catch* a marlin? Dillard was lucky, but you could wait for weeks . . ."

"Not here, Peta. Not in the season in a boat equipped with every possible device for locating fish, crewed by experts, concentrating on just that one kind of fish. Anyway, so you do wait weeks. Months even if you have to. And you wait for the right kind of person. A senator. A Richard Burton. A Margaret Thatcher. Even the President of the United States. Why not? No reason he mightn't enjoy a bit of game fishing. You wait. It's worth it. What did it weigh that fish that Dillard caught?"

"Over seven hundred pounds."

"Seven hundred pounds. Right. That could take, what? Up to two hundred kilos of cocaine? Have you any idea of the street value of two hundred kilos of cocaine. It's about thirty-six million dollars! Thirty-six million dollars! That's worth waiting for, isn't it? Waiting a year for if you have to."

Petronella smacked the side of the speedboat in irritation. "How many times do I have to tell you, Sergei?! There can't be an ounce of cocaine in that marlin!"

"And I tell you it's full of the stuff."

"Then have the police in. Smash it up."

"So we find the cocaine. But where's the proof Minahero had a hand in it? When he's got you ready to swear black and blue he's never been within yards of the thing?"

"As he hasn't. Well . . ."

"Well, what?"

"Well he helped put the rope round it. And he helped put it in the coffin. But that's all. After that he was nowhere near it."

"Coffin?"

"One of those two refrigerated compartments. You remember they put your dolphin in one of them? Do you mind if I smoke?" And ironically, "Of course there's the risk it might draw attention to us."

"You're feeling bitchy. That's good. That's very good. Go on."

She lit one and threw the match fizzing into the sea. The night was calm, humid, moonlit, exquisitely beautiful. The speedboat rocked gently with small chuckling sounds. The fenders squeaked interminably but quite softly against the pier wall. Music from the Deep Water Bar drifted to them. There was a smell of salt and seaweed and mangroves. A light on the end of the pier throwing a pool on the water had attracted a small garfish. Occasionally a larger fish, a hunting tarpon perhaps, smashed the surface and filled it with phosphorescence which gradually died away. Somewhere a night gaulin cried.

"You said he helped put it in the coffin."

"Yes."

"How did they do that? Exactly?"

"Well, they had these slings. Lengths of canvas with handles . . . well, handholes, each end. They slipped these under the fish and then the four of them . . ."

"Four of them?"

"Minahero. Ota. O'Kano. And Miyako. The one we called Fido."

"Where was Fujita?"

"On the bridge."

"All the time?"

"Yes."

"You're sure?"

"Yes. We never actually stopped. Anyway I could see him all the time. There wasn't a speedboat in the way."

"Right. So they slipped these slings under the fish, lifted it up and dropped it in the coffin."

"Yes." And then she remembered. "No. What they did was to lift up the fish and turn it round until it was pointing in the opposite direction. And then they lowered it." She was thinking aloud. "Now why did they do that? Was it the straps? No. No, they were . . ."

"Straps?"

"There were two sets of straps with buckles. And they strapped the fish in place so that it wouldn't be damaged."

"And you're saying they could have put it in the easy way and they could still have strapped it in?"

She nodded. "Yes. Yes, they could have."

"And then they put the covers on?"

"Yes."

"And the next time you saw the fish was when they took the covers off?"

"To have it lifted out."

"And of course it was pointing in the same direction?"

"Yes."

"Did Dillard have anything to say about it?"

"Yes." She spoke very quietly. "He said it looked bigger. Made a joke about it."

"You bet it looked bigger!" His voice was vibrant with triumph. "Because it was another fish altogether. My God it's brilliant! Absolutely brilliant!"

"But . . ."

"Just a minute!" He was thinking hard. "When I saw you Minahero was away. For two whole days. Ostensibly fishing off Bimini."

"Yes."

"Well he might have done a bit of that. As an alibi. But you can bet your bottom dollar that wasn't how he spent most of those two days. He spent most of them collecting that marlin, which Dillard believes he caught, which was handed over to him in mid-ocean somewhere packed full of cocaine, mounted but not painted and shoved in that refrigerated hold."

"There wasn't room for two. And we'd have seen it."

"No, you wouldn't. Because that hold's got a trick bottom . . . No." He put up a fist and whipped it round like a boxer doing an uppercut. "Don't you see? Those straps? Why those straps? Have you ever heard of anyone strapping a game fish in a compartment before? Never. But if you've got to turn a fish upside down in a hole in the floor of a cockpit filled with people the last thing you want is for it to go thumping on the floor and everyone asking if you've got a poltergeist aboard! My God, though, you've got to hand it to the sod! It's devilish, devilish cunning. You pick up an already mounted fish that's filled with drugs and hang it by straps in the bottom of a reversible compartment. Then you go fishing, keep your fingers crossed you catch one near enough the same size to fool the guy who's caught it when you do the swap. If you do, and you're so lucky he's a Dillard, you fuzzle him with booze . . . Right?" Petronella nodded. "Tell him what a clever guy he is. Keep him occupied. And meanwhile someone presses a button that turns the whole thing . . ."

"*Abekobe!*"

"What?"

"*Abekobe!* It's what Minahero said when he told them to turn the marlin round."

"And we don't need a dictionary to know what it means, do we? But let me finish. Suppose after going to all that trouble you don't catch your marlin, or one near enough to do your swap, what then? Do you commit *hara-kiri?* Not a bit of it. You just shrug your shoulders and say better luck next time, chum. But if you do catch your fish and it's near enough to swap then there's just one other thing you've got to do to keep your shirt tails clean. Get rid of the fish you *did* catch."

"You have to be right," said Petronella.

"What does that mean?"

"Fujita had been complaining the engines weren't running as smoothly as he liked. Immediately after he'd dropped us, he and Minahero took *Dai Nichi* out on a test run."

Roff chuckled. "And that poor old marlin which Dillard went to so much trouble to catch was fed to the sharks for supper!"

"Like Kress," said Petronella soberly.

"Yes," said Roff. "Just like Laurence Kress."

He put his hand on hers. Their faces were very close and in the bright moonlight, for all the strain, she looked as lovely as she had ever looked. It would have been the greatest thing in the world to have thrown off the mooring ropes, started up the engine and roared away into the night, leaving the whole of their earlier lives behind. It would have been the greatest thing. But it was not a possible thing.

"Now you've got to go back," he told her.

She was calmer that she had been. Able to reason. "Why? When there's nothing else for me to do."

"But there is." He was speaking unhurriedly, quietly but clearly, so that she should not miss a word. "In that mounting shed there's a marlin which everyone thinks is just a refrigerated fish awaiting mounting and painting up. But in fact it's already mounted. And not mounted as it was in the days of the old taxidermists. These days a mount's just a plaster base covered with fish skin or scales and with the various bits and pieces, bill, fins, tail, glass eyes added on, and then the whole thing painted to look like the original before it died. I know because I made it my business to find out. Inside that plaster cast is enough cocaine to create God knows how many new addicts and enough pay off to blow up scores of innocent men and women. It's up to Shapland what happens. When he knows, which he will before morning, maybe he *will* raid that shed. But I doubt it. And I'll tell you why. That cocaine's no use to Minahero until it's in the States and the plan's to let Dillard act as furniture remover because the chances are a hundred to one against anyone examining a senator's trophy when he docks in his own home marina. And even if they do and find the stuff, how are they going to prove Minahero put it in? That it wasn't someone else who did the swap? Okay. So it's ashore. It's only *now* Minahero wants to get possession of it and that in some way which doesn't muck up his chances of a repeat performance next year maybe. How, I don't know. Only Minahero knows. And that's where, unless I miss my guess, Shapland will come in. From the moment that fish is landed it's going to be tracked as carefully as a Russian intercontinental missile and sooner or later it's going to lead Shapland right up to Minahero's door. Providing . . ." And he paused, very deliberately. "Providing nothing has happened and no one has done anything to put Minahero on his guard."

"Which, for example," she said bitterly, "going off with you in this speedboat, forgetting the whole filthy business, trying to start a brand new life, would do?"

"Well it would, wouldn't it?"

"But what about you turning up like this? Dillard'll have seen you . . ."

"And one or two strangers may have heard you calling out my name? Yes. But I don't think it's too difficult. I'm still besotted. I've slipped over to try to bribe you back. Made you a better offer. Promised you the moon. But you've had all this before and nothing ever came of it. So you've sent me packing with a few choice words and fleas in my ears. But the whole thing's got you pretty uptight. So instead of going back to Dillard you go straight to Minahero and tell him you've had enough of being treated like a bitch on heat. You tell him that ten minutes back Roff sneaked into the Deep Water Bar and you sent him about his business but you're damned if you're going back to Dillard who can't keep his sweaty hands off you. Okay you've helped him catch his damn marlin like you were supposed to but that's the end of it. That's all you're going to do so far as Dillard is concerned. And if he, Minahero, I mean, doesn't like it he can lump it too. Lay it on good and strong. That there are plenty more fish in the sea where he came from. Etcetera. Etcetera. Etcetera. So far as he's concerned it'll be probably be par for the course. He'll have had it before from other women every time they couldn't take any more of his excesses. There's no reason on earth why he should connect it with what he's up to."

"And in the end I don't walk out on him, do I?"

"No."

"I stay close to him because that way through Wilberforce, or Le Clerc or someone or other I can keep in touch? Let you know Minahero's movements?"

He shook his head. "It would be easier to say yes, but I'm not going to. Shapland doesn't need to know Minahero's movements. Only the marlin's. But you stay with him and be exactly the same with him as you've been up to now because if you change, for no good and obvious reason, he's going to find one."

She looked away from him and stared across the moonlit water to the faint fringe of trees across the other side of the harbour. It didn't look like the sea but like a lake because the way the land lay the mouth to the ocean wasn't visible. She wondered vaguely if, when he left, Sergei would have any problem with the reefs or shallows.

"You realise what you're saying, don't you?" she said, not looking at him. "The idea was I'd stay here to keep Dillard happy so he'd go on trying to catch his fish. Well he's caught it and I've given up keeping him sweet. So what do we do now? Me and my *tomodachi?*—that means friend. Why we go back to Grand Bahama. Back to Minahero's fun and games. To dressing up like a bloody geisha, to . . ."

He shot out a hand.

"Why?" she cried angrily. "Don't you want to hear it?"

"No."

"I have to put up with it but you don't have to listen to it?"

"I can't bear it," he said.

"But I can?"

"You have to."

"What happens to me afterwards?"

He shook his head. "I just don't know."

"Or care?"

"I care enormously."

She looked at him full face. "I suppose you know I love you?" And, when he didn't reply, "You once said you loved me."

"I did."

"But not any more. Whores are not for loving are they, Sergei? And don't answer that. Because whatever you said, I wouldn't believe you."

She became clipped and practical—a totally different woman. "All right, I'll do it. Help me out, will you?"

He went ashore first and helped her out. For a moment they stood facing each other so close their bodies all but touched. But then Petronella stood away. And forced irony when all she felt was pain.

"What will you do afterwards, Sergei, if you pull this off?" she threw at him. "Go back to Anita and develop retirement homes for pensioners? Or become a new James Bond!"

And she turned abruptly and walked away into the night.

He watched her for as long as it was possible to see her. A faint trace of her perfume lingered until a small breeze shifted it away. Then she was gone from sight. He went quickly down the steps, threw off the mooring ropes, started the powerful engine and roared off away from Dragon Cay. Walking past the club-house, heading for the marina where *Tsuki* lay, Petronella heard the engine fading and saw the blazing headlight racing across the water, picking out the channel between the marker buoys.

SIXTEEN

"Yes, sir," said Dillard. "Yes, of course." The hand holding the telephone receiver was shaking, the other gripped the edge of the desk so tightly that the knuckles showed white. Clara, disbelieving, hovered close, hoping to catch the drift of things.

"Should be some time tomorrow," she heard her husband say. "No, I don't know exactly. Is it important? . . . From who? . . . But . . . Yes, Mr. President, I am . . . Of course . . . What! I don't believe it! . . . When are they arriving? . . . I see . . . Yes, naturally . . . I was going to throw a little party next week and I invited him . . . Well, no. He's got this English girl who's living with him. I invited her too . . . Yes, sir, I think so . . . As it is? Yes, sir . . . Lieutenant Goodson . . ." He signalled wildly to Clara, making motions she didn't understand. Hurriedly he put his free hand over the mouthpiece. "Paper! Pencil! Quick!" he hissed. She shoved at him a pad with a ballpoint pen clipped to it which, in fact, had been easily within reach of his hand. "Lieutenant Goodson," she heard him repeat as he wrote it down. "And the other name, sir? . . . Chapman? . . . Oh. Shapland! . . . I understand . . . You can rely on me, sir."

He rattled the receiver down on its rest.

"Well?" demanded Clara explosively. "What was all that about? What did he want?"

He stared at her dully, as if seeing through her.

"Rodney!" she cried angrily, each syllable spaced out. "What did he want?"

He shook his head. "I can't tell you."

"You can't tell me?"

"He told me not to. To tell no one."

"I'm not no one. I'm your wife."

"I'm sorry, Clara." He was like a paper bag with all the air squeezed out of it.

"The President of the United States calls you personally," she berated him disbelievingly, "and you won't tell me what about?"

He answered wildly, trying to find the way to silence her without divulging what he'd been told.

"It's nothing directly to do with him. It's that . . . well someone, someone very important asked him to ask me to give my complete co-operation on a matter of national . . . well international importance."

Clara grabbed the pad. "Goodson? Shapland? Who the hell are they?"

He hesitated, wondering if he could tell her just sufficient to keep her from haranguing him.

"They're the only people I can talk about it to," he said eventually.

"Who *are* they?"

"I can't tell you."

"What the hell have you been up to, Dillard?"

"I haven't been up to anything."

"The President of the United States calls you! And you tell me you've been up to nothing? It's something to do with this damn fishing trip, isn't it?" He nodded. "Well, I'm your wife and if you're in trouble it's gonna affect me too, isn't it? I'm entitled to know what the hell it's all about?" And, before he *could* have answered, "And what's this about a party next week? You never told me anything about it."

"Well you'll be busy with the wedding and I thought . . ."

"You thought, baloney! Thursday! That's when it's gonna be, isn't it? When I'm off in St. Paul. And who's this English girl? You think I'm an idiot, Dillard? You think I can't put two and two together?"

"If you want to know," he answered desperately, "this English girl is the property of one of the men I was inviting to the party." For all his confusion and discomfort he was grateful beyond words that after all he'd gotten nowhere with Petronella Harrington. "And the party's to celebrate that fish I caught."

"What the hell's that fish got to do with the President telephoning you?"

"Nothing," he lied. "Nothing at all. And I'm not in any trouble, Clara."

"I don't believe it," Clara answered flatly. "I just do not believe it. You're a senator and what do you do? Take yourself off fishing for best part of four whole weeks. No wonder you don't get anywhere."

"I got to be a senator . . ."

"On my money and my daddy's backing! Where the hell . . . ?" But she realised she was straying from the more important point. "Now, you listen to me. Rodney Dillard, I'm *going* to know what this is all about. Who's coming to this party? What happened down in the Bahamas?"

"There'll be two men coming this afternoon. We've got to put them up. They're a sort of . . ." It was excruciatingly embarrassing. How the hell could you not tell your wife?

"A sort of what?"

"Bodyguard." He might just as well have said they were assassins.

"Bodyguard!"

"For Christ sake, cut it out!" he yelled suddenly, goaded beyond words. "I've been ordered not to tell you. This English dame's nothing to do with me. If you want to know, she's the floozie who belongs to this Japanese guy who owns the boat I caught that marlin on. And like it or not we've got two guys from the CIA coming to keep us company . . ."

"From the CIA!" It was all but a scream.

"Yeah. The CIA." He found satisfaction in it. "And there's nothing I can do to stop them coming. And if I could tell you what it's all about, I would, but I can't, so will you kindly shut up, Clara!"

"I certainly will not. Now, Rodney Dillard, you hear this . . ." It went on for quite some time.

2

The marlin was two days late arriving and was carried into the apartment by two brawny men who neither could give, nor were interested in giving an explanation for the delay. It was housed in a huge, well-made packing case. Following Dillard's instructions, they deposited this in his study, required him to sign a receipt, accepted an overgenerous tip without undue gratitude and departed. Carrying out his orders to the letter, Dillard (having locked the study door against the possibility of Clara, out playing bridge, returning) dialled a number on his private line.

"Lieutenant Goodson," he said to the girl. And when Goodson came on, "It's arrived."

"Yes, I know. We're watching. Have you opened it?"

"No."

"Do so. I'll hold."

The crate was carefully screwed down. Dillard fetched a screwdriver and undid the screws, which turned easily enough. He took off the lid and stared at the beautiful fish resting on short lengths of battens and held in place by strips of canvas. He picked up the telephone.

"Lieutenant Goodson?"

"Is it yours?"

"It looks like mine."

"Have you taken it out?"

"No. I wouldn't be able to by myself."

"What were you going to do when it arrived?"

"Get some carpenters to come by."

"You've arranged for them already?"

"Yes."

"People you've used before?"

"Yes. They did my study."

"Get the carpenters and call me when they've put it up."

Clara arrived before the carpenters. "So that's it, is it?" she said, eyeing the marlin as balefully as the fish in its crate eyed the world which had taken its life away. She knew by now what it was supposed to contain; worn out by her tireless inquisition, Dillard's resolve had finally collapsed and now an extra layer had been added to his unease—what his wife, for all her assurances, might have let slip to her friends.

"You didn't say anything, did you?" he asked anxiously. "To Beth and . . . ?"

"Of course I didn't! It'd be all over New York by now. What sort of fool do you think I am?" She was still staring at the fish. "That's the one you caught?" she said, unknowingly echoing Goodson's query.

"I think so."

"Don't you know?"

"They all look much the same. Except some are bigger than others."

"And that weighs seven hundred pounds?"

"Seven thirty-seven. Well, it doesn't now, of course. They just keep the skin and the fins and things and put them on a plaster cast." He bent and managed to raise one end of the crate off the carpet. "It's damn heavy, though."

"Well it would be if it's filled with drugs." She looked round nervously as if wishing she hadn't used the words. "The sooner we get it out of here the better."

"We'll be all right . . ."

"And the sooner we get rid of them, the better, too." She nodded her head in the direction of the spare bedroom where the CIA men were housed. "And if you think . . ." She broke off, frowning, still looking at the fish.

"What is it?" he asked. "What is it, Clara?"

"It's broken."

"Broken?"

"The fish. Look." She went round the end of the crate so that they were facing each other across the length of it. "It's broken here." She bent to touch the fish just above its huge forked tail.

Dillard came round and saw she was right. There was a definite crack clear across the mount.

"Maybe that's where they put the drugs in," said Dillard. "Maybe that left a weakness. Well, it's not much good . . ." But then he remembered that he hadn't told Clara everything.

"I've got to make a call," he told her.

"Make it then."

He thought about it and decided that he could. "For God's sake don't cough or anything," he begged.

"If you hadn't known what was in it, what would you have done?" said Goodson.

"Contacted Minahero. I promised to anyway."

"Promised to what?"

"Let him know that it had arrived safely."

There was a long silence.

"Then you'd better do that," said Goodson. And after a moment, "I think we can relieve you of Bews and Salaman. No one's going to come bothering you."

It was two hours before Dillard got through to Minahero at the Pompano. He knew it would be a problem keeping his voice natural so he decided to fake anger.

". . . the damn thing's got a crack clean across and the tail's almost off!"

"Oh, I am sorry. It has obviously been badly handled."

"Badly handled, nothing! It's still tied down with bits of tape."

"That wouldn't stop it cracking if it was dropped."

"Look, Minahero, I know these people. They're a first-class Florida outfit I've used a dozen times. I was there when they unloaded it from my boat and I told them what was in it and I watched them put it in the truck. It wouldn't have come out again until it got up here. For God's sake, it's the same damn crew!"

The voice of the Japanese man was easy, untroubled, reassuring. "Well then I'm very sorry, senator. Let me think. Yes. The best people in New York are Todd & Snibbe. A very well-established company. I will telephone Mr. Snibbe and explain. I will ask him to collect the fish and repair it at my expense. You will not know it has been damaged. Please touch it as little as you can . . ."

"It's still in the damn crate."

"Good. Very good."

"When will I get it back?"

"I will explain to Mr. Snibbe that you must have it for your party. That is, let me see, next Thursday, is it not? Oh, and by the way, you're lucky to have caught me. I have to come up to New York rather earlier than I thought and

I am catching an evening flight. I will telephone you sometime tomorrow . . ."

3

Shapland, who had flown in on a lightning visit, came up to Roff's room in the Plaza—which Roff was entitled to regard as quite a coup.

"Why the hell can't we talk this over in the bar?" Roff said. "Why does it always have to be this hole-and-corner stuff?"

"We have our reasons."

"And I've heard that before," Roff said. "And I don't believe it. I think you've got yourself so involved in it, you've got secrecy indigestion."

"If you want a drink," Shapland said, "they'll send one up."

"I do want a drink. Do you?"

Shapland thought about it. "Yes, all right. I'll have a whisky."

"My God!" said Roff. And ordered drinks. "Todd and Snibbe," he said. "I take it you've had them checked out?"

"It's puzzling. They're quite reputable."

"So was Kress. Until you knew him."

"Yes."

Shapland sipped his drink as if it were a duty.

"Why didn't Minahero simply hijack it or organise trans-shipment of the damn fish himself?" Roff said.

"Why ask me when you know the answers?"

"I was asking myself. You've got his line tapped?"

"Permanently."

"Nothing?"

"Beyond the fact that he's arriving in New York tonight, which we could have got from Dillard, nothing. But when a man assumes his line is always tapped . . ." Shapland didn't bother to finish but got to his feet and going to the window stared out at the evening light over Central Park.

"Sit down, Shapland," Roff said. "You're making me nervous."

"I don't like New York. I never feel at home here." But he came back and sat down again. "It's being collected tomorrow," Shapland said abruptly. "You're entitled to be in on it."

"Will you be?"

"I'm going back tonight."

"Missing the kill?" Roff taunted him.

"I am not a policeman. Todd and Snibbe are sending for it at eleven. Goodson's . . ."

"Who is this Goodson?"

"From the Federal Drug Enforcement Administration."

"A policeman?"

"Sort of. He will be in an unmarked police car opposite Dillard's apartment and there'll be others at intervals along the route."

"Sirens and all?"

"You're an unpleasant fellow," Shapland said. "Do you want to be in that car or not?"

"I want to be in that car."

"Then I'll arrange it." He stood, his drink hardly tasted. "If," he said, "there are no drugs in that fish you will not be popular."

"There's a lot things about this business that aren't all that certain," Roff answered. "But that that fish is crammed with junk is the one bloody thing that is!"

SEVENTEEN

Through the rear window in the blue Chevrolet parked on East Sixty-fourth Street, Goodson, beside the driver (an un-uniformed policeman named Pittsie), and Roff in the back would be able to see the Todd & Snibbe panel van when it arrived. It would have been more comfortable being further west on Sixty-fourth, across the other side of Park Avenue, but there was always the risk they might be held up by the traffic lights and lose it somewhere heading up to the taxidermist's.

Goodson had a large-scale map of the immediate area on his knees and marked on this were the locations of the various back-up cars. The purpose-equipped cab which was to shadow the panel van had its hood open and a mechanic in oily overalls working on the engine and was parked two or three spaces ahead of them, its driver sitting comfortably inside smoking and reading a newspaper. Accordingly no fewer than eight police cars were stationed at strategic points all switched on to the frequency of the transmitter in the cab, with the blue Chevy following. There were also about two dozen officers in plain clothes and other cars, marked and unmarked, strategically located so that in effect the entire area east of Central Park as far as the East River could be rapidly sealed off.

At eleven-twelve, a white van, with the legend TODD & SNIBBE stencilled on in blue on the visible side, was spotted travelling south along Lexington Avenue directly ahead, catching the lights and going out of sight only to re-appear a few minutes later turning right off Park Avenue, having apparently made the journey west to park via Sixty-third Street. The driver stayed in the cab of the van but his mate got out and spoke to the doorman, went inside, re-emerged, signalled to the driver who, turning his head, spoke to someone behind him and almost immediately the double van doors at the rear were opened from the inside and two men in matching green overalls descended and, leaving the van doors ajar, went into the apartment building.

"Okay," said Goodson, a thin man with stiff wavy white hair and cold ice-blue eyes. "Spread it."

The driver switched on the transmitter. "Griffin calling. Subject just arrived to collect. Do you read me?"

Various voices responded indicating in various ways that they did.

"Standby then," the driver said and flicked off the transmitting switch.

"Well, Mr. Roff," said Goodson, "we shall soon find out if you've got it right."

Roff turned his head and caught a sinew somewhere in his neck. He jiggled his shoulder and the pain slowly ebbed. Goodson was watching the apartment building through the driving mirror.

Roff thought about Petronella. Minahero had arrived at JFK the previous evening and she had been with him. They had taken a taxi which had been tailed only for the tail to be lost in the heavy evening traffic. Some hours later exhaustive enquiries had revealed that the taxi had dropped them at the Pierre, where it was later confirmed they had a suite booked under the name of Nimoto. The suite was two-bedroomed, which was comforting. Further enquiries had elicited that they had been served a light supper in their rooms and that while Petronella hadn't left the suite, Minahero had done so by taxi which set off northwards, crossed Central Park by one of the transverse roads, and had again been lost, this time because of a traffic block at Columbus Avenue. Conceivably, if he was on his way to Todd & Snibbe, the taxi had doubled back through Central Park. Well, as Goodson had said, they would soon find out. But meanwhile Petronella took precedence in his thoughts. He could have taken her away from Dragon Cay. Instead he had sent her back. It could, he mused, have been a good thing between them. A thing good enough for a lifetime perhaps. Maybe even at the end of Dragon Cay it could still have been a possibility. Now, for sure, it was over and he was forever marked and she was forever scarred. At least when they had taken Minahero she would be freed. At least . . .

"Here they come," Goodson's hard voice cut across these deliberations. Roff resisted the temptation to turn his head. Farther along Sixty-fourth

Street he saw the two men with a woman exercising a spaniel turn and walk slowly back towards the taxi. The mechanic straightened and sticking up his thumb slammed down the hood. A man with a briefcase at the corner of Lexington put it down on the sidewalk so as to consult a diary taken from his pocket. Pittsie switched on and barked, "Subject loading." Goodson was watching through the mirror all the time. "It's going in," he said. The taxi driver had folded his newspaper and was exchanging words with the mechanic. Their chat was interrupted by the men and woman with the spaniel. The taxi driver looked doubtfully at the dog and shook his head. The woman said something to one of the men and both of them got into the taxi leaving her and the dog standing on the sidewalk. One of the men talked to her through the open window of the taxi.

"Okay," Goodson said, "they're pulling out."

"Subject leaving Sixty-fourth and Park, heading east," transmitted Pittsie.

The panel van passed as he started up the engine and the taxi pulled out behind it with the Chevrolet following. At Lexington the lights were red and there was sufficient blockage for them to lose both van and taxi. But they caught it up again with a couple of cars in between by the time they got to Third and by the time they had crossed York and done a left northwards on it at Rockefeller University, both were well in sight.

This, thought Roff, somehow feels a bit too simple. Twenty blocks and we shall be there. But as he listened to Pittsie's running commentary—"Griffin crossing seventieth. Subject still in view proceeding north on York"—he was aware his heart was thumping and his hands were clammy.

"Okay, Pittsie." Goodson's eyes were glued to the white panel van perhaps eighty yards ahead. Roff was baffled. If Goodson was not a policeman his manner and behaviour certainly indicated that he was. Nothing was ever explained.

The lights were red at Seventy-ninth with a lot of traffic cutting down to the East River Drive. In between them now were a couple of buses with the taxi sandwiched between them and the van in front of both. If he wants to throw us, all he has to do, thought Roff, is turn off somewhere fast. He hadn't the least idea where in New York he was. But Pittsie knew.

The lights changed in their favour.

"Mistofsky, do you read me?" he called suddenly.

Mistofsky came in. "Sure, Pittsie, I read you."

"We're stuck at Seventy-ninth and York. Subject just made lights. Maybe we won't. He's white with blue lettering, Todd and Snibbe."

There was hooting and klaxon horns. A police car, nothing to do with the operation, went sirening somewhere nearby.

"Christ!" said Pittsie. "We've lost him!"

The taxi had vanished also.

Roff felt the cold of sweat drip from his armpit.

The lights were green and red and green again before the block got sorted out.

At Eightieth the bus ahead did a right turn and York Avenue was clear without a sign of either the van or the taxi.

Pittsie was busy. "We've got one parked on Eighty-fourth," he advised Goodson. "If he's turned down where he should, he'll have seen him." And transmitted, "Lapidus, Pittsie here, do you read me?"

"Yeah, Pittsie," came crackling back. "I read you."

"Subject should have just passed you. White panel van lettered Todd and Snibbe. Confirm."

"Sure. Just went by." Roff wondered how they could be certain of deciphering it correctly, it seemed so crackly. "But the van was plain."

"Which side you parked on?"

"Downtown."

"Okay, Lapidus. That figures."

He switched the microphone out and commented in an aside to Goodson, "It's okay. It's just that he's only lettered one side."

They were now at Eighty-fourth and the driver swung them right towards Gracie Square and Carl Schurz Park bordering the East River. The taxi was pulled in to the kerb.

"Okay!" Pittsie exulted into his microphone. "Subject's here okay. I guess you boys can take it easy."

They pulled in behind the taxi, whose driver got out and spoke to them through the window. Ahead of them the expressway traffic was thundering into and out of the tunnel. It was a cold grey day with a sharp wind blowing off the river. Diagonally across was the wood which was Carl Schurz Park.

"Where are they?" Goodson asked.

"Down," said the cab driver pointing to a ramp to an underground garage in a building on the downtown side. "Harris and Zimmerman followed them in. Hold it." There were sounds coming from the Yellow Cab. He left them and they saw him talking on his intercom. He came back. "They're unloading," he advised.

"Let's go see," said Goodson.

They bundled out of the Chevy and made their way down the ramp. It proved to be a high and extensive underground garage which served business premises above and so was unusual in this largely upper-class residential area. There were quite a number of vans parked in it and it had a huge, old-fashioned elevator for transporting merchandise upwards. Close by this, its back end towards them, was the Todd & Snibbe panel van. Its driver was just in the act of closing the rear doors while the other three were manhandling the crated marlin into the elevator. There was a small glazed office by the bottom of the ramp close to where they stood in which a man and a girl in jeans were talking, heads close together, studying some sort of account book.

Goodson went to the window.

"Todd & Snibbe?" he inquired.

The man looked up. "Oh. Yeah." He stuck a thumb upwards. "Second Floor. Two-seven." He altered the angle of his thumb. "Use that elevator." And he went back to studying his ledger.

Roff was watching the merchandise lift. He saw the lattice gate swung shut and watched the crate with two of the green-overalled men standing either side of it start heading slowly upwards. The third man was talking to the panel van driver through his door window.

"Fetch them over," said Goodson to Pittsie, nodding to Harris and Zimmerman, who were standing apparently arguing over a street map they had spread open on a car hood.

"We're going up," Goodson said to them, when they'd come over. "Harris, you come with us. Stay here, Zimmerman; Pittsie will give you the okay when we've verified it and then you can call it off."

The four of them crammed into the small private elevator, which was located on the opposite side of the garage to the merchandise lift, and went up to the second floor and exited into a lobby with a double door opposite and a single door one end and a staircase up and down at the other. On either side of the double doors the names of the companies which used the floor were painted. Todd & Snibbe apparently rented the left-hand side only. They went through. Beyond the double doors was a large open space in which were stacked cartons, boxes and crates. Directly ahead was the merchandise lift and on either side were doors leading to various offices. A counter with a flap barred their way. Behind the counter was a girl.

"Yeah?" she enquired, scanning the four men facing her and finally picking on Roff for preference.

"Todd & Snibbe," he suggested.

"Who shall I say?" Her hand was moving towards a switch on her exchange.

"Say nothing," said Pittsie, flipping open a wallet to disclose his badge.

"Okay," said the girl as if calls by policemen were an everyday occurrence. "Second door left."

"Stay here and see she doesn't use that thing," said Goodson to Harris.

Goodson led the way, lifting the counter flap and lowering it when all of them except Harris were through. Roff, his heart pumping furiously, was trying to work out the plan which no one had vouchsafed to him. Ahead, half hidden by a large deal crate, he could see two extra men helping those in green overalls get the marlin out of the merchandise elevator. So far so good —the stuff had arrived. If Minahero was here there was no way out for him. Except possibly by fire escapes, the only exits were down this elevator or past where they were standing. By now, presumably, around the block were sufficient plainclothes police to detain all within the building and Minahero, if not here, as and when he showed.

Goodson strode to the door the girl had indicated and threw it open, disclosing a small office in which a girl was busy typing. Off it was a door of frosted glass.

"Watch that thing, Pittsie," said Goodson nodding to the fish, now deposited. "See no one touches it." The green-overalled men had gone back into the elevator which had started moving down.

"Yes, sir," said Pittsie.

The typist, a trifle alarmed at the sudden unannounced entry of four men into her tiny office, had yet to pull herself sufficiently together to ask their business.

Goodson gave her no time.

"Mr. Snibbe in there?" he asked—somewhat unnecessarily, thought Roff, considering that his arrival in the building would have been first checked.

"Yes, but . . ."

"Never mind." Goodson turned to Roff. "Okay?"

Roff nodded. Goodson threw open the door to Snibbe's office. Afterwards Roff was to wonder what exactly he had expected to find when Goodson threw open that door and what he had expected Minahero's confederate to be like. Whatever these things might have been, they could hardly have been more at variance with what that open door disclosed: a fair-sized room with a sufficient number of mounted fish, although none of great size, to remind him forcibly of the Deep Water Bar on Dragon Cay; an office notable for its rather frowsty look: an old leather armchair with scuffed armrests, a bookcase with the volumes anywhere, a tired carpet and, in a corner, an old dog which raised its head in a half enquiry before lowering it again; on Snibbe's desk an emptied coffee-cup and a half-eaten biscuit; on the floor around his feet, seen under the old-fashioned desk, some crumbs as if he'd fed the dog.

And Augustus Snibbe, a rather scholarly-looking man, with a high forehead and deep-sunk dreamy-looking eyes raising his head from some papers and regarding this intrusion with mild indignation.

As camouflage for a vital part in an international drug-running syndicate it was brilliant.

"Good morning, gentlemen," Snibbe said in a faint, weary voice.

"Where's Minahero?" Goodson said.

Snibbe showed surprise. Not the surprise of a man taken off his guard, but the beautifully delivered surprise of an actor playing his part superbly.

"I have no idea," he answered.

"You're lying. He spoke to you an hour back."

"Indeed he did." There was a pause. "You gentlemen seem to know a great deal about my business."

"Yep," said Goodson. "Like you're taking delivery this morning of a stuffed marlin for repairs?"

"Correct. But really, gentlemen . . ."

"Can that!" said Goodson crisply. "Pittsie!"

Pittsie came in, brushing past the secretary who had risen and was standing amazed at these goings-on.

"Badge," said Goodson laconically. Pittsie showed his badge. "Okay," said Goodson. Pittsie put his badge away and withdrew. Goodson shut the door. The girl, her shape blurred by the frosted glass, could still be seen, hovering.

"You're all policemen?" said Snibbe looking from one to other of them.

"Not exactly," Goodson answered.

"Well," said Snibbe, with surprising aplomb, "do sit down." He gestured with a pale, thin hand to the armchair.

"Never mind that!" said Goodson. "How long have you known Minahero?"

"Let me see," mused Snibbe, making a steeple of his fingers. "About three years."

"Regularly stuffing the fish he sends you?" The irony was crucifying.

But Snibbe took it as a straightforward question.

"Oh no. Most of my work is freshwater fish. As you see." He collapsed the steeple to gesture. "I have done one or two small repairs for friends of his. I believe this one has been damaged in transit. But may I enquire . . ."

"And when it comes, what've you got to do?"

"Repair the mount and then return it to . . ." He began to search amongst the papers on his desk.

"To Senator Dillard," Goodson stated.

Snibbe raised his head. "That's right."

"It's arrived."

"Yes. They called me from downstairs."

"Let's go take a look at it."

"Of course."

Snibbe rose to his feet and came from behind his desk. At once the dog uncoiled itself from the large rug-softened basket where it lay and stiff-jointedly followed him. They made quite a procession going through the two offices and across the storage area: Snibbe, the dog, Goodson, Roff and Pittsie. There was no one else in the area now except the girl at the counter who had swivelled round to watch these strange proceedings and Harris who was chewing gum with the indifference of a policeman who has seen everything before.

"Open it," said Goodson curtly. And as Snibbe started to walk away from them. "Where d'you think you're going?"

Snibbe turned and regarded Goodson with mild reproof. "I need tools," he explained. "If you look you'll see it's screwed down." He went to a small cupboard and opening it took out a screwdriver, came back, bent and, unhurriedly, undid the screws and took off the lid.

Prepared as he was, Roff was astonished at the size and beauty of the enormous marlin as perfect—apart from the broad crack just above its tail—as when it had been a living, magnificent hunter of the deep-blue tropic seas. He stared at the huge belly and only now conceived the huge quantity of cocaine which could be stored within it. He marvelled at the wonderful craftsmanship which could so utterly conceal what had been done. The thought flashed across his mind: Peta should be here. By God she should be here!

"Now hear this, Snibbe," he heard Goodson say. "We're opening up that fish."

"Opening it up?" His self-control was quite amazing.

"That what I said. And then we're waiting." He looked at his watch. "Twenty to," he said with satisfaction.

"You mean he *is* coming?" Roff said surprised. "Minahero?"

"At twelve. Right?" His cold eyes raked Snibbe's mild ones.

"That is correct," Snibbe said.

Roff wondered why, if a telephone call to Snibbe from Minahero had been intercepted, no one had told him.

"The building's lousy with police," said Goodson to Snibbe meanwhile, "so don't try anything." He turned to Harris. "Okay, you go see Zimmerman and tell him they can call off everything but waiting for the Jap and when he gets here, close it up. Then come back up here. Okay?" And, as Harris left, Goodson wagged a finger at the girl by the counter. "Make that board busy. And don't try making calls."

At that moment one of the two men who had helped unload the marlin entered from the room next to Snibbe's suite.

"Remember what I told you," Goodson reminded Snibbe.

"These men are all policemen, Henry," Snibbe said inaccurately. "You had better go back into the mounting room and stay there until I tell you. And tell Geoff the same."

"Don't move!" barked Goodson. He strode to the door of the mounting room and glanced around it, making sure there were no exits. "Okay," he said. "Do that! And don't try making calls."

"But . . ."

"It's all right, Henry," Snibbe said soothingly. "There's just a big mistake somewhere so please do what I say until it's been sorted out."

Frowning, the man withdrew, closing the door behind him. Meanwhile Snibbe's secretary was at her door, listening amazed to these proceedings.

"Go back in your room, Ruth," Snibbe said mildly, tidying up. "Don't use the phone."

The door closed on Ruth.

"Now," said Snibbe, as if he were in charge, extraordinarily impressive for all his tired, thin voice. "Will you kindly explain what this is all about?"

"Don't give me that," said Goodson. "You know what's in that fish."

"Oh," said Snibbe, as if suddenly he understood.

He looked down at the fish, lying in its crate at their feet. And suddenly he bent down and tapped it with two knuckles. The fish rang with a hollow sound. Snibbe straightened. "There's nothing in it, you know," he said.

The bottom fell out of Roff's world. It was impossible! Yet the ring was hollow. He looked from the fish to Snibbe's smiling face, to the suddenly uncertain Goodson. He bent down quickly. The dog he had forgotten growled but made no movement from Snibbe's side. Roff rapped the fish. The rap rang back, confirmingly. The mount was empty.

"Undo it!" he called at Snibbe. "Quickly!"

"Certainly," Snibbe said, and going back to the cupboard withdrew a pair of enormous scissors and with these cut the canvas ties. He put the scissors down on the floor beside him.

"It's a very fine fish," he observed professionally. "What a pity it's been damaged." Roff realised he was quite enjoying the situation.

"What?" said Goodson, perplexed by the turn of events.

"The tail. I really don't know how it could have happened. It's well enough secured."

In a blinding flash of intuition, Roff knew exactly—or at least was 90 percent certain. There was just one thing to do to cover the odd 10 percent. Steeling himself, he said to Snibbe quietly. "Mr. Snibbe?"

"Yes, sir?"

"Do you mind if we lift that fish out?"

"Of course. Where shall we put it? On that bench?"

"Maybe." Roff went to the end of the crate to which the long bill pointed. "Ready?"

He put his hands down and around and wide apart under the head. Snibbe put his just below the marlin's belly.

"Lift!" Roff said. And it was as he had expected, and feared. They raised it with comparative ease. The plaster cast was empty. There were no drugs in the void. Had it been filled with cocaine, they could hardly have lifted it.

"All right," he said to Snibbe. "Let's put it back."

And it required all his self-control not to drop it. He wheeled on Goodson. It didn't matter who heard what. There wasn't the time. "Come on!" he cried.

Goodson stared.

"For God's sake, don't you see?" Roff shouted. "They've switched it! Like they did on the boat! It's still in that bloody van! And God knows where that's got by now!"

2

The crisis at least explained one thing, who Goodson was—at the very least a senior agent of one of the groups into which the Federal Drug Enforcement Administration was divided, more likely of even higher calibre. After a scamper down the stairs (the elevator was busy, possibly with Harris returning) in an endeavour to stop the panel van leaving the garage—only to find that Zimmerman had faithfully carried out his instructions to call off everything except apprehending Minahero when he arrived and that the van had pulled out just a couple of minutes earlier—after that scamper, Goodson had raced up again and effectively taken over Snibbe's office as temporary headquarters. Snibbe himself, accepting the events of a remarkable morning with considerable aplomb, had taken the old armchair; the dog was back in its basket; Roff paced with something to say and as yet no chance of saying it.

"Okay," Goodson said, "So go with it, Bluey. And get the NYPD to cover it . . . Yeah, I know exactly what they think of us, but they'll do it just the same . . . Check. White GM panel van with Todd and Snibbe in blue letters off side, plain near side. Plate Number PCB 593. Driver and another guy in the cab and two more in the back, but you can't see them. Okay? . . . Right! Do it now!"

He put down the receiver, and raised his ice-blue eyes to Roff.

"Mr. Roff,"—he was exaggeratedly polite—"don't you think maybe you've caused enough trouble already? On your say-so we laid on a whole group of Federal Drug Enforcement Administration and a big slice of the New York Police Department's Bureau of Narcotics labour and mechanical resources to grab some Japanese guy who according to you was coming here to pick up a load of junk which it turns out isn't here at all. And now when I'm trying to re-orient maybe twenty, thirty cars and God alone knows how many policemen and detectives, all you keep doing is waving your hands and trying to interrupt me!"

"Finished?" said Roff.

"Sure. Have your say," Goodson said. "But make it short."

"A white GM panel van registration number PCB 593 with Todd and Snibbe in blue letters on offside only. That's what we're looking for?"

"Right."

"Mr. Snibbe. You use a white GM panel van?"

"Yes, sir."

"Lettered Todd and Snibbe?" Augustus Snibbe's nod was like that of a schoolmaster approving a pupil working out a problem by stages. "Offside only?"

"No, Mr. Roff. Both sides."

"Of course."

Goodson waved a hand. "So they only did it one side."

"They did it both," said Roff.

"They did it both nothing. Lapidus . . ."

"Said there was no lettering on the nearside. Which there wasn't when he saw it. Because when he saw it there wasn't lettering on any side."

"We saw the bloody lettering!" He was losing his cool.

"When it was parked outside Dillard's. Yes, we did. That was offside lettering. And, as you seem to have forgotten, we saw the lettering when it passed in front of us down Lexington Avenue before they did their right turn to take them along Sixty-third so they could go up Park and turn into Sixty-fourth Street. That would have been on the nearside."

"That's right," said Goodson guiltily.

"It's very simple once you get to learn how Minahero's mind works," Roff went on. "He used a van lettered Todd and Snibbe to make the collection look genuine from Dillard's point of view. But at this end, as he had undertaken to deliver the marlin . . . right, Mr. Snibbe? . . . as he had undertaken to deliver it, he could hardly deliver it in a Todd and Snibbe van."

"So he switched vans. Is that what you're saying? That's baloney! They didn't have the time."

"They didn't need the time." Roff paused. "Because all they had to do was press a switch somewhere which rolled narrow panels painted Todd and Snibbe one side and plain white the other through one hundred and eighty degrees. Just as they did when they switched the marlins on Minahero's fishing cruiser."

For fully ten seconds Goodson stared at Roff with an expression which,

starting out derisive changed through appreciation to positive alarm. He
seized the telephone and dialled a number in such haste that he made a mess
of it and had to start again.

"Bluey!" he bawled, on getting through. "That van! It isn't lettered! Have
you got that? It isn't lettered! . . . Yeah, I know that's what I said. But now
I'm saying it isn't . . . Right! No, Todd and Snibbe! . . . You think I don't
realise how many goddam plain white vans there have to be in New York
City? But at least you've got its number! No! No, you don't. Not necessarily.
If they can flip a sign they can flip the license plate! . . . No, I can't. There
just isn't time . . . What are you supposed to do? Stop every white panel
van between Sixtieth and one-oh-six and Central Park and the river. And stay
tuned to Griffin solid!" He slammed down the receiver. "How far is it from
Sixtieth to 106th Street?" Roff asked. And when Goodson failed to answer.
"How far, Mr. Snibbe?"

"Over two miles. Maybe nearer three."

"And from Central Park through to the East River?"

"Half mile? Three-quarters, maybe."

"And how many white panel vans in two square miles of New York City,
would you guess?"

Snibbe smiled.

"Jesus!" objected Goodson, looking at the ceiling. "Who started this goddam circus anyway?"

Roff nodded. Unlike Snibbe he wasn't smiling. "I know," he said. "I did.
But one has to face realities. And the current reality is that your chances of
stopping the right van aren't very good. Maybe it's already going through
your cordon. Maybe it doesn't even need to. Maybe it's heading for somewhere inside the area you're trying to cordon off. In fact just about the only
hope we've got is that it's going somewhere outside the cordon and has still
some way to go and that somehow we can get a line on the district it's
heading for."

"Like how?"

Ignoring Goodson, Roff threw open the door to the secretary's office.

"What's the telephone number of the Pierre?" Roff called to her.
"Quick!"

The girl was all fingers and thumbs with the directory but got him the
number.

"838-8000," she said.

He hurried back and dialled the number.

"Mr. Nimoto's suite!" he demanded. "Hurry! It's urgent!"

Pray God she's in, he thought. Pray God she can help us somehow. If she
can't we're finished.

Petronella came on. "Yes?" her voice was listless.

"Sergei . . ."

"Sergei! Oh my God . . ."

"Listen! There isn't time to explain properly. Minahero fixed a fake van to collect that fish from Dillard then switched it *en route*. We've lost track of it completely and . . ."

"He's calling himself Nimoto here . . ."

"Yes, I know. For God's sake, Peta, don't interrupt me. Every second's vital. That van's heading for somewhere where Minahero's going or more likely already gone. If we could narrow it down and those drugs haven't already gone to ground, we've still got a chance. Not much of one but still a chance."

"But Sergei, he doesn't . . ."

"Confide his business to you. Of course he doesn't. But maybe someone came to the suite . . . ?"

"No."

"Met him in the lobby? Maybe he made some phone calls?"

"He was up here all the time. No one came up except the waiter. He did make a couple of telephone calls the moment we got here yesterday but both in Japanese."

"Oh, Christ! I never thought of that."

"Just a minute!" His heart almost stopped beating at the change of her tone. "There was something he said in English! I remember because it sounded strange, suddenly, amongst all that Japanese to hear English spoken."

"Right! Think! For God's sake, think! What was it?" There was a pause which Roff broke himself. "Peta . . ."

"I'm thinking, Sergei. For heaven's sake . . ."

"Sorry." He possessed himself in all the patience he could contrive.

She *was* thinking. Sitting in an armchair in the delightful sitting-room of the luxury double suite which overlooked Fifth Avenue. Trying to recall out of all she'd overheard through the opened door of her bedroom when Minahero had made his calls. Calls which had been staccato, terse, obviously to the point. All in Japanese. Except . . . except . . . What was it he'd said? And then it came to her. It came crystal clear as if she was hearing it spoken now.

"Sergei!" she said excitedly. "I remember. It was . . . it was 'Mary's Park.' It sounded so strange, 'Mary's Park.' Amidst all that Jap—"

He interrupted. "Mary's Park? You're sure."

"Positive."

Roff looked at Goodson. "That mean anything to you? 'Mary's Park'?"

But Goodson was already on his feet, grabbing at his map. "Mott Haven!"
He moved so quickly from the desk as to send the chair he'd already stood up
from crashing backwards. The dog looked up indignantly. Snibbe stayed
where he was. The secretary alarmed by the crash came hurriedly to the door.
Goodson elbowed her aside and ran out of the suite towards the counter of
the storage area. Petronella was asking, "Sergei! What was that? Are you all
right?"

"It's all right. Don't worry," he reassured her. "And you're fantastic!" He
slammed down the receiver and raced after Goodson.

The dog stared soulfully after him, then settled down. Life in Augustus
Snibbe's office had resumed its normal speed.

3

"What is it? Mott Haven?" Roff asked Goodson.

They were back with Pittsie, speeding, breakneck, northwards along the
East River Drive.

"South Bronx, north of 138th! Here!" He jabbed a finger into the map
torn in his hurried grasping of it in Snibbe's office. Roff, off the back seat,
looking over his shoulder, saw an area perhaps a mile in diameter which
Goodson had ringed round in red. "That's Mary's Park." Goodson's thin
finger moved upwards an inch or so to an area shaded green.

Pittsie's radio was going all the time, tinny, squawky and sometimes plain
unintelligible. Instructions had been circulated to close in an area bounded
by 138th Street downtown and 149th uptown and Willis Avenue and Southern Boulevard west and east. Without exception every white panel van in this
area was to be tailed to its destination. If it left the ring, it was to be allowed
to depart unhindered.

With Goodson, map in hand, ordering their route, they left Willis Avenue
by East 142nd Street.

There were no fewer than five white vans under surveillance in their immediate area.

"Yeah. Just grabbed a space outside Wilson's Garage . . ."

"Heading north up Jackson Avenue . . ."

"Check that one out. If he's been there more'n ten minutes, forget him."

"Your signal's lousy. Repeat . . ."

"I said he's opposite the cemetery. There's two guys in the cab and two
just got out of the back. I can't see in."

"That's interesting. What's your location?"

"Corner of St. Ann's and East one-four-oh. Do we move in on 'em?"

"No. Hold it. Could be . . ."

"Could be nothing. They just unloaded. It's roses all the way! Where the hell d'you get roses this time of year?"

"Okay, Pittsie," Goodson said. "Park it."

Pittsie did so. Mary's Park was across from them on their left. Ahead was Jackson Avenue. By comparison with midtown the traffic was light, the vehicles shabby.

"What do we do now?" said Roff.

"Tell 'em where we are, then listen. Okay, Pittsie, I'll take it." Goodson took the microphone. "Griffin calling base. Griffin to base. Do you read me?"

The reply came back. "We read you, Griffin."

"We're parked on St. Mary's Street between Beekman and Cypress Avenues. What's new on the one at Wilson's Garage?"

"He just went to the men's room. You can forget him unless we extend the area."

"Nope. Anything new?"

"Just had a call from Rix of four group. He's in a drug-store and there's a white panel van parked across and two guys just leaning against it smoking. That's by the Mitchell Houses."

"Tell him to keep in touch but it's too far south. Anything else?"

"Yep! Ferrari's pounding it on Concord. Reports white panel van pulled down into an empty lot by a big old abandoned warehouse 'bout five minutes back."

"What's it doing?"

"Not doing anything."

"How many in the cab?"

"One."

"Forget it."

They listened to other reports; some interesting, some not. Then base came back.

"Griffin, do you read?"

"We read. Got something?"

"Sure have! Ferrari's just come through again. Four men just came walking round the corner."

"So what? Four men came walking?"

"These are Japanese guys."

"Jesus! Where's this warehouse?"

"Corner of one-four-four and Concord."

"We're on our way!" Goodson took the mike away from his mouth. "You got that, Pittsie?"

"I got it," Pittsie said, pulling out.

"It figures," said Goodson as if the scenario were his own invention. "They dropped off three and now they've going to do another switch!"

They drove along St. Mary's Street, crossed Jackson and turned left at Concord Avenue. The warehouse, gaunt, its fire escapes rusting, its windows blocked up solid, blackened where part of it had been fired, crumbling, was across from them on their left. Just beyond it was the entrance to the empty lot with a ramp running down to it. At one time, probably, it had been the basement of some building long since demolished, perhaps another warehouse. They slowed as they drove past but with the width of the road they couldn't see down into it.

"Make a U, Pittsie," Goodson said. "But keep it slow."

Pittsie went as far as 145th Street and made his U to come slowly back. As they did so a black Cadillac emerged from the lot followed immediately by a white van. The Cadillac did a wide left along Concord travelling in the opposite direction to them, closely followed by the van. Roff quickly turned away and at the same time raised a hand to hide his face. In the front passenger seat was Minahero. The driver of the van and the man beside him were Japanese.

4

Goodson had the mike. "Bluey, we're on to them! Do you read me?"

"Yeah, Lieutenant, I read you," came crackling back.

"Get this. Minahero's in a black Cadillac, plate number PKE 5237, heading north up Concord Avenue. Another guy is driving and we didn't get a line on him if he's a Jap or a Caucasian. They're being followed by a white panel van with two Japs in the cab and maybe one, two more in the back. We're tailing but we had to do a U and we're a coupla blocks back. The way they're heading they could be making for Westchester Avenue and out or doubling back downtown. You gotta saturate Melrose and Morrisania. Yeah, better Hunt's Point too. And alert all cars that the tailing's over. They've got to hit. Do you read that? Hit!"

"We read."

"Spread it, then! And get us some reinforcements. We can't do it solo."

Goodson switched out and at once base could be heard transmitting on the all-cars radio for everything within any reasonable distance of Mary's Park to close in. Specific instructions were being rapped out to named vehicles to head for vital crossing points Westchester and Third, Westchester and East 163rd Street, Southern Boulevard and East 149th Street and others. Roff had a mental picture of an office somewhere with maps spread out on desks, key points being circled, agents jabbering down microphones, locations being charted, telephones ringing, group bosses hurrying from their private offices to be where the action was, stenographers taking notes, the air thick with tobacco smoke, acrid with sweat, crackling with atmosphere.

Meanwhile, by comparison, the quarry was giving no indication they had the least notion they were under surveillance—and indeed with the Chevy unmarked, neither Goodson nor Pittsie in uniform and Roff hurriedly turning his head the instant he recognised Minahero, there was no reason why they should have been suspicious. In fact everything pointed to the contrary. With effort the Cadillac and the van might both have made the lights at 147th Street; instead they slowed circumspectly to a halt, allowing the Chevrolet to make up ground so that now there were only a couple of cars between them and the van.

"Do any of those guys know you, Roff?" demanded Goodson.

"Minahero does."

"Okay. Well, be ready to duck down when we get close."

"What's the plan?"

"We just stay with them. As long as we stay with them, it'll all be closing in. What we've got to watch is we don't lose them at the lights or at a traffic block and we don't do nothing that makes them think we're tailing." He switched on the mike. "Griffin calling base. Subject now crossing one-four-nine still heading north. Where the nearest car you got?"

"Corner of Cauldwell and Westchester."

"Facing?"

"Uptown."

"Have him . . ." Goodson was thumbing the map, ". . . Have him take a right at one-six-oh and pick up Westchester. Subject should coincide if heading . . . No. Cancel!" Goodson's voice became almost shrill. "Subject turning right ahead of Westchester on one-five-two!"

Roff watched the Cadillac turning in leisurely fashion and after it the van. Pittsie swung round after them, perhaps a hundred yards behind.

"Listen," shouted Goodson, mike close up against his mouth. "That car you got on at Cauldwell and Westchester. Is it marked or unmarked?"

"Marked."

"Okay. Have it keep going till it hits one-six-three, then do a right far as Prospect Avenue. Subject still in view and heading for Prospect about six blocks south of one-six-three."

But Pittsie cried, "They're turning off."

"They can't be," said Goodson. "There's nowhere makes sense for them to go."

"Unless they've arrived," said Roff glancing at his watch. "It's two minutes to twelve. That noon appointment Minahero fixed with Snibbe was camouflage to hold anyone who might have been tapping his phone at Todd and Snibbe's until that panel van had got to where he wanted it."

"That figures," Goodson admitted. And he was broadcasting, "Subject just made a right into Foley Street! They gotta be heading for Southern Boulevard . . ."

"No, they're not," Roff cut in quietly. "They're pulling into that garage."

"Jesus!" cried Goodson. And with admirable presence of mind, "On the floor, Roff!" Roff did as instructed. "Keep going, Pittsie," he heard Goodson order. "Keep going nice and slow. Look straight ahead. I'll watch the mirror. And what you do is this: take a second right, then two more rights which'll bring us back on Saracen and you cross and find a place to park as near Saracen as you can. Okay?"

"Okay, Lieutenant," Pittsie said.

Watching through the mirror, Goodson glimpsed the Cadillac turning into the garage forecourt followed by the van and then with Pittsie having to pull out to pass a parked truck lost sight of them.

"Griffin calling, do you read me?"

"We read you Griffin."

"Subject just pulled into garage on Saracen, south side. I'm manoeuvering to park Brock and Saracen north side. Flood it, Bluey! Got that! Flood it! All you got. And get an outer cordon round the area."

Pittsie shrieked the Chevrolet round the first of the corners. Roff sat up again. Pittsie shrieked round the second corner missing a pedestrian by inches as he swerved out hastily to avoid a parked vehicle facing them, then swerved in again to avoid ramming a car heading straight at them in what had turned out to be a one-way street. Horns blared. Pittsie made his final right, and, seeing he could make it, crossed against the red and pulled to an empty space on Brock Street. They were perhaps a mile from where they started—it seemed much further.

Goodson threw open the offside door and stepped out into the road.

"Jesus!" he said. "We've lost 'em."

Roff got out from the nearside rear and stared diagonally across towards the garage. There was no sign of the Cadillac; no sign of the van. There was just a very ordinary garage which sold petrol and did servicing. A couple of drivers were filling up their tanks from the forecourt pumps. There were vehicles in the service bay receiving attention. But no Cadillac. No panel van.

"They must have done a turn," said Pittsie head out of his window, neck craned round.

"Do you think they spotted us and used the forecourt to shake us off?" said Roff.

Goodson stared inimically at the garage. With his left hand he stroked his chin, thoughtfully.

"Got it!" he said at length.

"What?" said Roff.

"Nothing to stop you driving clean through that service bay."

Roff followed his eyes. And Goodson was right. The service bay was busy but all the vehicles receiving attention were on either side of it leaving an open corridor through the centre easily wide enough for the Cadillac or van. And at the end were sliding metal doors, closed across was what obviously an opening leading either to a further workshop.

"Okay," said Goodson thoughtfully. He got back in the car. Switched on the mike. "Griffin calling, do you read me? . . . Now hear this. Subjects believed holed up in rear of service bay to Branson's Garage, Saracen Street 10-F map reading. Now do this in this order. Put blocks both ends Abbey Street and Saracen Avenue, St. Stephen and Brock unmarked if you can, but marked if you have to to do it quick. I will wait with Pittsie, corner Brock and Saracen. Station marked cars Southern Boulevard facing uptown and down between Saracen and St. Stephen and same thing Foley Street. Advise when in position. Meantime get all the dope you can on Branson's Garage, previous history, anything suspicious. Okay? You hear all that . . . ?"

They got back in the Chevrolet to await developments. Close by the traffic on Southern Boulevard and beyond that on the elevated Bruckner Expressway thundered by. It was a cold, cheerless day. The owners of the cars which were filling up in Branson's Garage were swift to pay and slam shut their doors against the weather. The garage kiosk was a cheerful island; from the service bay came the sound of hammering. Traffic flowed, pedestrians walked. Altogether it was a very normal scene. It was hard to believe that just beyond those sliding doors inside a mounted marlin was enough cocaine to meet the immediate needs of a several thousand addicts or, capitalised, to finance a revolution, the hijacking of a few airliners, the seizure of a score of hostages or the bombing of a dozen targets.

5

"You know the guy. How do you figure it?" Goodson was showing a respect towards Roff previously lacking.

The preparations had been completed; the lines of escape shut off. If the Cadillac and the van *were* beyond the rear doors to the service bay, there was no possible escape for Minahero. Some seven or eight minutes of belly-gripping tension had passed since Goodson had issued his instructions. At the beginning motorists had come to fill their tanks, check their oil and tyres, buy cigarettes and candies. But there would be no more motorists calling from now on; no more pedestrians. The roads had been blocked off. Police cordons were holding back out of sight, and harm, a growing number of curious passers-by. Directly across Brock Street on the downtown side of Saracen was a police car with four uniformed officers in it ready and waiting; two others in Abbey Street straddled it.

"I don't know how to figure it," Roff admitted. "Either they've gone in there to switch that fish to some other vehicle or to split up the drugs."

"They'd have been out and scrammed if it was another switch," contributed Pittsie.

"And I can't see them sawing that fish open to get the stuff out in full view of anyone who happens to walk in," said Roff. "Not Minahero. Everything's planned and worked out to a tee."

The operation from start to finish flashed through his mind. The development of a tourist complex geared especially to deep-sea fishing located on the Colombia-to-Miami run. The secret adaptation of a fishing cruiser to allow marlins to be switched; the inclusion of a mounting shop without which the switching would never have been possible; the elimination of Laurence Kress to ensure that it was built. The rigging of the weighing gear so that the mounted marlin palmed on Dillard although weighing far, far less would show seven hundred pounds. The patient waiting for a visitor sufficiently respected by the authorities for his trophy to pass the customs unchallenged. Minahero's readiness to pimp, if necessary, his new-found mistress to keep Dillard longer on Dragon Cay. The requested confirmation from Dillard that his fish had arrived in good time for his celebration party. The deliberate selection of the perfectly respectable Todd & Snibbe as the proper place for its repair and return—and returned to Dillard it would be and no one would ever have been the wiser there had been a switch. The mock up of a panel van identical to Todd & Snibbe's and the device to show and then expunge their name. Even that noon appointment. Everything had been thought out, mulled over, thought out again. And at almost every stage, even if through some unexpected occurrence the cocaine had been discovered, Minahero could claim convincingly he was not personally involved.

In every stage till now.

Surely, surely, he would not be standing in open view, while packets of cocaine were taken out of that fish's belly and passed around.

And a new thought occurred to him. "There's one thing I'm certain of," he said to Goodson. "That garage is clean."

"How d'you figure that?"

"Because that's the way he works. Dragon Cay is genuine. Dillard's above suspicion. So are Todd & Snibbe. When it comes down to the nitty-gritty, the important things, he relies on Japanese."

"They weren't Japs drove that van to Todd & Snibbe."

"So he switches them. What did they have to do? Drive a van with a fish in it . . ."

"Two fish."

"Doesn't follow. The second one could be in a concealed compartment. We haven't been inside that van. What else do they have to do? Press a button to switch a sign. Dump the van in a parking lot and clear off. It's a bit peculiar but they'll have been paid enough not to ask too many questions. No, Goodson, I'd bet my bottom dollar, yours too if you like, that whoever owns that garage hasn't the slightest idea what's going on in that back workshop."

"So we just go and ask the proprietor what he *thinks* is going on?!"

"Exactly," Roff said.

They crossed Saracen and then crossed Brock on the downtown side. Before they left the Chevrolet, Goodson had held a roadside conference with other officers out of view of Branson's Garage and had advised base the way he was going to play it. He and Roff were a couple of businessmen with a proposition. Or salesmen maybe.

"Is Mr. Branson about?" Roff enquired of the black youth in the forecourt kiosk.

"Ain't no Mr. Branson." The youth's thoughts were elsewhere; he was puzzled by the sudden drying-up of customers.

"The owner then?"

The youth flicked a thumb over his shoulder indicating a fat-faced man with grey hair, a thick moustache and heavy horn-rimmed spectacles standing by the opening to the service bay talking to a mechanic. "In the suit."

"What's his name?"

"Gallacher."

"Thank you."

They walked towards Gallacher with such obvious purpose that happening to see them heading his way, he broke off his conversation.

"Morning?" he queried.

"Mr. Gallacher?"

"Yes."

"Can we have a word with you?" Roff was conscious of the doors to the back part of the service bay. Shut they might be but there could be a spyhole somewhere. But he'd worked it out with Goodson, he'd open the conversation as his limey accent would be disarming.

"Well, I'm a bit busy." Gallacher changed his mind. "Better come inside. It's warmer."

"Out here!" Goodson spoke automatically, instinctive in authority, forgetting his role.

The good-natured eyes behind the horn-rimmed spectacles widened, making the frames ride up perceptibly.

"Now just a minute, mister!"

"I'm sorry," Roff apologised as courteously as he could. "But it is a private matter. I promise you," he lied, "we won't keep you a moment."

Gallacher turned towards the mechanic. "Watch us, Bill," he said. "If there's any funny business, you know what to do." He turned back. "Okay. But be quick about it."

When they were out of earshot of the service bay, Goodson took over. "First thing so you know, Mr. Gallacher, we're police officers."

"Oh?" Gallacher did not sound too convinced. He flicked a thumb—rather after the manner of his black forecourt assistant. "Him too?"

"Second thing," said Goodson, ignoring this, "there's police cars at all four intersections. One. Two. Three. Four." With each number, he pointed to a corner. "And there's back-ups. See those guys over there?" He pointed to three men by a parked car across the street apparently deep in discussion. "Cops."

"You have identification?" said Gallacher, clearly puzzled, but not alarmed.

"Sure." Goodson produced a badge which Gallacher appeared to accept as convincing evidence. Roff wondered why. Anyone, he thought, could knock up something which looked like a badge to the uninitiated. He supposed it was film and television influence.

"Back there?" said Goodson, putting the badge away. "Back of that service bay. Behind those doors. What's going on?"

Gallacher shook his head. "That's my business," he said.

"See here!" cried Goodson. "We don't have time to go through the fancy stuff. We ask the questions. And if you know what's good for you, you answer them. What gives behind those doors?"

"I've told you," Gallacher replied with commendable calmness, "that's my business. And I don't know any law that requires me to say what my business is just because some cop shows up and asks it. So if you want to know what's going on in there, you'd better get yourself a search warrant because I'm not telling you."

"And all those cars ringing the joint?" Goodson snapped, catching the thumb gesticulation. "You think that's playtime?"

"I don't care if you've got the whole damn Army . . ."

"Now you hear this, Gallacher, and hear it good . . ."

"Just a minute, Lieutenant," Roff cut in, putting a hand on Goodson's arm. "Hold it."

Goodson calmed. "Okay, Roff," he said. "You've got just thirty seconds."

"That'll do." Roff addressed the garage proprietor. "Mr. Gallacher, inside that workshop there's a black Cadillac which drove in ten minutes back with a Japanese gentleman in the passenger seat and that was followed by a white panel van with at least two more Japanese in it? Is that right?"

Gallacher grinned. "No harm in agreeing to that," he said. "You can ask anybody." He waved a casual arm.

"If I was to tell you that there isn't the least possibility that anyone inside that workshop will be allowed to leave . . ."

Gallacher considered. "Just a minute." He went to the kiosk. "Joe," he said, "just walk as far as Abbey Street and see if there's any police cars near the corner."

They waited while Joe did as requested: Roff impatient, Goodson quiet but fuming, Gallacher composed.

Joe came back. "There's two," he said laconically. "One both sides. No wonder no one's buying gas." And he went back into his kiosk.

"Okay," said Gallacher. "I don't know who's put you up to this but someone's face is sure going to be red by the time you've finished." And he addressed Roff, as if Goodson no longer existed. "It's rented out. Has been for about . . . be about three months now. To Hal Bardini. You heard of Hal Bardini?" Roff shook his head in puzzlement rather than denial. "Races cars," Gallacher explained. "Not all that well. Also owns a Cadillac. Black. It was him drove Mr. Nimoto in."

"Go on," said Roff, steeling himself.

"Bardini's got a car in there he's working on. Seems Nimoto's backing him. Wouldn't figure myself he's doing anything but waste his money but it's not my business. So long as they pay the rent . . ."

"You mean that for the past three months there's been a car in there . . ."

"The car came in about . . ." He pursed his lips. " 'bout six weeks back. Seems they had some customs problems."

"It's a Japanese car."

"Sure. A souped-up Honda."

"And the mechanics who come to work on it are all Japanese."

"Correct."

"And it's . . . well, your staff aren't supposed to go in there?"

Gallacher was no longer grinning . . . "Seeing as how you know so much about what's happening, I can't see why you've got all these police cars blocking up the place and keeping away my customers."

"You'll see," said Goodson. "All right. We'll check up on what you've told us later. Now clear the place. You've got two minutes to get everyone who works for you out in the street. Then we're going in." And he turned to walk away quickly back to Pittsie.

EIGHTEEN

Roff had had a bottle of scotch and some splits sent up in readiness. Peta threw off her shaped leather jacket, disclosing a chestnut and white dog's tooth suit which went superbly with her titian hair which had been done into a bun as if she wanted to undervalue her attractiveness. She looked tired and drawn, yet still beautiful. She lit a cigarette and watched him pour them both stiff drinks. It was about six in the evening. "All right," she said. "Tell me."

He put the scotch on the table by her armchair. "Have you ever heard of Attu Isle?" he asked. She shook her head. "In the Aleutians. It was the first place taken by the Japanese the Americans took back. There were two thousand Japs on it and the Americans used ten times that number and a massive task force. It took them three weeks to retake it. When they did, they didn't find a single one alive. That's how it was at Branson's Garage."

"They're all dead?"

"Yes."

"You saw it happen?"

"From a distance. They wouldn't let me go too close." He laughed without mirth. "But they gave me a gun. A Police Special .38 they called it. It weighed a ton."

He went to the window, drink in hand, and stared down on Central Park, watching the lights of the traffic moving swiftly along the park drives and transverse roads, reflecting off the rain-swept streets, conscious of the vibrancy of this remarkable city, its contrasts, its variety, its excitement, its poverty and wealth which often missed rubbing shoulders by a mere block or two. Thinking of its apartment buildings, its houses, offices, garages; its shops, hotels, cafés—of how in each small cell, in each place to live or work, in each one of several million units which made up the teeming city, men and women were living their lives out, lives which, to each of them, were in their way as complicated as his own and Peta's, as Goodson's and Pittsie's, as had been Kress's and Minahero's. For the immediately pressing problem, be it to do with triumph or disaster, filling the mind, bulks larger than the catastrophe of an entire nation. A city may well be the sum of its individuals but to each of them that city is no more and no less than what it has to offer.

He turned from the window and sat on the corner of the double bed facing Peta.

"Someone else took over, from Goodson," he told her. "I never even learnt his name. He had a walkie-talkie in one hand and a revolver in the other. With him was a policeman with a loud-hailer and there were about, I don't know, thirty, forty more backing up. They put cars across the forecourt exits and there were others across the road. Branson had got all his men out to safety."

"But they must have known all this was going on?" said Peta frowning.

"That's what I kept saying to myself and yet all there was, was this iron door. Just an iron door and yet somehow it looked sinister. As if any moment it would be thrown open and . . . and we'd see something dramatic: a bunch of Japanese behind a machine gun; even an armoured vehicle charging out! But nothing happened. Nothing at all. It was just very quiet. Just this policemen giving instructions through his walkie-talkie and listening to replies. No traffic, no pedestrians—just masses of uniformed men standing by ready to storm the place. And it was very raw; which made the waiting longer. And then this policeman with the loud-hailer stepped forward about a yard or so. I don't know why. But he stepped forward so that he was standing quite on his own and told them to come out one by one with their hands on the top of their heads and that they'd got just two minutes and then the police were coming in."

"Did they come out?"

"I thought they were going to. After all there was nothing they could do. They hadn't a chance in hell of escaping. The door slid open one end. Not very much. Two or three feet. And this racing driver, Hal Bardini, was standing there with his hands on his head. A swarthy fellow with oiled hair. Young. Probably in his twenties. He stood there for a moment with his hands on his head and then he started walking slowly towards us. But he didn't get far. There was a shot, just the one, and he fell forward on his face. Dead. I assumed it was one of the policemen had got trigger-happy. But it wasn't. One of the Japs had shot him in the back."

He drank a little of his scotch and then went on.

"When they shot Bardini it was obvious no one was going to give themselves up and I wondered if I was going to witness a real shoot-out. You know, one of those scenarios where everyone is hiding behind a car and now and again popping up his head to take a bead on someone and shots are whanging about the place. But it wasn't like that at all. It was all done very sensibly. This policeman in charge . . . a great bull of a fellow he was . . . sent for some tear gas and when it came he had a couple of his men go up on the roof and smash some glass rooflights and then they poured the stuff in from every angle. And then half a dozen cops wearing masks got ready to go in. Real cowboy and Indian stuff it was, with them, guns at the ready, creeping along the side up to the angle where that door was still open . . . Lord knows why they didn't try to close it? . . . and a few more crawling along the roof . . . And then there were four shots, just four. One after the other. So then they rushed it. And there were the four Japs—all with neat holes through the front of their heads and their brains blown out."

"And Minahero."

"Still alive. Just. You know what he'd done? Disembowelled himself. With a genuine *hara-kiri* dagger. It was on the floor beside him. You never saw such a mess."

Peta put her hand up over her eyes as a sudden wave of nausea swept over her. "God!" she whispered. "Oh my God!"

She heard the creak of springs as he left the bed and for a moment imagined he was coming over to comfort her. But then she heard him refilling his glass.

"I wouldn't be too sympathetic," he said, not looking at her, busy with his drink, "killing himself in such an aristocratic manner was probably the high point of his life. Especially dying slowly in front of the police knowing that with Bardini dead it'd be that much more difficult for them to get a line on the original suppliers and all the rest of the mob tied up with something on this scale." He came back and sat on the bed again.

"It had been pretty cleverly worked out," he told her practically—and she knew he was doing this to ease the shock of it. "Inside the workshop they'd erected some screens around this Honda as if it really was having some very special treatment no one else was allowed to peek in on and they'd carried the marlin behind these screens so that if anyone stuck their head unexpectedly into the workshop they wouldn't see it."

"What had they done with it? Sawn it open?"

"Nothing so subtle. They just gave it one clout with a sledgehammer."

"How much cocaine was there?"

"Goodson figures not less than a hundred kilos, maybe more. It was all in neat plastic parcels. About twenty of them. Different sizes to fit the fish."

"A hundred kilos," Peta mused.

"Say twenty million dollars' worth street value. Maybe more. Maybe much more."

"And how were they going to get it out?"

"In the Cadillac. It had been specially prepared." He chuckled. "I bet Minnie insisted on that. And the funny thing is that if instead of trying to stow it in all those crafty little compartments they'd simply chucked it on the back seat they could have been in and out in about two minutes flat and, who knows, maybe got away with it."

"And Minahero's payment?"

"In a suitcase. You never saw so much money. I bet they're still counting it."

There was a moment or two of silence, then Peta said, "So you end up the blue-eyed boy? The fellow who got it right all the way along."

She wondered why she spoke so meanly, but Roff understood and forgave her. A void stretched ahead of her. She had volunteered for a task without appreciating the demands that task would make upon her. No matter how important her part had been proved to be, now it was played out she could only view it with disgust.

"What I did," Roff answered, "was to use my common sense. What you did was to sacrifice yourself. Without you Minahero would still be alive and well and living in Grand Bahama planning his next shipment."

"I know all that," she said wearily.

"Yasuo Minahero saw himself as a kind of reincarnated *Daimio* and had built up around him a bunch of samurai with the same crackpot point of view; men he could utterly rely on, who would carry out his orders implicitly and, if the balloon went up, kill themselves rather than be taken prisoner. I bet he persuaded himself every time he had sex with a Western woman he was revenging himself on his country's enemies. But it's a strange thing, sex. The ways it works. The way men twist their minds to make it work, the risks they take. It's extraordinary how weak even the toughest of men can be when it comes to sex, how they lay their whole careers, families, principles, on the line and lose the lot! But we were lucky because Minahero had this weakness while you had the guts to see it through. And because you did, a lot of innocent people who would otherwise have been slaughtered won't be and a lot of youngsters who would have got hooked on drugs aren't going to get hooked."

"Give me another drink," Peta said.

He fetched it for her.

"It was a good try, Sergei," she said, taking it from him, "but, you know, you haven't helped at all because I just can't get a glow on as a public benefactress when all I've done is whore."

"Act the part of a whore."

"Whore. First with you. Then with Minahero. And I would have whored with Dillard only he happened to catch his fish before I had to."

"You weren't a whore with me."

She laughed. Harshly. "That first time you saw me, posing by that swimming pool in Tucson—was that any different from standing in a window like the prostitutes do in Amsterdam? And it worked, didn't it? I got you into bed with me which, after all, was the original object of the exercise."

"I don't believe it."

"You don't want to believe it. What do you think I said to Shapland when he asked me how, if he took me on, I could make sure you didn't chicken out before I got my hooks into Minahero?"

She lit another cigarette.

"There was a time when I could have taken you away from Anita, Sergei. I could have said to you when we were about to dock in Grand Bahama, let's not do this, let's go on and on and on. Let's find a new world together. And you'd have come with me. Even that last night on Dragon Cay, when we were sitting in that motor boat you'd hired, maybe I could have found the way. Maybe it still wasn't too late." She blew smoke in the air, looking at him through the cloud, calmly.

"But," she said, "when I went back to Minahero for another week and when that was over, somehow everything was different. Because I was different. I could excuse myself about the first week because it was all so weird and unexpected and because it seemed possible I might learn something I didn't know. But I couldn't excuse myself for going back for more when the only purpose in it was to stop him suspecting he'd got a maggot in his woodwork . . ."

"But it wasn't like that, was it, Peta?" Roff argued. "It was you being with him, overhearing that telephone call, gave us the one essential bit of information we had to have. Without that he'd have got clean away with it."

She nodded. "From your point of view, yes. But not from mine. You see, back on Grand Bahama, in that damned bit of Japan he'd created, I just let him use me as he chose. And I didn't really care." She laughed softly. "Funny, isn't it? I went into this to get rid of a lot of hang-ups and I've come out less free than ever."

He looked deep into her green eyes, remembering very clearly the first time he had looked into them and found them cool, appraising perhaps, but candid, frank, straightforward—in a word, ingenuous. But now there was wariness, knowledge which had not been there before, the first hint of cynicism.

She stubbed out her cigarette and got to her feet. "For all the talk," she said, "it's what you do that matters not the reason why you do it. You take a boy and teach him how to use a gun for the very best of motives and then you send him off to use it. And you never see that boy again."

He stayed sitting on the bed looking up at her. "There's something else, isn't there?" he said.

She nodded. "I had a call this afternoon. From Shapland."

"Something else he wants you to do?"

"Yes."

"And you're going to?"

She smiled, sadly. "Would you take me away, Sergei, if I asked you to? Would you get a taxi with me to JFK and catch the first flight taking off to anywhere? Start afresh? Never come back again? Because, you know, you only have to ask me." She stretched out an arm for her jacket. "But you won't. Not because of what I've done, but because of what I've done has done to me. Because I'm become a different person. Like that boy they gave a gun to." She put out a hand. "No, don't get up. If you get up you'll touch me and I couldn't bear it." She reached the door, opened it. "One of these days," she said, "your telephone will ring like mine did this afternoon. And you'll have to make a decision. As I had to."

"And what should I say?"

"You should say no," she told him. "But if you say yes? Well, who knows?"

She closed the door behind her. He went to the window wondering if he'd see her go. But it was dark outside. And anyway the portico cut off the cabs. He sat in the chair, still warm from her body, and drank the drink he had poured out for her she hadn't touched. Then he picked up the phone and asked the operator to get him his San Francisco number.

ABOUT THE AUTHOR

Charles Russell is the pseudonym of a man who has been a World War II fighter pilot, prisoner of war in a camp near Hiroshima, travel agent, surveyor with offices in London, Trinidad, and Jamaica, property developer, impresario, author, and playwright. His first novel was published in 1964 and since then he has written eight more novels, numerous short stories, and three non-fiction accounts of the war in the Far East. He also has to his credit a dozen plays performed on West End and provincial stages, or for radio and television in the United Kingdom and abroad. As an impresario he has presented many works by other playwrights on the West End and provincial stages. This is his second novel for the Crime Club. He lives in Henley-on-Thames, in England.